Eden

Will you survive a new plague?

J. Sharpe

the consumer or reader of this material. Any perceived slight of any individual or organization is purely unintentional.

The resources in this book are provided for informational purposes only and should not be used to replace the specialized training and professional judgment of a health care or mental health care professional.

Neither the author nor the publisher can be held responsible for the use of the information provided within this book. Please always consult a trained professional before making any decision regarding treatment of yourself or others.

First, a small gift

I want to thank you personally for buying this book. You are about to go on an epic and thrilling ride. As a thank you, I want to give you something. You love to read, otherwise, you wouldn't have bought this book. So let me give you a free story. To get access (and to stay in touch with me and my work) simply go to my website www.jsharpebooks.com and sign up for my email list. Don't worry, you can always unsubscribe if you're no longer interested.

Writing a novel is fun, but it also can be a hard and daunting task. Especially to make sure a lot of readers will find it and read it.

My dream is to be a full-time writer. I've traditional published 13 books so far in The Netherlands but still have a day job. Now the time is right to publish my books in other languages to, like this one, and chase my dreams furthermore.

And you can help me with that a lot.

If you like this book, then please leave an honest review afterward. I love to read what you think.

For now: enjoy this rollercoaster.

J. Sharpe

Preface

I'm a believer as much as a non-believer and mostly the type of person that thinks 'seeing is believing' – which puts the whole issue of faith into a rather strange perspective, according to me. Sometimes I envy people who are true believers, because, in my opinion, a firm belief in something is the only thing that can bring absolute peace to your soul. Mostly parents raise you in certain religious beliefs, or sometimes people change their minds about the divine as they go through life. Whatever the case, I hope there is something up there. No one wants to live just one lifetime, but I will only know for sure when I see Him.

I'm also of the opinion that you should read a book for fun, which is why I'm warning people in advance. My story isn't meant to sacrifice sacred cows, but some scenes could be deemed offensive to readers, especially to people of faith. If you think that this is you, maybe it is wise to put the book aside now.

In case you don't, I wish you a pleasant reading experience.

-1-

I woke up in a dark, stifling room.

Still groggy with sleep, I stared at the floor. Drool dribbled down my double chin and splattered onto my naked upper leg. The fact that it was a naked leg only occurred to me after a few more seconds. Which wasn't surprising – my head felt like a bunch of elephants were playing musical chairs inside my brain. Everything was spinning, and with each beat of my heart my head nearly exploded. A haze danced in front of my eyes. A cold draft covered me like a blanket of ice, chilling me to the core of my soul. My body shook uncontrollably. My feet – which seemed rooted to the spot on the icy, concrete floor – felt numb, and my nipples would have made great clothes pegs. The blinking light didn't make the situation any better. On. Off.

Light. Dark... it was driving me nuts. In short:

This was not exactly what I'd call a glorious awakening.

Where am I? What happened?

I moaned. Without thinking, I tried to raise a hand to my throbbing head, but I didn't get far. A jab of pain in my wrists sent a rush of adrenalin through me, dissolving the haze and making me more alert. The throbbing faded into the background, and the elephants turned to mice. In the glare of the strip light above me, which challenged the darkness with every flicker, I saw that my arms were tied behind me against the chair. I didn't just see it – I *felt* it. Thick, chafing flax rope was strung across my body from shoulder to thigh in the shape of an X, fixed to the same chair, and cutting into my flesh with each movement I made.

Not quite ready to face reality, I tried to wriggle free. Pointless, of course.

What the hell is this?

My heart was hammering like crazy. The temperature couldn't be more than forty, and yet I was sweating like a pig. I tried once more, putting all my strength into it – to no avail, but I wouldn't give up. A sharp pain lanced through me. My anger forced the pain to the background. Yanking on the rope, I got to my feet – or at least, I tried to tell my limbs to do so. It was a big mistake. My legs were also tied to the chair, and when I tried to pry them loose and stand up straight, I lost my balance. The chair started to tilt to the side, the two left legs lifting up from the floor, and I hit the floor with a thud.

At once, the elephants were back and I saw stars.

I struggled to sit up, but after a few seconds I was out of breath and I just lay there on my side, cursing myself for my stupidity.

All this time I'd managed to silence my surfacing panic, more or less. I once read somewhere that you can only keep a clear head if you suppress your panic, which could be the difference between life and death. There's a fine line between the two, the span of mere seconds, which I know from experience. But my fall caused me to lose that control. My body shook. "Help! Help me!" My cries echoed off the plastered walls of the bare room.

Then I saw her.

Naked, just like me. Long legs, bare stomach, full breasts. She was on the opposite side of the room, sitting on a chair, but she wasn't tied to it. I gasped for breath, wanted to beg for her help, but couldn't utter a single word. The silence that ensued was deafening. I don't know what frightened me more – that silence or the woman.

On second thought, I take that back. The woman was definitely more frightening.

7

Her long, brown hair was tangled and dirty. Her amber-colored eyes were filled with sadness. And how I knew that this person was *me*, I still don't know today. I just knew. My eyes might have been able to deceive me, but I *felt* it, deep within me.

"How..?" I heard myself stammer. The strip light – off. On. Light. Dark.

The woman didn't reply. Was that a tear rolling down her cheek?

"What the hell is this?" I ground out.

Silence.

The woman's left arm started to move. Because of the damned blinking light – and the fact I was still lying on my side – the image of her moving looked even more sinister, like a stuttering silent movie. A gun in her hand. Frame one: the gun near her thigh. Darkness. Frame two: the gun close to her waist, her eyes filled with tears. Darkness. Frame three: the gun pressed against her neck, her mouth slightly agape, her head hesitantly shaking no, her tears. Darkness. Frame four: the gun against her temple.

Jesus, no.

"Wait!"

A bang, so loud it seemed to shatter my eardrums, while the sound of the gun clattering to the floor was pushed into the background.

The strip light. Off. On. Light. Dark.

In the glare, I saw the body – *my* body – lying motionlessly on the floor. Blood ran toward me like a meandering stream of water.

I screamed.

What are your options when you're tied to a chair on the floor in some dark hole? That's right – you don't have any.

It took me a good, long while before I'd calmed down somewhat. As calm as any naked, tied-up girl who'd just witnessed – from up close – her double committing suicide with a bullet to the brain could be, anyway.

Close your eyes. Take a deep breath. Don't look at the body.

8

That helped – a little. But I wasn't sure the darkness was any better.

As controlled as I could, I inhaled the damp air. A sickening feeling came over me and only got worse when I started to consider what usually happens to a person's body once that person is dead.

Rigor mortis, decomposition, maggots...

Don't think about that, I urged myself. *By that time you'll be long gone.*

God, I really hoped I was right about that.

How long was I there on the floor, eyes closed and controlling my breathing as carefully as I could?

Seconds? Minutes? Hours? It felt like a lifetime was passing me by.

This is all a joke, a nightmare. Once you open your eyes for real, the body will be gone and you'll find yourself spooning with Mark in your very own bed.

I opened my eyes.

The strip light: off. On. Light. Dark.

My inner voice was a liar.

Soulless, wide-open eyes were staring at me, seemingly watching me. Which was nonsense, of course. On the other hand, it was just as nonsensical to wake up tied to a chair, facing someone who looked just like me and had a death wish. Because that's what it had been, right? Someone who just *looked* like me? Surely there was just one me. I hadn't been cloned and as far as I knew I didn't have a twin sister. Maybe I should grill my parents about it – if I ever got out of this bizarre situation. It wouldn't be the first secret my dad had kept.

Of course you're not that woman. The mere thought is ridiculous. She just happens to look like you.

Naturally. Of course, it was just a coincidence. What a load of horse crap. What the *hell* was going on?

My eyes darted across the room. I half-expected cameras mounted to the walls.

9

Because that's what it had to be, I reasoned. *One big, fucking joke. Well, haha. LOL supreme. Now could someone please show up to get me out of this mess?*

I knew it was no use lying to myself.

Okay, think. How did you get here? What's the last thing you remember?

It was a simple enough question. And yet, the answer came to me in fragments. It wasn't that I couldn't remember – because I certainly could – but it was like looking at a flickering movie reel, like my mind was being influenced by the wavering light.

Mark, pushing me up against the wall passionately. His hands sliding through my hair. His lips on mine. The shudder that ran through me the moment he pressed his warm body against mine. In that last memory, we made love, but something wasn't right about that picture. We were crying. Why on earth were we crying?

I racked my brain for the answer. The cold enveloping me didn't help. My body was shaking so violently that I almost started to think it was the floor that was trembling, not me.

"*… so sorry. We've detected metastasis from the primary carcinoma…*"

Mark's voice, whispering dejectedly: "*How long before she…*"

The doctor's voice, calm, clinical: "*Hard to say. Months, perhaps a year.*"

God, how I wanted to jump up from my chair and smack him in the face. There was no emotion in his tone. That hack was telling me my life was over like he was having a casual chat about his mother-in-law. But the reality was that somehow, it made sense. This was his job. He might have to conduct conversations like these on a daily basis. Wouldn't we all raise our emotional shields in that case? You had to not to lose your mind. But fuck it, this was *my life* we were talking about. I was special, wasn't I?

Funny, that. This feeling most of us seem to have – that we're different. Immortal, even. We always know death is waiting for us, but only when you actually turn that corner do you realize just how fragile life really is.

The realization that I'm still walking this earth and have the ability to write this all down while he, along with billions of other people, drew his last breath a long time ago… it's almost comical in a sinister way.

In my memory, I couldn't move as I sat there across from the doctor. His words rained down on me like the blows of a sledgehammer. Mark's hand in mine. He almost had to carry me out of that hospital.

I didn't tell my family. *Couldn't* tell them. I'd cross that bridge later, I reasoned, once we'd dealt with it ourselves. Made our peace with it as best as we could. But whether I actually did or not – I couldn't remember. The mental images didn't reach that far. Nor did I remember anything that might explain my naked presence in this room. Had I been abducted? And if so, why?

I shook my head. It wasn't important right now. I had to find a way to get out of here.

Think.

I tried, I really did. And I launched so many attempts to free myself that the skin under the ropes got raw from trying.

Just admit it, darling. You won't get out of this without help.

So I did the only thing left to me at this point.

I cried for help.

-2-

During the first few hours, I still had the idle hope that someone would hear me and rush to my aid. I mean, *if* I had been abducted – and that seemed likely, although I didn't have the faintest clue why – then someone knew I was here. Obviously, someone had to have been around to tie me to this chair. And there had to be a reason.

Did I have any enemies? Yes – the Colombians maybe, who might be trying to get to my father by hurting me. But wasn't this a bit far-fetched for a simple act of revenge?

The answer came to me immediately. *No, it wasn't. They were very much capable of doing this.*

But maybe it had nothing to do with those guys and I'd just been at the wrong place at the wrong time. Besides, if my abductors wanted money, they'd be in for a nasty surprise. My parents weren't exactly poor, but they weren't rich like the Hiltons either. Not anymore, at least – not since we'd been forced into a different kind of life seven years ago.

I'd stopped shouting by now. I didn't have the strength for it anymore. Nor could I muster up the strength to hold up my pee any longer. For minutes, I tried really hard, with sweat beading down my temples and my bladder feeling like it was about to pop like a balloon. At long last – and with heated cheeks, even though there was no one around to witness the act – I let it out. The urine felt warm on my bare legs.

My throat felt like sandpaper. Swallowing was sheer torture. My stomach rumbled and contracted painfully. I'd been here for God knows how long. If I didn't get something to eat soon, I'd faint. Not to mention some water.

As a recent medical school graduate, I knew you could last on your fat reserves for quite a while before the body started consuming itself. I saw two potential problems with that in my case, however. First of all, I was a measly 130 pounds, so I didn't have a lot of fat reserves. Secondly, extreme cold could drastically shorten that survival time. On a positive note, I wouldn't have to worry about starving to death at all. No human could survive without water for more than three or four days, so I'd succumb to the effects of dehydration much sooner.

But surely it wouldn't come to that? Surely *someone* would find me before that happened? Undoubtedly people were looking for me. I may have been dying, but I hadn't been forgotten, right?

The smell pervading the room made me gag every now and then, even though – strangely enough – I was starting to get used to it. The moldy smell of before didn't stand a chance against the stench of my own urine. And if I wasn't found soon, the reek of the decomposing body would only add to my misery.

A shiver ran down my spine. I felt dirty. Here I was, strapped to a chair and lying on a concrete floor in a puddle of urine. I wasn't going to last much longer.

My gaze drifted to the lifeless body once more.

The strip light. Off. On. Light. Dark.

"Who were you?" I whispered. I made sure I spoke out loud every now and then. The sound of my voice kept the loneliness at bay, even though I'd lose that fight in the long run. Immediately I stopped talking. Speaking started to hurt my throat too much.

The woman didn't react – of course she didn't. If she winked at me now, I'd suffer coronary arrest on the spot.

Why had she taken her own life? Was it her own choice, or had she been forced by someone?

So many questions, so few answers.

Why did you do this to me? You could have helped me – released me.

Anger thundered through my veins. That was a good thing. It chased the cold away, if only temporarily.

And where has it gotten you, huh? You're dead. What's the fucking point of death for anyone?

A new thought came up. *What if that woman was the one who tied me to this chair?*

A single word bubbled up in my throat, had to get out. I clenched my fist and yelled as loudly as I could, ignoring the pain in my throat. "Bitch!"

I really shouldn't have. That word wasn't the only thing that came out. Bile, slime. My stomach contracted, heaved, and pushed up the burning substance.

This was the one-to-last stage, I realized. The next stage would be shock, but I had no way of stopping it.

I vomited…

… and lost consciousness.

-3-

I jolted awake. Voices in the dark. Far away. Laughter. It was coming closer.

"… sure no one will find us here?" A girl, giggling.

"This building has been abandoned for years." A boy. "And even if someone were here… doesn't that add to the excitement?"

A thump. A high-pitch cry of pleasure.

"I've waited for this for so long." The boy.

"Shh. Kiss me."

I wanted to scream, clench my hands into fists and beat the floor with it, but I didn't have a single shred of energy left in my body. I was toeing the line between life and death. I knew organ failure was imminent because I couldn't breathe properly and my stomach hurt like hell. Maybe it was better this way. I was terminally ill. Even if someone found me and I was nursed back to health, that health was only relative. I'd have a few more months to live. Months of gradually deteriorating, leading up to my death in some hospital bed. Wasn't this a better way to go?

Just get it over with.

I opened my eyes. Slowly, as though my eyelids were caked with glue. The strip light had finally given up it's blinking – thank God – and in the darkness, I was no longer able to see the body.

That's where the logic ended. Why couldn't I smell

the decomposition of the body? Hadn't I been here long enough for me to start smelling it? Hadn't the rot set in yet? Impossible.

Your nose has gotten used to it.

No, that wasn't the case. Something else was going on…

The laughter died away. The sound of receding footsteps. The sound of my last hope to be found walking out of here.

Get it over with, I thought to myself again.

Death wouldn't come.

My eyes fell shut and I lowered myself onto the bed of semi-consciousness. How long was I there? Seconds, minutes, hours?

A door – what door? Why hadn't I seen a door before? – swung open, casting a blanket of light over me.

Giggling. "Maybe this is suitable…" The girl.

"What are we going to…"

"Jesus!"

Shrieking.

Footfalls hurrying toward me. Warm hands on my skin, a finger against my jugular vein.

"Is she…"

"Not yet. Call 911."

"Who would do a thing like that?"

"Iris…!"

"Yeah, yeah, I'm on the phone right now."

I vaguely registered the girl walking off. Even though I knew she had to be close, it felt to me as though she was in a parallel world. Then I heard her voice. Panicky. Alarmed. "… a girl. Naked. Tied up. Please come quickly…"

"You'll be all right." This time, the voice was closer to

17

me.

I doubted he was right.

"What's your name?"

"Meisner," I managed to utter, surprising myself that I was able to perpetuate the lie I'd lived for seven years even under these circumstances. "Anna."

A hand gently squeezed my shoulder and shook me to keep me awake. "The paramedics are on their way."

Despite trying to convince myself of the opposite before, I was still grateful that they'd found me. I didn't want to die like this. I tried to thank the boy and fling my arms around this complete stranger to have a good, long blubber. But all I could do was mumble.

"Save your strength."

I tried to take in his appearance, but to me he was just a hazy blur.

What happened after that is not as clear in my memory. I think I must have passed out, only to momentarily wake up minutes or even hours later and slip back into an unconscious slumber again. It was a vicious cycle I just couldn't seem to break.

I do recollect a few things, such as the sound of the sirens, and the rain hitting my face. The gray sky above as I was wheeled out on a stretcher and taken to the ambulance. I vaguely recall opening my mouth to catch a few drops of rain.

The next thing I remember: I woke up in a hospital bed. Wires and tubes running in and out of my skin, connecting me to several machines. A heart monitor reported my heartbeat with annoying, beeping sounds. Figures around me. My vision was still out of focus, which made them like nothing more than vague blurs to me. I assumed the blurs were doctors.

There were voices surrounding me, even in the moments that I lost my battle to stay awake. Sometimes they sounded terrifying, sometimes comforting. I had to trust these voices. What other choice did I have?

This is how I stayed in a partial slumber for days, until someone woke me up and I saw the man at the end of the bed. At that moment, my world was about to change again – into a sick rollercoaster.

-4-

I heard the voices before I saw the people around my bed.

"She's still weak. We can ask her some questions, but make sure to keep it brief."

"Have you found out more about her condition?"

"No, we're still awaiting the final test results. But what we found so far has baffled us."

"Can you explain it?"

"No, we can't. It's like a miracle. If she is indeed *that* Anna…"

"I don't believe in miracles."

Someone gently shook me by the shoulder. "Miss Meisner?"

Slowly, I opened my eyes, looking around me dazedly. I felt the kind of exhaustion you feel when you've slept for too long – for weeks, it seemed to me. My vision had returned to normal and for the first time in forever, I felt like I would win the battle with my drooping eyelids.

From my position in the bed, I could look outside through the window on my left. Fluffy clouds drifted across a blue canvas. Beams of sunlight penetrated the glass and caressed the duvet I was under.

"Miss Meisner?" The woman's voice again. "Anna?"

I turned my head. The room was empty apart from the IV drip to my right, a chair in the corner, and the two people next to my bed. Underneath the covers, my body was beginning to wake up too. Without me consciously telling them to, my fingers contracted. They touched my body and I noticed I finally wasn't naked anymore. I was wearing a nightgown.

A woman in a doctor's coat looked at me inquisitively. She was skinny, with sunken cheeks and dark-red hair. She smiled at me, but it was clearly forced.

A shiver ran across my back. What was the matter with me? I felt good – healed and clean, even. My stomach no longer rumbled, my lips were no longer chapped. Then why was this woman looking at me as though something was horribly wrong with me?

"How are you feeling?"

I shrugged, trying my best to sit up.

"Wait." The doctor helps me to an upright position and propped a pillow against my lower back. For a second, the world spun around me, but it soon subsided.

"How long was I out?"

The doctor pulled up the duvet a bit. "You've been in the Moreno Hospital for the past two days. Can you remember what happened?"

I nodded. "Woke up, was strapped to a chair. A woman was sitting across from me. She looked like me, *was* me. She shot herself in the head…" The words came out haltingly. My tongue felt like a thick, leather rag.

The man at the end of the bed interrupted me. "Hold up… a woman? Shot herself in the head?"

I took in his appearance. He was wearing a black, leather jacket and jeans. With his mutton-fists, almost square head, and typical goatee, he looked like an ill-conceived Lego doll. His badge flashed on his belt.

The doctor took my hand and pumped it lightly.

"Anna, this is chief inspector Rogers. He has a few questions…"

"Can you tell me a little bit more about that woman?" The police inspector walked over to the side of the bed, staring me in the eyes intently.

I put a hand to my forehead, as though that would help me to push back the headache fighting its way into the foreground. "What else do you want me to say? You've found her body, haven't you? She was lying in the same room I was kept in." I shot the doctor an inquisitive gaze. "Where was the room, anyway?"

"Inside an abandoned apartment building on the edge of town. It was on the demolition list, but…" She looked at the police inspector with a question in her eyes. He nodded and took over once more.

"Ma'am, apart from you, the room was completely empty." There was an undertone of something in his voice. He didn't believe me?

In shock, I turned my head to face him. "What..?"

"Calm down, Anna." The doctor put a warm hand on my arm. "You've been through a lot."

I yanked it away. "What's that supposed to mean? That I made it up?"

"No, but both your mental condition and your physical condition were terrible when you were found. Maybe you hallucinated about this woman."

"In other words, I made it up. But that's nonsense!" I yelled. "She looked just like me. She was real!"

"Anna, could you tell us in your own words what happened, according to you?" Chief Inspector Rogers asked.

I sighed. My head was about to explode. "Do I have to do to it now?"

"Living through these experiences again might be too harrowing for her right now," the doctor protested. "I'm not sure whether…"

"Dredging it up might be too much for some time to come," the inspector reacted flatly. "There's an ongoing investigation, so I…"

I raised my hand in the air. "Fine, All right." I'd rather be left alone, but it was clear the inspector would only leave after I'd told him my story. *Let's make it quick, then.* "What do you want me to say? I woke up in that room, tied to a chair, with the woman across from me."

Rogers whipped out a notepad and a pen and started scribbling. "What did she look like?"

"I just told you – like me. Like I was looking into a mirror."

"Could it have been one?" the doctor suggested, looking at the inspector. "A mirror, I mean."

Rogers shook his head. "That room was completely empty apart from the chair they'd tied her to." His eyes swerved back to me. "And what else?"

"What do you mean?"

"How did you end up there?" He bit out the words without emotion. Or was I just imagining that? Surely he couldn't be that big an asshole.

"Do you remember who tied you up in that place, honey?" The doctor's voice did sound compassionate and understanding.

The police inspector sighed in irritation. "Ma'am, does the patient require any immediate medical attention?"

'The patient?' For real? Yep, my first hunch was spot-on: he really was an asshole devoid of human emotion.

"No, but…"

"In that case, would you be so kind as to leave us

23

alone for a few minutes?"

The doctor looked at him, her eyes ablaze. "I'm not going anywhere. Not before I tell her…"

"Could you at least do me the courtesy of not interfering?"

"I was just trying to help." The doctor shook her head before walking around the bed and positioning herself near the window, her arms crossed. "Jackass," I heard her mumbling under her breath.

"Ma'am?" Rogers fixed me with his stare.

"What?" I didn't want to do this anymore. I wanted to go home and leave all of this behind. And I definitely did *not* want to answer any more questions coming from this blockhead. Never in my life had I longed to see Mark more than I did now.

In response, the jerk decided to engage in a staring contest, pen and paper still in his hands.

"No, I can't remember how I ended up there," I snapped. "Trust me, it was the only thing on my mind as I was wasting away on the floor there. Now could you leave me in peace?"

"What's the last thing you do remember?"

"Being home, lying in my boyfriend's arms."

"Boyfriend?"

I nodded. "Mark."

From the corner of my eye, I saw the doctor whipping around to make eye contact with the inspector, who momentarily granted her that favor before turning his attention to me once again.

"And when was this?"

"Me being home, you mean?"

Rogers nodded.

"Hell if I know. I don't know how long I was kept in

24

that room for. Days, I'm guessing." I looked at the doctor for affirmation, who nodded at me, still with the same bafflement in her eyes. "So a few days ago, I suppose?"

That seemed to be the last straw breaking the camel's back. The doctor made a beeline for me. "Anna, can you tell me what today's date is?"

"Ma'am..." Rogers warned her.

"To hell with you, Inspector. Come back with your round of Twenty Questions later. Apparently, she's far worse than we thought." She searched my eyes and forced yet another smile. Jesus, that woman deserved a Raspberry Award. "Anna, what's today's date?" she repeated.

"What the hell kind of question...?"

"Please, Anna."

My fists clenched of their own accord and I felt rage coursing through my veins. "What the hell does it matter? I'm done with this shit. Obviously, there's more going on than you're willing to tell me. So please, just spit it out. I'm..."

"The date, Ma'am," Rogers insisted.

"You really don't know when to stop, do you?" I shook my head. "Some time at the end of April. Excuse me for not knowing the exact day. That's what being locked up in a gloomy room for days on end does to your memory. Shocker, right?"

"And the year?" the doctor asked.

"Year?"

Rogers sighed. "The year we live in."

"Two thousand fifteen, of course."

Again, secretive eye contact between the doctor and the inspector. Exchanged looks that gave me the creeps and took away my biggest securities.

My voice was suddenly no louder than a tentative whisper. "Isn't it?"

The doctor took my hand and squeezed it lightly. "Anna, it's 2017."

Wide-eyed, my gaze volleyed between her and the inspector, looking for the tell-tale sign of a mouth curling up when a bad actor is trying to pass off a lie as the truth. But I didn't see anything. Anything at all. "Don't be preposterous."

Rogers put down his notepad and pen, close to my feet on the bed, and retrieved his cellphone from his inner pocket. "Read the latest headlines, sweetheart. It's all online." He addressed the doctor next: "I think you might be right."

His voice was a murmur in the background. My fingers danced across the keys of the phone and my eyes scanned the headlines, determined to prove these two idiots wrong. But all the places I looked only seemed to support their story. "I don't get it."

"To be quite honest," the doctor piped up, "neither do we, Anna. You're a medical miracle."

"A what?"

"Once we knew your name, of course, we traced you by looking at medical files from before. You do remember being very ill?"

"My cancer, you mean? How could I forget?"

"Yes, the cancer. How long did you have to live, according to the doctors?"

"I'm sure you know the answer to that, doctor. It must be in my file."

"I'd like to hear you say it."

I sighed. "A year at most, if I was very lucky."

The doctor nodded. "Not only have we fast-

26

forwarded two years, but we also can't detect a single cancer cell in your system anymore."

I sat up and felt the pillow slide out from between my back and the bed. "Excuse me?"

The doctor nodded. "Now do you understand why I called you a medical miracle?"

The look in her eyes – this was no joke. She was being serious!

My body started to shake uncontrollably. One moment I was cold, the next I was hot. "I don't understand," I stammered. "Please tell me what the hell is going on with me."

"That's the million-dollar question," the doctor replied apologetically. "We don't know. We have no medical explanation, nor do we have…"

"Nor what?"

Rogers took over. "We were hoping you could provide *us* with some answers, Miss Meisner. If that's really your name."

I gave him a startled look. *Could he know?* But no, that was impossible. This guy was just a local police inspector. The secret me and my family were hiding was only known to the highest national authorities. We'd been trained not to talk about the life we had before ever again. To never use our real names again, not even among ourselves. You never knew who was listening in. After all these years I'd gotten so used to my charade that I even called myself by my new name in my own mind. I did that on purpose so I'd never slip up.

Play along, Anna, I thought. "Why wouldn't I…"

"Two years ago, Anna Meisner was terminal," the man sternly interrupted me. "With only months to live."

"I know perfectly well what state I'm in, Inspector," I

27

hissed.

"And she's been missing for the past two years."

"Missing?"

Okay, I hadn't seen that one coming.

Rogers nodded. "Overnight. Disappeared off the face of the earth."

"But that's impossible." I felt woozy. The headache started to pound again. "I was with Mark just a couple of days ago. Ask him. He'll…" I fell silent, looking around the room. No flowers, no postcard, not a single sign that Mark or whoever else knew I was in the hospital. "Where is he?" I whispered. "Where's Mark?"

The two people at my bedside shot each other a look. At last, the doctor spoke up. "Anna, there was a car accident. According to eyewitnesses, you and Mark Smith were on your way home after a birthday party. Your car collided with another one. Only two bodies were found – your boyfriend's and the other driver's. They never found yours."

"Correction," Rogers cut in. "Anna Meisner's body was never found. I don't know who this young lady is, but…"

"Don't be ridiculous, Inspector," the woman hissed. "We saw pictures of Anna. This girl doesn't just say that she is her, she *looks* exactly like her, too."

"True, but your research shows…"

"Yes, which is why we'll keep doing tests, Inspector. There has to be an explanation for this."

Thousands of questions tumbled through my mind. White spots blurred my vision. For just a second I considered telling them the truth, but I bit my lip. First of all, because my secret identity couldn't possibly have anything to do with my present bizarre situation, and secondly because I couldn't help feeling this was all orchestrated somehow. The reason for us to assume new identities and literally burn our past behind us, could very well be known to these people. They could be using it to draw me out. But most of all I mulled over what they'd just told me. Because what if it *were* true? "But… Mark…"

The doctor: "Anna. Mark's been dead for over two years."

-5-

Two days later I found myself at the police station. I swapped out the nightgown for an old pair of jeans and a red shirt, which they'd given me in the hospital. The questions were repeated, but now in a more bureaucratic fashion. No notepads and pens this time around. Everything was recorded on camera. And this time there wasn't a friendly doctor around either – someone who believed me, or at least pretended to. Apparently, her services weren't needed. Apart from some dehydration symptoms, I was as healthy as a fish. Well, physically at least.

The tiled interrogation room was dark and seemed to come straight out of a movie set, including the infamous mirror wall and the usual wooden chairs and table. On the other side of this table were two men, one of whom was Rogers. The other one – he'd introduced himself as Chief Inspector Bernard – was a bald-headed man who was so muscular his uniform was bursting at the seams. My guess was he praised God on his bare knees every single night for this job at the police force because the look in his eyes – I don't think I've ever seen anybody look that vacant in my lifetime – convinced me that no other workplace would have allowed him to get a position at the top.

"What's your real name?"

I heaved a sigh. We'd been over this at least three times. "Anna Meisner."

"You know we'll be staying right here until you tell us the truth." Bernard didn't look up from his notes. It was like a game of chess with similar moves every time. A round of questions was fired at me, and once I'd answered them all, he'd launch into a new round with more or less the same questions posed. Not only did he want to know my name, but he also inquired after my age. I'd wanted to say 'eighteen', then realized I missed two years, so that would make me twenty years old. So bizarre! He wanted to know how many direct relatives I had – four: mother, father, little brother, sister – where I lived – in the suburbs – what I was doing here – which was a damn good question – what had happened – why don't you look at those notes properly, you dick – and so on, and so on. It was driving me nuts. So half of the answers were lies, but I had good reason to lie.

"I'd be happy to give you a different name if that makes you happy, but that would *really* be a lie." I folded my hands and tiredly rested my elbows on the table. I decided to try a different angle. "I don't understand why you're keeping me here, calling me a liar. I mean, they fixed me up at the hospital, did just about any test they could come up with in order to establish what the hell is going on with me. Undoubtedly they took my blood, too."

"So?" Bernard prompted.

"Blood. DNA? Proof that I'm speaking the truth!" I knew the witness protection program had done a thorough job of erasing every detail of my previous life – and my family's.

"We can only determine your identity with DNA if

you have a criminal record," Bernard replied. "And during the investigation we conducted, it was revealed that you can't possibly be Anna."

"Excuse me?" *What a load of bull.* "What investigation? And what *did* it reveal, then? Who am I?"

"Nobody."

"Nobody?"

"A Jane Doe. Not a single name pops up in the database when we run the data."

"What?" I shot him an incredulous look. "How's that even possible?"

"That's a very good question. All the system comes up with is the name of Anna Meisner."

"And yet you still doubt my story? I heard you have photos of me. Or actually, photos of Anna."

"We have those in our possession, yes."

"So? Do I look like me?" I snipped.

"Spitting image, but that doesn't prove anything."

"Excuse me?"

Bernard folded his arms in front of him and nodded confidently. "Whoever you are, you're not Anna Meisner."

"What makes you so sure?" This guy was putting my back up, I was boiling with rage inside. I'd have loved to yank him out of that chair, drag him across the table and stomp him in the face. Which was indicative of the state of mind I was in – before this all happened to me, I was never this aggressive. Strange, that: what it does to you to be called a liar. I restrained myself with great difficulty.

"What do *you* think?" he said.

"I guess the cancer should have eaten me alive during the two years I've allegedly been missing?"

"Bingo."

Rogers tapped Bernard on his hairy arm. "Maybe we should give her time to come to terms. Let's grab some coffee and come back later."

I wasn't under the illusion that I was highly intelligent, but I wasn't stupid either. It was glaringly obvious that these two were trying to play good cop, bad cop, in the hopes that I'd eventually start to trust Rogers more and tell him what he wanted to hear. Unfortunately, the man was about as good at acting as the doctor at the hospital had been. I wasn't falling for it. Still, his idea wasn't half bad. Every minute that would spare me from being subjected to their barrage of questions would be a blessing at this point.

However, Bernard completely ignored him. "What was your connection to the two teenagers who "found you"?' He air-quoted the last two words.

"No connection." It took me a minute to let his question sink in. "Why the hell would you think I'm somehow connected to them?"

"Because you were the only three people present in that building."

"Ever heard of *coincidence*, Inspector? Those two were simply looking for a place to get it on, and I'm very happy to have ruined their horny plans."

"They could have had sex at home, too."

"You're not really big on the romance, are you? You've never been young?"

To my surprise, that got a chuckle out of Rogers. Bernard shot him a withering look, which prompted Rogers to get up and walk over to the door. "I'll get us something to drink, then. Glass of water, Jane?" He looked at me probingly.

"My name is *not…*"

The door slammed.

Just great, I thought. *Now I'm stuck with this wacko all by myself.*

"The fact is, Ma'am, I don't believe in coincidences," Bernard droned on.

"What are you getting at?"

"Maybe the three of you planned this whole thing. Or was it some kind of sex game gone wrong?"

"I was starving, dehydrated, and almost dead!"

"You wouldn't believe the lengths people go to for a bit of attention."

"You're one sick puppy, you know that?"

Bernard shrugged.

"You asked them the same idiotic questions?"

"The boy and girl are being held for questioning at the moment, yes."

On impulse, I looked around me, which was ludicrous, of course. "Are they here? In the same building? I haven't had the chance to thank them."

"So this wasn't some kind of set-up?"

"Of course it wasn't! What the *fuck* are you thinking?"

"I don't know what to think, Ma'am. That's exactly my problem."

I shook my head. In order to contain the rising pressure of a headache, I pinched the bridge of my nose between my thumb and index finger. "So let me get this straight: you think I'm in cahoots with the boy and girl who found me, that we all agreed to them tying me up naked because that's my kind of kink, after which they – what, forgot about me or left me there for days on *purpose*?

"The possibility exists."

34

"In your mind, maybe."

"Admittedly it's a long shot, but..."

"Gee, you think?"

"And I assume you can't give me another explanation?"

"No other explanation besides the truth, you mean? Why would we even engage in such a game? What's our motive, Mister Police Officer?"

Bernard sighed.

I didn't understand where he got the gall. If anyone was entitled to a long-suffering sigh here, it was me.

"You don't want to know what kids get up to these days to rock social media."

"Even *if* that were true: I spent days there without food or water, chilled to the bone. That alone can play havoc with your mental health."

"Is that how you want to play it?"

"I don't want to play at *anything*. I know as much as you do." Clenching my fists, I continued: "Dammit, you arrogant prick. Try to be in my shoes for a moment. Not only was I strapped to a chair for days and confronted with my alter ego committing suicide in front of my eyes, but I also somehow lost two years of my life. Plus, the cancer's left my body, and... and..." There it was at last: my point of no return. Postponed, but now hitting me irrevocably and with full force. Tears streamed down my cheeks. My stomach felt tight and my throat constricted. Words came from my mouth in a whispered stammer. Although we'd lived a lie in the past few years, at least it had been a normal lie. A normal life. Our identities had been faked, of course, or they'd have found us. We hadn't been too gung ho about it either. It was at the suggestion of the FBI! But this... this was a different kind of animal. Where had the last two years gone? How could I be cured? It just didn't add up. *And Mark. The love of my life. The one who just knew me as Anna and still loved me. Killed in an accident that should have resulted in my death as well.*

Back at the hospital I'd borrowed someone's phone and looked up images of the scene of the accident. Never had I been more shaken up by simply staring at photos.

Behind me, the door opened once more. From the corner of my eye, I saw Rogers enter the room, holding three cups in his hands. He sat down next to Bernard, put the cups down, and slid one across to me. My throat felt raw and swollen from emotion. Thankfully, I picked up the plastic cup and took a few sips of water.

"Now do you understand why we don't believe you're Anna?" For the first time, the Chief Inspector's voice sounded compassionate and friendlier.

I replied so swiftly that I almost choked on my water. "No, I don't understand how you can believe it's *not* me. Apparently I'm missing a chunk of two years from my memory, the same amount of time I went missing. Why would I think I'm delusional? That I'm *imagining* I'm Anna Meisner?" I looked at him, wiping the tears from my eyes. "What's the reason?"

"We're only trying to puzzle the pieces together, Jane," Rogers replied. "Like you pointed out yourself: you're supposed to be dead. That's harsh, I know, but it's true." He looked at Bernard searchingly. "You want me to show her the rest, too?"

Bernard nodded.

Rogers plucked a photo from his breast pocket and slid it toward me across the table. "You recognize this house?"

36

I gasped for breath when I saw the picture. It was my living room, there was no doubt about it. Everything was there: the dark-brown sofa, the black coffee table, the bookshelves and painting on the wall. Even though they were mostly blocked out by the guns, revolvers, knives, swords and hand grenades lined up in the room. In between the makeshift arsenal was a dead body.

"Joey?"

For the first time, the cops threw each other a baffled look.

"How..?" Tears rolled down my cheeks.

"After the disappearance of Anna Meisner and the death of her boyfriend, her younger brother lived in her old house for a while," Rogers said, suddenly sounding hesitant. "Bodies were found in the rest of the apartment building, too. The killings seemed random. But everything points to the murders starting in that one apartment. Witnesses described a young woman with long, brown hair looking suspiciously like you fleeing the scene. Just before the bodies were found."

"Hold up," I stammered. "Surely you don't think…"

"Unfortunately, we don't know what to think," Bernard complained. "Fact is: you're our only suspect."

"But that doesn't make sense! Even if I were the one you were looking for, why would I own up to being Anna Meisner? What would be the point?"

Bernard nodded. "That's what we're trying to find out."

-6-

Another cop – one wearing black pants, black shoes with thick soles, and a small pimple on his nose (I was noticing the weirdest of things right now, possibly because I had suing these bastards on the back of my mind) – escorted me from the interrogation room.

"Put her in cell five," a young woman behind the reception desk called out. "That one's available."

"Can I make a phone call there?" I asked. I had to talk to my parents. I longed for a fatherly hug and his voice telling me this was all one big misunderstanding. That he was on his way to take me home. In a way, I still had this feeling someone was about to jump out from a hidden corner and shout *Smile! You're on candid camera! Just kidding. Haha-fucking-ha.* "If anyone can tell you for sure who I am, it's my parents."

"You really believe we didn't think of that?" the officer replied. "We called them straight away when you were in the hospital. They were vacationing in China and of course they were flummoxed to hear that someone claiming to be their missing daughter had been admitted to the hospital over here. They were willing to book the first flight home, but most flights from China were called in the past few days due to bad weather."

"You're joking."

"I'm not. Apparently violent storms are a real

problem over there at the moment. Just your luck, huh?"

"But they're on their way, right?" Hope floated in my stomach.

The officer nodded. "I think they're scheduled to land in a few more hours."

"How about a lawyer?" I wanted to get in touch with the people in the witness protection program. They probably didn't know I was here, or they'd have gotten me out a long time ago. I was sure of it. Maybe they could explain to me what the hell was going on here. "I assume I'm entitled to phone my lawyer?"

"Someone's on his way on your behalf. We called him as soon as you were brought here. But this is upstate New York, young lady. We're not in a hurry like the people in NYC. My best guess is he'll be here tomorrow morning at the earliest. Until that time…" He escorted me to a row of day cells. Most of them were occupied. The next-to-last cell was empty. The officer opened the door.

"Now what?"

"Now you get in there."

"I'm not stupid," I snapped. "I mean, for how long? Will I be charged with certain things? You don't honestly think I'm connected to those weapons and all the dead people? And what about my little brother? Is he really…"

"It's late. They'll inform you about our next course of action in the morning."

"You can't just lock me up in here!"

"Can't we?"

"No, of course not."

I was shoved in the back, tripping forward into the cell. Behind me, the police officer slammed the door shut. "I guess we can."

And that was that. End of story. No one was going to tell me anything at all. Not tonight, anyway. With tears burning in my eyes and a runny nose, I sat down on the bed, which was the only thing in this small room apart from the toilet. Thousands of questions and images were tumbling through my mind.

Okay, recap: apparently I've lost two years of my memories. Nobody believes I'm Anna. And not only was my apartment used to store shit loads of weapons, but it was also the place where they found my brother's body. Witnesses saw someone who looked just like me running away from there right after the murders.

Joey… dead?

It all sounded ridiculous, even to me. How could they possibly think I had anything to do with the whole thing? How did they expect me to believe any of it?

The internal questions didn't help. I had to block them out but realized I'd lose the battle before it even started.

This isn't really happening. I'm not here. It's a misunderstanding that will be set right first thing tomorrow. They'll walk in here and apologize to me.

That night was terrible. I'd never felt more lonely, sad and confused. I didn't even know a person could cry this much. Peaceful snoring and voices mumbling to themselves next door carried into my own cell. Outside, the wind was howling along with me. At long last, I drifted off to sleep, but only due to my mental and physical exhaustion.

I was awake before the first light of day brightened the floor of my cell. Not much later, I heard the sound of footsteps in the hallway and the cell door swung open with squeaking hinges. I was sitting on my bed, my knees were drawn up to my chest and my arms circling my legs. My back was against the cold wall. I was dazed and completely worn out. Ever since I woke up I'd been rocking back and forth with a blank mind.

Bernard pinned me with his sickening gaze. He pointed to the door, whispering: "Hurry up, we don't have much time."

Surprised, I cocked an eyebrow. "Excuse me?"

"The guards are dead, but it won't be long before someone finds them. It's almost morning."

My breath hitched. "Is this some kind of test?"

"Not at all," the inspector told me. "Are you going to hurry up or not?"

I remained where I was. "I'm not going anywhere. My parents will be here in a few hours and so will my lawyer. They'll…"

"Don't try to tell me this isn't all an act, soldier."

"An act?"

"With Rogers present, I couldn't really speak freely, but I recognized you immediately. We can sense what the other is thinking, can't we? We were being watched before, so I had to play by their rules." He shrugged. "No matter. This works for me too."

"You've lost me."

"I was afraid you might say that." Bernard clucked his tongue disapprovingly. "It would actually be smarter to just kill you, but I want to give the person inside of you another chance."

Startled, I looked down at my body. *Inside of me? What's he talking about? This guy is stark raving mad!*

"I'm talking to that person directly now." Bernard took a threatening few steps in my direction. "Everything has been set in motion, but I hope you can

41

gain control once more. If not, you're useless to the cause and we'll be coming for you too."

I didn't see the blow coming. Pain shot through my head like a flash of white light. Then everything turned dark.

The next thing I remembered was waking up underneath a bench in what looked to be Central Park. I opened my eyes and stared up at the wooden slats and the gray sky above in confusion. Different scents and twittering birds made me turn my head. Besides the lawn and the flowers, I didn't see a soul. The park seemed to be deserted. No – that wasn't quite true. In the distance, I saw a young guy walking his dog. His eyes were glued to the display of his cellphone and he hadn't seen me at all.

One hand pressed to my throbbing head, I scrambled to my feet from underneath the bench. My legs swayed but I managed to stay upright. It took me a while to realize that I was no longer in the cell, even though I didn't understand how that was possible.

"We had to play by their rules. No matter, this works for me too."

"The smartest thing would be to kill you, but I want to give the person inside of you another chance."

"Everything has been set in motion, but I hope you can gain control once more. If not, you're useless to the cause and we'll be coming for you too."

Thousands of feelings passed through me.

It may sound strange, but the first thing that occurred to me was that I had to find my way back to the police station. After all, my parents would go there to visit me, and my lawyer would be there too. I wanted answers, dammit, and maybe they could give them to me. But that was a stupid thought, I concluded. That lawyer knew me about as well as I knew him. I'd been missing for over two years, had been about to croak because of cancer before that, and was a suspect in my brother's murder, among other things. No – my parents would have just as many questions as I did myself. Besides, I'd be behind bars once more, and that prospect wasn't exactly appealing.

Sure enough, sooner or later they'd track me down and drag me back to prison, pushing me for information about the person who set me free – if they hadn't found out already. They expected me to show up because I might plan to find my parents and they were waiting for me at the police station. But until that time, there was no point playing right into their hands – I wanted to use my newly-gained freedom to set the record straight and make plans.

One thing was clear to me now, at least. There was more to this whole story than I could remember. And I intended to put the pieces of the puzzle in my brain back together again.

-7-

Plagued by disturbing thoughts, I exited the park and strolled through familiar streets. Cars and people passed me by, not paying attention to the confused twenty-year-old in their midst.

Irrefutable proof of me missing two years was all around me – on the billboards, on the front page of newspapers being sold by newsagents. And yet it couldn't be true. I refused to believe it. Every time I thought about it, a shiver ran through me and I almost started to hyperventilate. My vision was distorted, and every car, dog, or person passing me by seemed to be a terrible creature staring at me menacingly, ready to tear me to shreds and devour me whole. It was a Herculean effort on my part not to break down screaming. I had to be strong – lock these thoughts away in the recesses of my mind, or I'd go off the deep end.

Aren't you already there, Anna?

I had to get off the streets. Calm myself down. Almost stumbling over my own two feet, I went into the first store that caught my eye. A bell above the door announced my visit.

Everything was dancing. I felt nauseous. Closing my eyes, I inhaled deeply. A musty smell penetrated my nose. The air was dry, as though it was filled with thousands of particles of dust and ash. I gagged and opened my eyes again.

An antique store?

I was standing between faded sofas, wooden tables and chairs, lamps, candelabras, rugs. And books – whole stacks of them, so high and wide that they almost blocked out the sunshine coming from the ceiling light.

On the other end of the only aisle the store seemed to possess, I saw a set of eyes observing me in wonder. The old man they belonged to was wearing crumpled clothes – old and faded. His gray beard was also typical. He leaned his elbows on the counter he was standing behind. The blueish glare of the laptop next to him cast an eerie glow onto his skin. "You all right, sweetheart?"

I shook my head. Not to tell him no, but to clear my vision, which he took the wrong way.

"No, you don't look too well, I must admit." He walked around the counter. "Glass of water, maybe?"

"Could I maybe use your phone?"

"Excuse me?"

"Your phone. Can I use it?"

The man laughed.

"What's so funny?"

The store owner raised his hands apologetically. "I'm sorry, but a girl your age asking *me* for my phone – that's just hilarious. I mean, the minute you're born you're basically holding a cellphone in your hands. My fifteen-year-old cousin for example: she owns three, and…"

I felt the headache resurface again. "I lost mine," I lied.

He took another good look at me. The corners of his mouth turned down. "I hope nothing serious happened to you?"

I quickly shook my head, not feeling the need to

unburden myself to a complete stranger. "If you would be so kind…"

"All right, all right." He dug around in his pants pocket, pulled out his cellphone, and held it out to me. "But keep it short."

I nodded gratefully, walked over to him, and took the phone from him. The moment my fingers wanted to punch in the number, I froze.

"Sir," I started. "I…"

"Let me guess. You don't remember the number."

"No, I don't."

"Of course you don't. All numbers are saved to your contacts these days. You don't need to remember any of them, which is why today's youth is so mind-numbingly stupid. In my time, I can tell you, in my time…"

"Don't you have a phone book or something? You know, an old-fashioned one?"

"Of course not. I haven't had one for years. But maybe you can find it on the internet." He gestured at his laptop.

I walked around the counter as fast as I could. "Thank you." My fingers danced across the keyboard.

"What happened to you, girl?" the man tried once more. His voice dropped to a solemn, lower tone. "You weren't… touched by anyone, were you?"

Touched? Oh, Jesus. "I don't want to talk about it."

"Sorry." He sounded indignant. "Didn't want to pry." He turned away. "I need to rearrange some stuff in the front." And with those words, he left me alone, for which I was eternally grateful.

So – where to start? You could find practically everything online. Names, addresses, your relationship status, sex tapes uploaded by your ex years ago… but with private landlines few and far between. Even the phone book only listed companies. My parents used to work for a big energy provider. I considered calling them for a moment, but I could already imagine the fruitless phone call. *"Hi, I'm Anna. Your two employees' daughter who went missing two years ago. What's that? Ah, yes, that's right, I'm actually supposed to be dead. But anyway, could you give me my parents' current phone number?"* Nope, not such a good idea. I couldn't really ask to talk to either of them without telling the person on the other line who I was, because they weren't there – they'd been on vacation when the police notified them of my situation. I hoped they'd be back by the time I came round to visit them. Also, I didn't know if they still worked there. After all, two years had gone by.

What would you tell your parents if you did know their phone number? If the police divulged to them that a woman looking like me is suspected of killing your younger brother, they might call the cops on you themselves.

No, they wouldn't.

Are you sure?

No, I wasn't. But I would soon find out because I was going to visit my parents no matter what.

Running out of options, I tried to log in to my Facebook account as a last-ditch effort in the hopes it was still active after two years. I typed in the password and luckily I was able to log in. My eyes skimmed the messages on my wall, and some of them weren't even that old yet. People who only knew me through friends and didn't know I was missing had congratulated me for my birthday last February. But I also saw a message from Joey on my timeline, more than a month before his death. *I miss you, Sis* were the only words. My eyes welled up

47

with tears. My heartbeat like a jackhammer and I started to perspire. "Miss you too, little brother," I whispered. When had I last spoken to Joey? To me, it felt like last week, but in reality, it had been many months ago.

So bizarre.

At the bottom of the screen, a chat window suddenly popped up.

Hey! This is my sister's Facebook account.

I couldn't believe my eyes.

How dare you hack into her account?

My fingers were trembling.

Hannah? I quickly typed back, afraid she'd sign out.

Who are you?

You're not gonna believe me when I tell you, I thought to myself. How was I supposed to break the news to her? The answer was simple: there was no good way.

You know what, I don't even care. Just take your paws off this account.

That final remark made me afraid she'd log out, so I just blurted it out.

It's me. Anna.

No response.

It took her a minute to reply: *Not funny, asshole.*

I know it's difficult to believe. I don't know what happened to me either. To be honest I've never been this scared in my life. Mom and Dad have already been alerted by the police. They know and they're on their way back from China to meet me at the police station. At least that's what was supposed to happen. By now they'll have heard I'm no longer there. I'm missing two years of memories, and... I swallowed, trying to control my breathing. This wasn't going to work. How the hell was I supposed to convince her? I had to get to the point, even though I doubted she'd respond to my next question as I typed it into the chat window.

Do you guys still live in Brooklyn Heights?

I also wanted to know whether they were still under surveillance, but we'd been taught never to discuss the witness protection program in public places. Which included messages on social media and emails. You never knew who was listening in, after all.

No response.

I only realized the store owner was standing behind me the moment I felt his hand on my shoulder. "Were you able to find that phone number?"

Like a young boy caught in the act of watching porn, I quickly clicked away the browser page.

"Unfortunately not." I handed the man his cellphone back. "Thanks for your help." And with those words, I ran from the store. I had no idea whether my parents were still living at the same address as two years ago, but there was only one way to find out – even though there was a good chance of police being stationed there to capture me.

Once outside, I suddenly screeched to a halt. On impulse, I rummaged through my pants pockets, as though I was seriously expecting to find money in them. With a sigh, I re-entered the store. The bell above the door jingled sofly. The owner looked at me with raised eyebrows.

"Any chance you could lend me some money for a cab?"

-8-

Not a word was spoken once I was inside the yellow cab toward Brooklyn. I felt tired, tense, and dozens of questions haunted me – just like the memory of Inspector Bernard's voice.

"Don't try to tell me this isn't all an act, soldier."

"It would actually be smarter to just kill you, but I want to give the person inside of you another chance."

A shiver slid down my spine.

A grumbling voice startled me. "Might as well have hitched a ride with that fella, Ma'am."

"Excuse me?"

The taxi driver jabbed a thumb over his shoulder. "That black car's been following us since you got in."

Alarmed, I looked behind me and spotted the car he was talking about. The driver made sure there were two or more cars between him and us. If the cabbie was right, it was a damn big coincidence that this car had followed us all the way across town. Too much of a coincidence? I decided to keep an eye out, half-expecting the car to turn into a side street and disappear. It didn't, though. Not even when I asked the driver to take a little detour.

I knew the cab driver had been kidding. He'd said it in a joking way. Maybe he'd just wanted to break the awkward silence in some lame attempt to have a chat with me, but I was beginning to feel paranoid.

It's the people who tied you to that chair. They're not done with you yet! Another thought popped up. *What if all of this is connected to your father? What if the Colombians are behind all this and they're the ones following you right now? You'd lead them straight to your parents' door.*

My heart thumped like crazy and my palms turned clammy. Just as I was about to get out of the cab near a traffic light and hurtle into a shopping mall – try getting to me when I'm part of a larger whole, you dipshits – the Volkswagen finally disappeared from view. I heaved a sigh of relief, shaking my head.

Jesus, Anna. If you fall into the trap of imagining things and being strung along by your own fantasies, you can kiss your sanity goodbye for good.

"Whoa. You look like you just saw a ghost," the cabbie said to me. "You feeling all right?"

I ignored him. I didn't think he deserved an answer after he terrified me with his comment, even if he only meant it as a joke. I saw him glancing into the rearview mirror to take me in and finally shrugging his shoulders as if to say: *Whatever.*

Our street in Brooklyn Heights hadn't changed much. The small neighborhood still contained the same brownstone houses crammed together, the same little park with the red slide across the street, and the same kind of trees. The familiar sight made me doubt my two years of absence once again, but I knew I had to stop kidding myself.

The cab parked in front of number 50. I mumbled a thank-you to the driver, paid him, and got out. As the car slowly rolled away, I stood there rooted to the spot to stare up at the house I'd lived in for years.

A whole movie reel of memories played out in my

mind's eye. Like ghosts, I saw visions of me and my siblings playing a game. We'd only been in this house for a few weeks and we still had to get used to our new lives, so we'd looked up in alarm at every unexpected sound. This whole FBI business had thoroughly shaken up our lives. We were whispering. The voices echoed forlornly and gave me the creeps.

A bit further down the road was my seventeen-year-old me – the girl who'd gotten used to living a lie. She was standing hand in hand with Mark. I remembered this moment so vividly. How could I not? It was the first time we kissed.

I felt the tears well up again. In an effort to suppress them, I closed my eyes and shook my head. When I looked back up, the images were gone.

There was no doubt that this was the same house I'd grown up in. So why were the drapes in the windows different, and why was the garage door green instead of red? Why was the whole front yard different? Okay, I told myself, a lot can change in two years' time. And yet I felt a tight cluster of nerves knotting together in my stomach.

Where are the cops?

Astonished, I let my gaze drift through my street. No one.

Isn't it obvious this would be the first place I'd go to? I can't imagine they haven't thought of this back at the station. Or am I missing something?

Just then, my ears detected the sound of an approaching car. Tires squeaking on the asphalt and the hum of an engine. I looked sideways and saw a black Volkswagen turn into our street on the other end, parking there. The sound was drowned out by three laughing kids rounding the corner on their bikes. They shot me puzzled looks, then kept going and cycled away from me. I barely noticed them. My attention was solely focused on the black car. Suddenly it all became clear to me.

Would the Colombians – or whoever tied you to that chair – be waiting for you here? No, it's the police, Anna. They tracked you down and decided to follow you. Or worse yet: what if that cop who set you free staged the whole escape together with the others and watched your every move, to see where you'd go? What if this whole thing is a set-up?

Was that the reason why they still hadn't arrested me?

I clenched a fist. Where did they get off? Did they honestly expect me to seek refuge in yet another house filled to the brim with weapons so I could go on another killing spree? Even *if* I were the killer they were looking for, surely I wouldn't be deemed that stupid?

This is probably their best chance.

Some part of me wanted to walk over there and confront them. Maybe they'd leave me alone once they realized they'd been made. And let's be honest, if they really were the police, those guys needed to be sacked pronto. I mean, if common people like me and the cabbie could spot them from miles away, they were putting the entire department to shame. But I decided to let them stew in their own juice. So they wanted to know where I was going and what I was up to? Fine. I had absolutely nothing to hide.

You really are being paranoid, Anna. It's just a black car parking on this street.

But it followed me!

There are more black cars in this world. How do you know this is the same one? Did you remember the license plate?

No, but…

And even if it followed you, that doesn't mean a thing. Maybe it's just someone who had to run errands downtown and now he's come back home.

That doesn't make sense!

It being the police, now that wouldn't make sense.

Hell no! It's the same damn car, I'm sure of it!

How can you be sure of anything after what happened to you?

Come on, I'm not crazy.

You tell me. You're the one debating with yourself.

I silenced my inner voice before heading for the front door of my childhood home to knock on the door.

God, I so longed for my mom or dad to open the door.

Footsteps on the other side. Mumbling. The squeaky door opened to a crack and an unfamiliar man faced me with a dubious look on his face. His skin was dark, a bald head, and a black beard that seemed to grow larger as he opened his mouth to speak. "Yes?"

I was shocked. My tongue stuck to the roof of my mouth like it was petrified.

The man narrowed his eyes and took me in.

"Jason, is that Amanda?" a female voice behind him piped up. "Tell her to come in. What with all that's happened, I think it's safer to stay indoors."

"It's not Amanda," the man replied.

"Then who is it?"

Those words shook me from my stupor. "I, uhm…"

"You need help?" the man ventured.

"Sorry," I stammered. "I'm looking for the Meisner family."

"Meisner? I'm sorry, they don't live…" The man paused mid-sentence and lifted his index finger in the air, as though he was telling me to be quiet. "Wait." He turned around to address the woman inside. "Honey? The Meisner's. Weren't they the people who used to live here before us?"

"No clue. Maybe. The name rings a bell, vaguely. Why?"

The man ignored her question and turned to me again. "Yes, I think that's it."

"What's what?"

The man nodded to himself. "We took over this house from them, one and a half years ago."

"But..." I stuttered, feeling confused. "My sister – she told me..."

"Your sister? I'm sorry, I'm not sure why..."

"You happen to know where they moved to?" I interrupted him.

The man cast an anxious look into the street behind me. "We don't talk, but I run into them every now and then when I'm doing groceries. I think they moved a few streets down. Now, if you don't mind..."

"Which street?"

The man shrugged. "No idea. Like I said: we don't talk. But if I were you, I wouldn't worry about that right now."

"How so?"

"You mean you haven't heard the news yet? It was broadcast fifteen minutes ago. And it seems to be getting worse by the minute. I urge you to get indoors quickly. It's..." The man shot me a dazed look, shaking his head before he slammed the door in my face.

Gee, thanks for nothing.

Completely stupefied, I turned around and walked back to the street. What the hell had he meant? I decided not to pay his words any heed. If it were truly important, I'd hear about it sooner or later. Right now I was conflicted about something else entirely.

"I think they moved a few streets down."

My eyes darted from left to right, inspecting each and every house. Did they move? Why? Was that even allowed? Had their identities been compromised? Were they in any danger? I couldn't think of another reason. But still – moving houses and staying in the same area? Wouldn't that defeat the entire purpose?

Okay, so now what? I debated with myself to ring the doorbell of every single house in the neighborhood. What other option did I have? Sooner or later, either my parents or my sister would open one of the doors.

Yeah, unless they happen to be out.

Even if they were out, this area was only small. *Sooner or later, I will find them.* That thought put me somewhat at ease.

But what will you do once you find them?

That was a very good question. I hadn't thought it through that far. What was I going to tell them? How would they react if their daughter, who was presumably dead, would show up on their doorstep? I hoped they'd be over the moon. And maybe they would be – eventually. Their first reaction would be one of shock and disbelief. And yet, I had to try!

At that precise moment, the air alarm went off.

-9-

The sound could shatter crystal. It was so high-pitched that it seemed to cut straight through my eardrums and mingled with the barking of dogs jumping up and down behind various windows looking out on the street, and the quacking of the ducks on the pond, now taking flight in a flurry of panic.

It didn't take long before the people living here broke into a panic, too. Within minutes, front doors were flung open and entire families carrying bags and suitcases legged it to their cars. Like they'd been waiting for the hammer to fall, and that air alarm had been the last straw, their cue to leave the sinking ship. It was bizarre, considering the fact that an alarm like this was usually raised to tell people to stay indoors. It made me cower with fear. I was rooted to the spot. What in all the hell was wrong for people to organize themselves into a mass exodus like this?

Not everyone made for the streets, however. In some houses, I saw people closing the shutters and all the doors in a hurry.

Despite everything, I couldn't stop myself from frantically looking around to maybe spot one of my family members. No luck, though.

"Hey, you. Get in here!" A young woman in her thirties with short, blonde hair was standing on the threshold of the house across the street. She was beckoning me inside. "It's not safe out."

"What's going on?" I asked.

"Just get in here," she replied.

I spurred on my legs to get moving. As I crossed the street and ran toward the woman, I looked up at the sky, half-expecting to see something horrible. Although it wasn't raining yet, the sky looked gray – almost black – and ominous.

In the distance, I saw two men getting out of the black Volkswagen. Both of them were holding cellphones pressed to their ear, and they ran into one of the houses. I was sure one of them shot me a threatening look before he disappeared from view.

I'd barely taken two steps into the hallway before the door was slammed shut behind me.

"What's happening?" I stammered.

A man dashed out of the kitchen, running in the direction of the living room. He was skinny, bald, and he was wearing round glasses. "It took the world just a half hour to go completely nuts!" Before he stormed into the living room, he abruptly halted midstride to stare at me, as though this was the first time he realized there was a stranger standing in his hallway. In surprise, he looked from me to his wife.

"I couldn't leave her out on the street, honey," was her reply.

Without responding, the man continued his run toward the living room.

The woman gently shoved me forward while mumbling her name was Carla and pushed past me into the living room.

I couldn't get in after her fast enough.

The room wasn't big as it was and seemed even smaller because there was a corner sofa crammed into it, plus a side table and a gigantic bookcase containing a large TV on the middle shelf.

Images flashed across the screen. At first, I seriously thought they were watching a movie – it had to be. The TV flooded the room with death and destruction. Forest fires, exploded cars, armed lunatics shooting people in the street. A newsreader appeared next, his eyes bulging with shock and his face white as a sheet. "… really don't know what to say…"

The next image was one of a large city – Paris, from the looks of it, although I wasn't sure. It lay in ruins, practically all the buildings had been destroyed. The few things still standing were crumbling walls rising from piles of shattered bricks. The air was gray with ash. Black flecks of something – burned bodies, most likely, but I pushed the thought away before it'd make me shriek with terror – drifted through the air. The news ticker showed us a text: *Third World War. Nuclear bombs dropped onto Paris and Washington – millions of casualties.*

I stared at the images with increasing alarm. My jaw kept dropping and my fingers clawed into my own palms, digging my nails into my skin. I started to tremble. If I hadn't absent-mindedly sat down on the armrest of the sofa, I probably would have fallen down on the floor. My hand pressed against my mouth, I ventured: "This is not happening, is it?"

The woman completely ignored me, mouth agape and her eyes glued to the screen.

"This is unbe-fucking-lievable!" the man yelled, pointing to the screen demonstratively.

"War?" I stammered. "Who… where..?"

59

Outside, the air alarm kept howling.

"That's just it," Carla responded, shaken from her stupor. Her tone was defeated and almost mild. "No one knows who started this."

"That's their party line," the man snapped. "Don't you believe those assholes in the White House don't have a clue. They wouldn't tell us, of course." He restlessly paced up and down the room.

Ignoring him, the woman continued with her gaze still fixed on the screen. "It looks like a number of countries fired nuclear missiles all at exactly the same time."

"A half-hour ago, everything was fine." He angrily gestured at the TV. "And now look what's going on."

"But that doesn't make sense," I exclaimed.

As though it was sinking in only now, Carla turned around to face her husband, unadulterated panic replacing her incredulity. "What if we're next, Hank? What if they nuke NYC too?"

"In that case, there's not a damn thing we can do about it. But even if they don't..." He walked back to the kitchen and returned with a roll of tape.

"What are you doing?" the woman asked, her voice cracking.

"Washington was wiped off the map. That's only a four-hour drive away. If the wind is coming from the southwest, the radiation can reach us here within days, and the weather forecast did say the wind was going to be quite strong."

"Jesus Christ!" Carla and I blurted out in unison.

I clapped my hand over my mouth, but ultimately I shook my head as something occurred to me. "No, a nuclear explosion would have generated an electromagnetic pulse which would have disabled all electronic devices. There's no way a camera crew could have filmed those images we just saw."

Hank seemed to consider my observation. "You might be right, but I'm not taking any chances," he concluded, nodding to his wife. "Go upstairs and close all the windows. I'll go around and stop up the chinks on the first floor."

Carla seemed about to protest, then thought better of it when she saw the look Hank was giving her. She trudged up the stairs.

I was wondering whether he wasn't taking things a bit too far. At the same time, I doubted his actions would be of any help if he was indeed correct. "Can I help you with something?"

The man seemed to have forgotten about my existence altogether. "Huh?" Again, he shot me a surprised look. "Well, yeah. Can you check all the windows and doors on this floor? Make sure the cracks are sealed, too."

At that precise moment, we heard gunshots, followed by screams and a lot of barking. The sound of shattering windows followed. It was barely loud enough to rise above the din of the fire alarm, but it still shook us both up. Muttering a curse, Hank rushed to the windows. My heart was beating way too fast as I followed him.

On the other side of the street, we spotted eight men walking side by side, toting guns while laughing and shooting at the houses they passed. They also shot at the people who were milling about carrying suitcases, making them scurry in all directions like horses on the run. Some managed to get away, but most of them got shot.

Two doors down, I saw the two men who had been in

the black Volkswagen bursting through the front door, guns at the ready. "Police! Drop your weapons." In all the hubbub, their voices were practically drowned out, but I heard them just fine. Fuck, I'd been right! Those two had really been on my tail.

I hate being right.

On the other hand – they were trying to save innocent people now. Didn't they deserve my respect for that?

They took cover behind parked cars and fired at the other men. Their aim was lousy. Despite the fact that the armed men didn't duck away, only two out of eight were shot – and one of them staggered back up soon afterward. The other six soon spotted the two cops and opened fire. The fight that ensued didn't last long. Do I need to tell you who won? I didn't think so.

"Carla, get your ass down here and bring my baseball bat," I heard Hank shout.

Carla's halting voice, hardly audible because of all the noise: "Why?"

"Get your head out of the clouds and look outside!" Hank threw me the roll of tape. "Go finish what I started."

"And what are you up to?"

Without a reply, he stormed into the kitchen once again, re-emerging soon after with a large butcher's knife in his hands. "If those thugs break down the door…"

Two women and one man wielding a baseball bat and a knife versus a whole slew of armed hooligans. Nope, our chances didn't look too good from up close. "Let's hope they don't."

I glanced out of the window once more and saw a man running away from a young boy who had been gunned down, screaming with rage. Shouting at the top of his voice, fists flying, he ran straight at the armed men. "My son! You sons of bitches!" I never heard a full-grown man yelling in such a high-pitched voice before. The fact he was charging at the shooters made five other men and women brave enough to kick into action as well. Maybe they thought they could be heroes, like those people stopping the terrorists from crashing that other plane into its final destination on 9/11. Of course, those heroes were no longer around to tell the tale, but that didn't occur to them at this moment. The only thing that mattered to them was to protect their friends and family.

Those people don't have the time to stop and think, girl. It's nothing more than a reflex.

Of course, what they were doing was utterly stupid, and yet I felt a certain admiration for their bravery. Part of that bravery was most likely anger mixed with a generous helping of adrenaline. All in all, they got quite far – the man crying for his son the furthest. Just when he was about to jump one of the shooters, he was shot in the head, flipping him backward and slamming his body onto the pavement. A few seconds later, the others were also lying motionlessly in puddles of blood.

Upstairs, I could hear Carla let out a muffled cry. She had apparently caught on to what was happening outside. She stormed down the stairs, looking pale as death. With a glassy, uncomprehending look in her eyes, she stared at us both. "Now what?"

"What we were planning on, and let's hope they don't enter the houses." Hank looked outside again. "They're not carrying bags or anything. They'll run out of ammo eventually."

I stopped the chinks around the doors with tape and

stayed as far away from the windows as I could. Not just because I wanted to avoid being seen by the shooters, but also because I didn't want to see the bodies.

"Hank! Look over there!" Carla's voice rose above the noise. Both Hank and I looked her way. She'd made a beeline for the TV and pushed up the volume so we could hear it above all the racket outside.

"…are advised to stay indoors and lock windows and doors. The police and the armed forces are trying their hardest to arrest as many of these assailants as they can, or take them down. The situation is under control…"

Liars!

Various burning towns and villages appeared on screen, where soldiers were crawling around battered streets covered in debris and opening fire on clusters of armed people. These weren't just men – women, children, and some fellow soldiers were among them! At first, I thought the army had lost it – that they were firing at innocent people – but then I saw the weapons in the hands of these children and their parents.

"Under control?" Hank guffawed. "Bullshit."

"So there are other lunatics with guns roaming the streets?" Carla restlessly paced the room.

"This is a national TV channel," I replied. "Which means they could be talking about the same phenomenon, nationwide."

"Nationwide? Have they all gone mental?"

"In the meantime, people are recommended not to drink any tap water," the newscaster droned on. "This morning, hundreds of people were admitted to the hospital with severe stomach problems. Tests concluded that the water had been poisoned. It is best to stick to bottled…"

Carla switched off the TV. "I can't take this anymore." She tottered over to Hank and fell into his arms. Each sob shook her shoulders.

Hank tried to console her but kept an eye on the window all the time to be on the lookout for those shooters.

As for me, I'd slipped down along the wall until my bum hit the wooden floor. I shook my head in disbelief and felt my heart hammering in my throat. My stomach felt like there was a brick inside. Every now and then, I had to gasp for breath because my body seemed to forget it was a basic reflex to breathe.

"Don't try to tell me this isn't all an act, soldier."

"It would actually be smarter to just kill you, but I want to give the person inside of you another chance."

It was a crazy thought, but somehow I started to believe this may all be happening because of me. Which was nonsense, obviously. How could the end of the world – which it increasingly started to look like – have *anything* to do with little old me? And yet, I could *sense* this was the case, as though a repressed memory was struggling to get to the surface, but couldn't quite make it yet.

I shook off the thought. I had to, or I'd lose it. Other thoughts popped up, however.

The first of which was: *my family!*

According to the man across the street, they still lived somewhere in this area. It was a Sunday, so the chance of them being at home was there. In that respect, those murderers outside couldn't have picked a better day for their carnage. But what if they were trying to run, like all the others? What if *they* were the ones who'd been shot at just now?

65

The second of which being: *those poor souls outside.*

Both thoughts gave me the strength to scramble up. Partly hiding behind the wall, I cast another look outside. No more shots were being fired, but I could still see those men. They were now strolling along a frighteningly empty street. The only sound that was audible now was some plaintive yammering and the barking of dogs – they'd taken out the air alarm in this area, but the one a little ways away was still going.

The men stepped over the bodies and turned the corner.

I hurriedly let my gaze drift through the street. A lot of windows in parked cars and houses had been shattered. The pavement was littered with suitcases, duffel bags, baby car seats, and dead bodies. I recognized the two girls who'd cycled past me not a half-hour ago. Now they were lying on the sidewalk, bleeding.

Dead?

I clenched my fist and swallowed down my emotions. My throat felt sore. Why would anyone do this?

I didn't see anyone looking like my parents or sister. It gave me a glimmer of hope. I made a decision. "Come on!" I rushed to the front door.

"What are you doing?" Carla inquired.

"I'm going outside, of course."

"You're *what*?"

"Are you out of your mind?" Hank replied.

"Listen." I tapped my left ear. "You hear those cries? Some of the victims will be dead, but they're not all dead. They need help. Besides, my family is out there somewhere…"

"So are those trigger-happy assholes."

"They rounded the corner. I'm not hearing any more

shots. Maybe they ran out of ammo like you said."

"Or maybe not and they'll be back. And if it starts to rain, it might be radioactive water coming down. You'll have an increased risk of getting cancer."

Been there, done that.

"Surely it'll take a bit longer than that?" Carla wondered aloud. "That bomb was dropped on Washington just one hour ago."

Hank shrugged. "Damned if I know. But I'm not going to take that risk. How about you?"

"We can't just leave them lying there! I threw back. "There are children bleeding to death, goddammit! I studied medicine. The least we can do is staunch the bleeding."

Carla and Hank remained frozen.

Incredulous, I shot them a derisive look. "Jesus! At least have the decency to call an ambulance."

"And you think it's gonna show up?" Hank hissed. "Just look at the news. The whole world is going to shit. ERs will be overflowing."

"We should at least try, right?"

Carla wiped away her tears and got to her feet. "She's right, Hank. They're our neighbors."

With a snarl, Hank jumped to his feet. "When will you get it through your thick skulls? It's every man for himself out there."

Startled, Carla took a step back. "This is not like you, Hank. Since when are you such a sadist?"

"Sadist?" He shook his head. "I guess you mean realist."

"Yeah, you know what?" I interrupted the two turtledoves and their bickering. "Go fuck yourselves. Just stay put. See if I care." And with those words, I threw open the door and ran outside.

I came to a stop in the middle of the road. Sitting inside watching the events safely from behind windows was one thing, but being smack in the middle of it was something else altogether. I could smell smoke, mingled with a strange, all-pervading odor that I couldn't quite place. In the distance, billowing smoke rose above the houses as though they were on fire.

The city!

The wind had picked up, as if it had decided to participate in all the craziness, and covered me like a blanket of ice. It started to rain softly.

It might be radioactive, I could hear Hank say at the back of my mind.

No, I reasoned. *Carla's right. It can't be here yet, can it?*

Howls of revulsion, cries of pain.

I hurriedly started to move, not having the faintest idea where to go, so I headed for the first two bodies I spotted. Two little boys were propped up against the tires of a Jeep, unmoving. I sank to my knees next to them. A few yards away was a man crouched and leaning against a tree. Bullets had hit him in the chest, legs, and neck. All of them had a glassy look in their eyes. Blood had colored the streets red. It was diluted by rivulets of rain and washed down to the sidewalk and down the sewer. I didn't have to check their pulse to know that they were dead.

I swallowed down the lump in my throat.

"Oh, God. No!" someone exclaimed close to me.

Adrenaline still pumping through my body, I looked up. A woman was sitting on her knees next to an elderly lady who was gasping for breath while staring up at the sky. Her flowery dress was red from the blood dripping from her abdomen.

Before I had the time to rush over to them, my attention was drawn by a male voice, belonging to a man who was hunched on the street two doors down, cradling a seemingly dead girl in his arms. A bit further down was a dog, squeaking so loudly at me that it seemed he was trying to say: "Come over here! It's my owner, he's not moving anymore."

Bile rose in my throat and I felt sick. Being a medical student, I'd seen my fair share of misery, but this... the horrifying reality of it all, the images on the TV, combined with the things I'd lived through in the past few days, made it very hard for me to pull myself together and let all things fall by the wayside except the here and now. On top of all that, these things had happened right in front of me. It was only when I took the time to really take a good look around that I realized how many victims there were, and how many of them needed help.

I couldn't do this alone.

Keep your mind focused, Anna. No matter what you do, don't lose control.

From the corner of my eye, I saw people shuffling out of their houses, hands pressed to their mouths and all blood drained away from their faces. Some of them emitted such shrill cries that they almost didn't sound human, whereas others lost all muscle power in their legs and simply sagged down on their porch steps, crying.

I felt a hand on my shoulder and turned around.

Carla's cheeks were streaked with tears, but at the same time, she looked as though she had some fight left in her. She kept looking over my shoulder, as though to check the shooters weren't coming back. "Our house is too small. We could shelter some of the wounded in our living room or in the attic, but not all of them, I'm afraid."

"But I thought Hank said..." I paused mid-sentence when I saw him behind her, picking up a crying, pregnant girl to carry her inside.

I wiped my tears away. "Most of them are dead."

"We can't just leave them out here, can we?" Carla said.

"I'm afraid we don't have a choice." I pointed to the other houses and was happy to see that other people had shown up to help the injured. "They might be able to harbor a few of the wounded, but I'm not sure they'd be willing to keep bodies in their..."

Again, I paused mid-sentence.

The barking of a second dog drew my attention to something further down the street. A Labrador restlessly ran in circles, right next to a Mercedes parked askew in the middle of the road. The pavement was littered with shards of glass, one of the tires was flat, and the car itself had a few dents, but I hardly registered it. Bullets had shattered the windshield and created three large holes through which I was just about able to see two heads.

I shrieked.

My legs felt like rubber. My heart skipped a beat. The world moved in slow-motion before completely grinding to a halt for just a second. All the sounds faded away. A heavy silence replaced the hubbub. It felt like my feet were sinking, sucked down further and further by quicksand until my ankles were lodged firmly in place. I couldn't move.

No, no, no!

Exactly when the world started to turn again, making the quicksand disappear and prompting me to move, I couldn't tell. But the next thing I remember is yanking the door on the passenger's side open and screaming with incredulity:

"Dad! Mom!"

My father's head had been knocked backward, his chin pointing up. Blood seeped from the wound in his forehead. A string of saliva was dripping from his open mouth. Part of my mom's neck had been blasted to bits. Her hands were tainted with red, which had probably happened when she tried to staunch the bleeding. Now, all she could do was lean against her dead husband's shoulder, her eyes wide open.

No, no, no!

I seized them both by their shirts and shook them back and forth. I hit my dad's cheek, hoping he'd open his eyes. I hurled and banged against the car door. Snot was dripping from my nostrils. My hoarse cries turned to sobs and a flood of tears. Everything inside me felt warm, burning.

The Labrador kept barking, trying his best to worm his way into the car to revive his two owners. I could hardly fend him off with my leg.

Stay away, I thought angrily. *These are* my *parents!*

The rain started to fall harder, the drops battering the roof of the car. Because of all the sounds, I almost missed the begging voice coming from the back seat.

"Help me."

With sweaty palms and a perpetual lump in my throat, I grappled for the headrest next to me. Eyes widening, I glanced past my parents. In between three haphazardly chucked-in suitcases, there was a girl.

Jesus... Hannah!

She was covered in blood and was pressing her hand against her shoulder, her face taut with pain. Her curly black hair was tangled, her glasses had slipped down her nose, but I'd recognize my little sister everywhere.

As soon as she saw me, her eyes turned big as saucers. She looked at me disbelievingly and almost seemed to forget the pain she was in.

For the first time in many years, she called me by my true name.

"Paula?"

-10-

2009

I was eleven when it happened. My mother had picked us up from school a few hours ago: me, my little brother and sister. As she was busy preparing dinner, we were bumming around on the sofa, bickering about which channel to watch. We'd been so involved in our fight that I didn't even hear the front door open. It was only when I heard my mom's surprised voice that I turned around to look.

My father stepped into the living room. His folded coat was dangling from his arm and he was carrying his briefcase in his left hand. He seemed perfectly normal, except for the look in his eyes. It was hollow – terrified, even. Ashen rings were visible around his eyes. His skin had a deathly pallor. He plonked down in the first available seat while shaking his head.

Joey and Hannah – those were not their names at the time, but to avoid confusion I'll stick to the fake names they'd be given later on – didn't notice at first that something was wrong. They were too young for that at the time. All they noticed was that their dad was home, so they tumbled off the couch in order to give him a hug.

"Hey, little rascals." My father's voice was barely above a whisper. He dropped his case on the floor and hugged the three of us.

"Daddy, are you all right?" Joey let go of my dad and

looked up at him in confusion.

"I'm afraid I'm not, kiddo."

Only now did I realize that my dad wasn't the only one to have come in. Two men in uniform had followed him in, both of them showing us a forced smile. Their eyes betrayed the horror that was about to descend upon us.

"Jacob, who are these men?" My mother's voice sounded shrill.

In the background, a laugh track poured out of the television speakers. My father wordlessly extended his arm, so Hannah could dump the remote control in his outstretched hand. He switched off the TV. "We need to have a talk. All of us."

My mother's gaze morphed from surprised into accusatory. She narrowed her eyes and her mouth pressed down in a grim line. "What have you done?"

"Where's Steph?" was my dad's only reply.

"He's been upstairs for hours," my sister told him, almost beaming with pride for betraying her older brother. Yes, I do have another brother, but there's a good reason why I haven't brought him up so far. "He's just been lying around on his bed texting with Kim. One weekend without her and he's practically heart-broken. I wouldn't be surprised if they moved in together soon."

Normally speaking, that would have gotten a chuckle out of my dad. But now he just asked for someone to call Steph down, addressing no one in particular.

"Steph, downstairs. Now!" my mom hollered, before anyone else had the chance to open their mouths.

It took a while before we heard footsteps. A door flew open. Steph sauntered down the stairs and stopped on the bottom step, a question in his eyes. "What's…" He fell silent when he saw the two uniformed men. Slowly, he stepped into the room. "What's going on? Did I do something wrong?"

"Not you, son," one of the men replied. His voice was low and his eyes were a bright blue color. "Your father did."

"Dad?" Steph moved closer, grabbing a chair from behind the dinner table so he could have a seat.

"Jacob, you're scaring us." My mom's voice trembled. "What the hell is going on?"

My father's hands were shaking. "Could I have a glass of water, please?" Only now did it occur to me that he hadn't looked anyone in the eye ever since he came in.

Steph got up again, walking over to the adjacent kitchen to get him a glass of water, which he put down on the coffee table in front of my dad. No one spoke. I held my breath. I don't think I'd ever felt a tension this heavy inside our house. What had my father done? Surely it wasn't anything serious? No, of course it wasn't. My father took good care of us. He worked a lot, but being an entrepreneur was hard work. That's what my mom always told us if he missed dinner. To me, 'home' wasn't the house we were currently living in – my father's dream house, the estate he bought one year ago. Home, to me, was still the small row house I'd grown up in, on the edge of town, in a neighborhood where I knew everybody. I kind of liked this house, too, but it was much too big for my taste. Eight bedrooms, three bathrooms, a cinema in the basement, a garage that could house up to four cars, a front view of the sea, and a golf court in our back yard. The transition had been too big for me. I was happy that the jewelry business was going so well and I understood why my father thought all this luxury would make us happier, but it didn't work that way. It was hard, leveling with the rich kids around here. I felt closer to Savannah, our housekeeper, than to them.

But every time my dad did come home, the slate was wiped clean. Because all those times he was truly there for us. He played games with us, laughed as he asked how our day had been, and tucked us in when it was time for bed. Always in a good mood, always sweet to us. Especially because of that, I couldn't imagine anything serious could be the matter. And yet, the shame on my father's face was telling enough.

He was clearly trying to pluck up the courage to speak up, to find the words. He clenched a fist, took another sip of water, but his gaze ruefully remained fixed on the floor. "I'm afraid I've made a big mistake."

"What kind of mistake?" Hannah asked.

Joey nodded at the two unfamiliar men. "Are you guys cops?"

"Something like that," the broadest of the two replied. He had a very round head. A pair of glasses were perched on his nose. It was obviously taking too long for him, because he turned around to face my mother before stating: "Your husband is being sued for money laundering and supporting criminal organizations, Ma'am."

"*What?*" Their eyes wide, both my mother and Steph jumped up from their seats.

"What's money laundering, Daddy?" Joey inquired.

"Criminal organizations?" I mumbled, aghast.

Hannah only managed to stare at my dad in utter bewilderment.

"Let's start out by saying I'm innocent." My father

76

shot the round-headed man a reproachful look. "I already talked to my lawyer and he says we have a strong case."

"I don't get it," I blurted out.

My father folded his hands. "It's like this: I've done some trading with people who turned out to be in possession of illegal funds."

"Why don't you just give it to us straight, Dad?" Steph asked, his voice trembling. "What did you do?"

"Diamonds," my dad sighed. "Jewelry, precious gems. I sold them for heaps of money to a select few and kept it out of the books."

"But you're a trader," Steph replied. "A jeweler. That's your job, right?"

"That's what I've been trying to tell the folks from the FBI."

"So, you're FBI?" I asked the two men.

They both nodded.

"Who did you trade with, Jacob?" My mother licked her lips and crossed her arms. "What kind of people are we talking about?"

"Colombians. More specifically: drug runners."

"Drug runners?" The words tumbled out of everyone's mouths in unison. Hannah was the only one who didn't seem to understand. It was like she was watching an incomprehensible tennis match, her gaze volleying between the people sitting on the left and on the right.

My mother gasped. "You're kidding, right?"

"This is no laughing matter, honey. But I swear I didn't know. They were just customers to me, customers with a lot of money. How was I supposed to know where they got that money from?"

"How can anyone?" Steph wondered aloud.

"It's a bit more complicated than that, son. I took payment in advance. Plus, I recommended a small airline to them, which makes it seem I knew what was going on at the time."

"And did you?" my mother wanted to know.

"Did I what?"

"Did you *know*?"

My father looked at her as though she'd slapped him in the face. "Of course not."

"Airline?" Steph repeated.

Another sigh. "It didn't occur to me why they were looking to rent a small plane. I thought they wanted to go on a sightseeing trip or do parachuting or whatever. I know it sounds naïve, but I never dwelled on the possibility that they might have something else in mind. I never stopped to think where the money came from either."

An awkward silence ensued.

"So in other words: this mansion, all those city trips, all the vacations, everything..." My mother gestured at all the stuff in the room. "It was paid for by drugs money?"

My stomach turned. I was too young at the time to comprehend the full extent of this, but I was old enough to understand the connection between selling drugs and doing time.

"There's no hard proof that I was in on the whole thing," my father continued as calmly as he could. "But the coin can come up either way in court. Though even if it's not down to the toss of a coin – those guys need to be stopped, and I may be able to help. So the FBI has made me an offer."

"An offer?" echoed Joey.

My dad nodded. "In exchange for a possible reduced sentence and the protection of us as a family – of all of you – I've decided to testify in court to implicate the people who got me into this situation."

"Protection?" I asked in shock. "You mean we're in danger?"

The man with the round glasses took over. "This is not just any drugs cartel, honey. They have connections. If they get wind of your dad being a witness in court, they won't hesitate to stop him, no matter the cost."

"No!" my mom suddenly exploded. Tears were streaming down her face. "I don't get it. All you did was sell them some diamonds and jewelry. How could you have known…"

"It's not that simple, darling. Especially not once they take a close look in court at what kinds of payments I've accepted from them in the past two years. It doesn't exactly make me look good."

"Jesus, Dad," Steph exclaimed. "How could you be this stupid? So naïve?"

"I'm sorry," he replied dejectedly.

Silence.

"Will you have to go to jail, Daddy?" Joey asked the question that was on everybody's lips.

"Until the trial, yes. A few months at most, maybe a little bit longer. It all depends on them being able to cross out my sentence by using the time I'm in protective custody." My dad nodded at the two men, who then proceeded to sit down on the sofa. "These guys are here to protect us, and to explain to us what will happen next."

The man with the glasses took over once more. "Let

me do some proper introductions. My name is Kings."
He indicated his colleague. "And that's agent Carlson."
He folded his hands. "Have you ever heard of the
witness protection program?"

We all kept quiet, as though the floor underneath our
feet had begun to shake and we were all waiting to be
plunged down into the depths. Except it wasn't the floor
that was about to give, but our life together.

"The what?" Hannah blurted out.

"Isn't that the program that helps people disappear?"
Steph inquired. "Really disappear, I mean. Like, they
wipe your data from all systems, you get a new identity,
and you move to a different part of the country?"

Joey looked around him with panic in his eyes. "We
have to move?"

"I'm afraid so, buddy," Carlson replied. "Your dad
loves you all very much. The people from the cartel
know this. They might use you to get to him."

"But I don't want to leave here," Hannah sobbed.

"We have to, honey." My father took her by the hand,
pulling her in and wrapping an arm around her
shoulders. He looked around, mumbling to himself:
"Everything we built up together – gone."

For the first time in my life, I saw tears in his eyes. It
made me choke up so much that my body started to
shake. He'd always been the one we could rely on, our
tower of strength. And now he'd taken that away from
us. He said he hadn't known, but deep down I knew he
was lying – that he'd gotten in deeper and deeper until
he couldn't get out even if he wanted to. Until they'd
catch him. That day had now come. But instead of anger
or hate, I could only feel sympathy and pity. I walked up
to him and hugged him close. "It'll all work out, Dad," I

whispered.

That's when my father burst out in tears.

-11-

The bureaucratic paper mill had been working for the past few days, it turned out, because it slowly dawned on us that these FBI agents weren't just here to protect us – they were here to take us away.

We could each pack one suitcase, nothing more. The rest of our personal effects would be shipped to our new address a few weeks later, wherever that might be.

There I was, in my room. My gaze darted from left to right. One suitcase only. What the hell was I supposed to bring? What couldn't I live without? Tough questions for an eleven-year-old girl. *Everything* was important. At long last, I packed some of my favorite books, as well as some cuddly toys and my laptop. I hardly had room left for clothes, which prompted my mother to take out half of what I packed afterward.

Everyone was dealing with the situation in their own way, but we had one thing in common: we hardly spoke. I wandered around the house, memorizing every little detail. It was true that I didn't yet think of this building as 'home', but now that I suddenly had to leave it behind, it hurt me more than I expected.

I passed the bedrooms belonging to my brothers and little sister. Joey and Hannah were busy filling their one suitcase each. Every item they packed seemed to cause an internal debate – was it important enough? They'd take it out, put it back in again, only to take it out a second time and chuck it in a corner of the room in frustration.

"How am I supposed to choose?" Hannah hissed.

Steph wasn't doing a thing. He was just staring into nothingness, sitting on his bed.

My mom was busy too, but her main task seemed to be to avoid my dad and help the kids pack. The times they did cross paths, she'd shoot my father a withering look. It would take years for their relationship to get back to what it was, more or less.

My father was really trying his best to help, but frankly, he was just in the way. He tried to strike up a conversation with Hannah and my mom but had difficulty finding the right words. In the end, he just sat down at the desk in his study.

That's where I found him – a cowering, little man looking lost, with tears in his eyes. I set my suitcase down in the hallway and approached him.

As soon as he spotted me, he quickly wiped away his tears. "So, packed and ready to go?"

I nodded, walking around the desk before taking his hand and pumping it lightly.

My father nodded back at me, his eyes still glistening. "I'm sorry, my girl. I'm so sorry."

"You're really going to prison?" It still hadn't quite sunk in yet.

"Afraid so."

"I'm gonna miss you."

He squeezed both of my hands. "I'm gonna miss you too, sweetheart. All of you."

We fell silent. I wanted to comfort him, but I didn't know what to say. It took me a long time to ask him the

83

question that had been on my mind for a while. "Can't we go back to our old house now?"

"I don't think so." My dad grimaced. "I understand why you're asking, but there's too many people there who still remember us."

"My friends live there."

"Exactly. Which would be a problem if we're all supposed to be someone else, don't you think?"

Disappointed, I hung my head. "I guess you're right."

He pushed my chin up. "No worries. You'll be okay in our new house, I'm sure of it."

"I hope so."

A few minutes later, we all gathered in the living room so Agent Kings could explain to us what was going to happen next.

"Jacob will come with us in a moment and will be serving his prison sentence in a safe location until trial. Hopefully, that will be all the time he'll need to do so you might see him back within one year."

Joey clung to my father's arms again. "I don't want you to go, Daddy."

"Me neither!" Hannah joined in, sobbing.

"There's no way around this, sweethearts." He turned around and looked from Joey to Hannah, staring deep into their eyes. "You both gotta be brave now. Can you do that for me?"

With glistening eyes and after hesitating for a beat, they both nodded.

The agent continued. "As for you, you'll be transported to Brooklyn, New York, and you'll all be given new names. It's very important you will not disclose this location to anyone, do you understand?" He gave us, the children, an intent look. "Not even to friends or family, not even in emails. Although this is not a must, it would be wise to call each other by your new names even when nobody's listening. That way you won't run the risk of making mistakes, and it'll be easier to adapt."

"I'll never manage," I told the man.

"You'll get used to it soon enough – you'll see. It's not the first time you're moving as a family, is it? Last time you also had to transfer to a different school where you had to make new friends. We'll make sure you'll all have plenty of opportunities to further your education. We purposely don't relocate you to no man's land so you'll have all the usual amenities at your disposal."

"Only this time they'll be burdened with a secret that will force them to pretend all the time," Steph added sarcastically.

"You're not the first family to be placed in the witness protection program," Agent Carlson replied. "Trust me, we know what we're doing. You'll blend in soon enough. Besides, we…"

I interrupted his pep talk, looking at Steph full of dismay. "What do you mean, 'they' will be burdened with a secret? Are you saying you're not coming?"

Steph hung his head before looking at the two FBI agents. The looks they exchanged made it clear to me that he'd been talking to them before this gathering. "No, I'm not."

"Excuse me?" My mother looked up in surprise.

"I got my life here, Mom. I'm in my senior year at college, I got a good job on the side, and I was planning on moving in with Kim in a couple of months. Which will now be a couple of weeks, I guess. I already told her…"

"I knew it!" Hannah broke in. "I told you guys that

Steph was planning this?"

"You'll do nothing of the kind. You will join your mother like the rest of your family!" For the first time today, my father's voice sounded booming. He shot the two men a withering look, as though they'd betrayed him. "You knew about this?"

"It's none of your business, Dad," Steph replied. "Especially not *yours*, since this is all your fault. I'm a grown-up. I don't *have* to do anything if I don't want to."

"It's a good thing you're moving," Carlson said, "but keep in mind you can't do anything stupid, okay? Whatever you do, don't draw attention to yourself. Stay under the radar. Don't open any accounts and so on in your real name."

Kings added: "And please be aware that you won't be able to see your family for a long time."

Steph nodded gingerly, his face ashen. "I know. And it's eating me. But if I do join you guys, I'll have to drop everything I built up here, including Kim. I can't expect her to drop her life either just to come with me. It's a tough choice to make, but this is what I want."

My throat turned dry. It felt as though someone had slapped me in the face. Steph was my big brother through and through. I could always knock on his door if something bothered me. He'd been the one to teach me how to patch a tire, how to play the guitar, how to sing. He couldn't just leave me behind, right? "Steph…" I stammered.

He took my hands. His fingers felt ice cold. "I'm sorry, Nightingale." He was the only one to use that nickname. He'd come up with it after I just kept singing him songs, and hearing it finally made something inside of me snap. It hit me like a ton of bricks. Steph wasn't just going to summer camp for a few weeks, like he used to. *We* were the ones leaving. And we were never coming back. Crying, I fell into his arms.

"We'll advise him on what to do and what not to do as soon as you're gone," Carlson went on.

"I don't know what to say," my mother said, dejection in her tone.

"There's nothing to say," Steph answered. He let go of me to approach my mother and give her a hug. "But this is goodbye, okay? Not farewell."

"How can you be so calm?" she sniffed.

Steph forced a smile. "I'm not. I'm just trying to keep it together, like all of us. But I can feel the mask slipping, so it's time you guys went on your way."

"He's right." Agent Kings got up and so did his partner. "The car's waiting."

We walked outside as though we were in a trance.

Saying goodbye had never been more painful, so I made it quick. I gave both Steph and my dad one final hug before I ran outside with tears in my eyes. Once I was in the car, I watched my parents saying goodbye to Steph one after the other, before saying goodbye to each other. I saw the way my brother and mother looked at my dad: full of reproach and disappointment at the same time.

A few minutes later, the car started to move and Joey, Hannah, my mother and I glanced backward, all four of us, to where Steph was sitting on the veranda, wiping away his tears and waving at us half-heartedly. A little bit further down, my dad was being escorted to a different car, like the alleged criminal that he was.

-12-

2017

The attic was illuminated by a dusty lamp, and the candles that Carla had placed on top of the table and some boxes. Shadows danced across the walls. It was two o'clock. The darkness accompanying the night, as well as the events of that day and the threat of who might be walking around outside, made us all hyper-alert and unable to get any shut-eye. Whenever we looked outside, we saw Manhattan lit up orange in the distance. Skyscrapers, apartments, and stores had to all be ablaze. The wind was in our direction, which caused the pungent fire smell to penetrate even the house.

The attic was clearly used for storage. Everywhere I looked I saw stuff fit for the junkyard. A faded sofa, various board games, trash bags full of clothes, moving boxes, empty cabinets. The only thing that clearly had a function here was the boiler. Every time someone was using the hot water, it kick-started with a lot of noise.

Just like the walls, the floor consisted of nothing more than wooden paneling. Every step we took on it caused it to creak ominously. It made me feel like it could collapse at any moment.

Four injured people were here, moaning, cursing, or crying amid the jumble on their makeshift beds made from piles of towels or airbeds. One of them was called Daisy. She was a very pregnant twenty-year-old and we all hoped her water wasn't about to break. The reason we were using the attic was because we had the most space in here – and also, it was a better vantage point for keeping an eye on the street. Another bunch of people was holed up in the living room. They weren't injured and were mostly just there because they were too afraid to be home alone. Most of them were in shock; they had lost loved ones and didn't know what to do with themselves.

A feeling I knew only too well myself.

For hours I was on auto-pilot while doing chores. It was a good thing. It enabled me to keep it together and not really take the time to let it sink in – what had happened not just here, but all over the world, not to mention to me personally. I'd have had a mental breakdown by now without my auto-pilot. I was focusing on the task in front of me and thought of nothing else. I darted to and fro and tried my best to comfort the injured, help them, calm them down. Fortunately, I wasn't doing it alone. Carla and Hank were there too, alongside a few friendly neighbors.

Disinfectants, Band-Aids, bandages, painkillers – Carla had stocked up on all of it. After I'd pulled on one of Carla's dry pairs of jeans and a clean shirt, I asked Hank whether he and a few other men were up to checking out the houses nearest to us, break in if need be, and take everything they thought we might need. We were especially short on bandages. Unfortunately, all they brought back was a small first aid kit, so I had to tear up a few shirts to dress the wounds.

They were doing the same thing for the injured in other houses on the street, but it soon became clear that no one possessed the medical knowledge I had, although it wasn't much use to me with the limited supplies I had access to. I surprised myself by shoving aside my own problems – along with the thousands of questions milling around in my mind – and taking charge. I appointed people who needed to look after the injured as well as they could – with my help, of course – and asked others to fetch help on the outside, which turned out to be in vain. Another group offered to stand watch in case the trigger-happy assholes decided to come back. This is how the entire street was turned into an impromptu emergency room.

Every round I made started and ended with Hannah. She was sitting on the floor in the living room, propped up against the side of the couch with a pillow to support her back. The white Labrador pressed up against her, his body extended on the floor while his head rested on her leg. His eyes darting from left to right looked exhausted and intensely sad. He was whining softly. Hannah stroked his head consolingly. Meanwhile, she had her pale face turned to the TV in the room. Carla had wanted to switch it off at first, but changed her mind when people begged her to leave it on. It was terrible, having to witness what was going on in the outside world, but being aware of it was better than sticking your head in the sand. The people who insisted ignorance was bliss – or couldn't handle knowing what was going on – simply didn't watch. The volume was turned down and hardly rose above the sounds that the people in the house were making.

The entire world seemed to be at war. The images on the screen showed us bombed and burning homes. Armed soldiers ran back and forth on top of the rubble. Tanks were rolling down the streets. Images of the White

House, covered in black soot and still smoking. Images of Chinese temples that had been leveled, of malls where people smashed windows in a blind panic, grabbing what they could – not just food or medical supplies, but also computers or monitors they would probably never get to use. It filled me with abject horror. I watched all this from the corner of my eye but tried to ignore it and put on a brave face.

Nervously, I tapped my feet on the floor. I looked around me and really registered the chaos surrounding me for the first time. The people, the mess, the caked blood. For a second, the world started to spin. What the hell had I ended up in?

Keep busy, Anna. Don't think too much about it.

Easier said than done.

I squatted down next to Hannah and inspected the wound on her shoulder. A stray bullet had only caused a graze, fortunately, but this was the second time already that I had to swap her soaked bandages – or actually, the strips of an old shirt.

"Jesus, you look like hell!" Hannah looked up at me in shock.

I shrugged as I tore up another shirt to replace the bandage. "I'm tired, scared, and confused. My clothes are covered in blood yet again, I'm in a stranger's home with masses of injured people, and the world seems to have gone to shit. Mark's dead, and so are Mom, Dad, and Joey. And I haven't even told you about my own adventures. Let's just say I've had better days."

"It was really you, then? In the Facebook chat?"

I nodded.

"So, what *happened*?" Hannah asked. "I mean, how can you be here? I thought you were dead."

91

"You're not the only one, apparently."

"But how..?"

I put a finger to my lips to shush her. "Once this chaos is over, I'll tell you, all right? Though I doubt you'll believe me. But I can't talk about it right now, I just can't. I just hope you don't seriously believe I killed Joey."

"Of course not, but..." Hannah saw the look in my eyes, then just nodded and stopped talking.

I petted the Labrador's head, which caused him to temporarily stop his whining and wag his tail. "What's his name?"

"Luca." Hannah looked down at the dog at the same time he looked up at her. She smiled faintly. The love in that reciprocal look was heart-warming. "He's five. We got him from the dog shelter a few years ago."

"He's cute."

Hannah nodded. "I can't think of a more faithful dog."

We fell silent for a while, watching the TV and listening to all the speculation that was going on. Everyone was trying to find a logical explanation for what had happened.

"It's those damn Russians." Peter, a retired teacher, pointed to the TV with a dismissive gesture. "I'm sure of it."

"Don't forget those guys in the Middle East," Julia reacted. She looked like a twenty-year-old crackhead who'd been knocked up in some dark and glum place. She was skinny, with rings under her eyes. Luckily she only had a head injury. With her – thankfully unharmed – baby, she staggered into the living room coming out of the kitchen. "A few years ago it was suicide bombers, and now they found a way to really make an impact."

In the corner, his back against the doorframe, was nineteen-year-old Max. The personification of the word 'nerd'. His spectacles were askew, the lenses scratched. It made me wonder why he was still wearing the thing. "It's the aliens. They have finally come."

Hannah grimaced. "Maybe he's right, you know."

"Excuse me?"

"Aliens. Maybe they were the ones who abducted you. It would explain why you disappeared off the face of the earth for two years."

"You really believe that?" I commented sarcastically.

"Nah." She carelessly shrugged her shoulders, making her flinch with pain. She clenched her teeth together and sucked in some air. "But to be honest, I don't really believe what's happening right now. I feel as though I'm trapped in a nightmare and I just can't wake up."

"Yeah, I get that."

Victor, a man in his thirties who lived three doors down, approached me. His black coat and long hairs were soaked with rain, but he didn't seem to care. Raindrops glided off him and landed on the floor. "You need anything else, Anna?"

I sighed. "I basically need more of everything. We'll have to find help soon, because we can't heal all the sick like this."

"I just got back. Two doors down they're already making plans for that. They're trying to figure out how to move the injured people into several cars. Frankly, I don't think there's a point. We just don't know what to expect outside this neighborhood. It might be dangerous out there. Besides..."

"We don't know whether hospitals are operational

anymore," I finished his sentence for him. "And even if they are, they'll have crammed patients into every nook and cranny. That's what Hank said. But we have to at least try, don't we?"

Victor looked away guiltily. "Maybe."

I decided not to enter into a discussion with him and quickly changed tune. "We'll need to get new supplies at the very least. We're out of painkillers and disinfectant."

"We found a few people who were willing to check out a block of houses further down the road, go on a recon mission. Hank's one of them. Hopefully, they'll come back with fresh supplies soon."

I nodded, pointing at Hannah. "Could you get her something to drink, maybe? If anything's left in the fridge, that is."

"You really think the water's poisoned?" Hannah inquired.

"I'm not about to volunteer as a lab rat. What about you?" Victor replied.

I shook my head. "Poisoned tap water… you know, maybe this is some kind of terrorist act. The one to end them all."

"Possibly." Victor was about to turn away when I grabbed his ankle. He looked back with a question in his eyes.

"Any chance you could play some music?"

"Music?"

I nodded. "Yeah, as a distraction." All the yammering, speculating, and sobbing was beginning to take its toll on me now that I wasn't busying myself anymore.

Hannah picked up on it. "Sit down for a while. You look like you're about to collapse."

I shook my head. "I can't. These people…"

94

"You won't be of any use to them if you're going to have a meltdown next."

"But…"

"Sit. Down," Hannah told me.

I took her in, really looked at her. It was bizarre to see how much she'd changed since I last saw her. It did make sense: she was now sixteen and in my absence, her body had been working hard to transform her from girl to young woman. Her eyes no longer reflected the light and gentleness that had been there a few years ago. Her chest was no longer flat – in fact, she was a larger cup size than me. Her face had changed too, although it was hard to put a finger on all the small differences. Sighing, I sat down next to her. "Hannah. I'm struggling to understand something."

"Join the club," she replied.

I ignored her cynicism. "Why did you all move?"

"You really don't understand?"

I shook my head. "It had nothing to do with the witness protection program, did it?"

"It was *you*. You were the reason, Anna."

"Me?"

"Of course. The old house reminded us too much of you."

"But why stay in the same neighborhood?"

"I still go to school in Brooklyn Heights. Or at least I did – I doubt I'll ever see a classroom from the inside again. Mom and Dad had jobs close by. It's a friendly neighborhood where everybody knows each other, and we got a lot of support from our neighbors." With a hateful glare in her eyes, she looked outside. "It was purely about that one house."

"I understand."

"But I don't," Hannah exclaimed. "You have to give me *something*, Anna. Throw me a bone here, because I keep feeling like I'm talking to a ghost."

I worried my lip, not sure whether this was a good idea, but in the end, I decided to give her a brief summary of all that had happened.

When I finished a few minutes later, Hannah shook her head in disbelief. "You were right."

I stared at her uncomprehendingly.

"It really is kind of hard to believe."

"Just as hard as dealing with the fact that I am now sitting next to you?"

She had to ponder that for a moment. "Touché," she said at last.

Silence enveloped us for a moment.

"They'd gone on vacation without you, right?" I asked.

Hannah nodded sadly. "I was going to go on a trip with a few friends in a couple of weeks. It would have been my first vacation without Mom and Dad."

"Didn't they call you?"

"What, to tell me that they'd been contacted by the police and they were on their way back home, you mean?"

I nodded.

"They tried, but I was at work and I hadn't found the time to call them back yet. So imagine my surprise when they were suddenly back home. Dad told me everything, but…" She fell silent.

"You never did forgive him, did you?" I asked Hannah after a while.

"Who?"

"Dad."

"Did you?"

I thought for a second. "I don't think any of us truly did."

"Mom surely didn't. After he came back to us, things never really went back to the way they were. We all pretended like it was forgiven and forgotten, but really, we were all just trying to avoid him."

I nodded. "Why do you think I was so eager to move out? Partly because of Mark, of course, but honestly I couldn't stand the tension at home anymore. And yet I've always felt sorry in a way. He was trying so hard to mend the relationship with us, and with Mom…" I swallowed, biting my lip to force back the tears I felt welling up. "Maybe we should have tried harder to forgive him. We all make mistakes."

Hannah hung her head. "And now it's too late." She took my hand and squeezed it. "I still can't believe they're gone and you're alive."

I squeezed her back lightly. "I know, honey."

Silence.

"Are we going to bury them?"

I sighed. "I can't bear seeing them right now. I don't think that's going to change in the next few days either, and I know we can't just leave them in the car like that, they don't deserve that, but…" I wiped away a lonely tear and took a deep, raspy breath.

Loud and quick footsteps on the stairs, followed by a cry. "Anna!"

I glanced up and saw Carla barging into the living room. She looked around searchingly before her eyes settled on me.

Luca barked.

I sat up. "What's wrong?"

"Have you ever been a midwife before?" Out of breath, Carla rested her hands on her upper legs while taking deep gulps of breath.

It took me a while before I understood the full extent of that question. "Don't tell me she's having it right now."

"Afraid so." She took my hand and hauled me into the hallway.

"Wait." Abruptly I came to a stop. "I've never done this before."

"You think I have?" Carla yelled. "None of us have. You're the only one who has basic medical knowledge."

"Let me help." Hannah got to her feet as well, just like Victor, Peter, Max, and Julia, who was still cradling her baby close to her chest.

Before I could respond, a shriek drifted down from the attic.

Shit!

Without thinking, I stormed up the stairs, the others in my wake. Luca was heading our troupe. Barking, he jumped up the steps. The sound of many footsteps on wooden planks echoed off the walls.

And then the so-called shit hit the fan – when sudden darkness descended upon us, which heralded the end of human civilization as I knew it.

-13-

"Holy shit!" My curse hardly rose above the din of the shrieking woman.

The burning city in the distance still cast a faint light into the attic through the windows. It made the darkness outside gray, rather than pitch black, casting shadows and enabling me to make out the shapes of the people around me, at least. Hannah was just behind me on the stairs, like Carla.

Petrified, we stopped moving while all holding our breath. The shrieking died away for a moment, as though the person emitting it had to pause for breath. The sudden silence seemed charged and caused my heart to beat like a trip hammer. Not one second later, renewed cries of agony started up again.

Very carefully, as though every move I made could set off an earthquake, I looked around me. In the darkness, I hardly recognized anything in the house anymore.

"Just great!" I heard Victor call out. "As if we weren't in enough misery already."

"What happened?" Peter wondered out loud.

"Isn't that obvious, genius?" Max quipped. "The electricity was cut." His voice contained barely hidden sarcasm. Something told me they hadn't been the best of neighbors to each other in the past.

"Of course it's obvious, you punk," the man hissed.

"But *why*?"

I imagined Max shrugging his shoulders and looking around him with fear in his eyes. "Maybe this is the part where the aliens are coming for us."

Julia tried shooing her crying baby. "Itsy bitsy spider climbed up the water spout," she started to sing softly. Her voice trembled, which was probably the reason why it didn't work. The baby kept crying.

Another scream coming from the attic, the sound curling itself around my heart like a squeezing hand.

"Are the candles still burning in the attic?" I quickly asked Carla.

Although I couldn't see her face, the panic was evident in her voice. "I want Hank. I want my husband. Where is he?"

"He's on a supply run," Victor replied. "He'll be…"

"Carla!" I interrupted, almost screaming. "The candles?"

"Y-yes," she stammered. "They're still burning."

"You guys got a flashlight somewhere?" Hannah asked.

"We don't use those kinds of thing on a daily basis, so no," Carla whispered despondently.

"Well, it would have come in handy now," I said. "You got any more? Candles, I mean."

"A few – not a lot."

"Get them and light them." I grabbed the banister and stumbled up as quickly as I could. "The more light, the better. Hannah, come with me. And the rest of you: I need stuff. Towels, water, cloth, anything you think might be useful during childbirth."

"How the hell are we supposed to know?" Peter protested.

"Use your imagination," Max yelled. His voice sounded faint, which clued me into the fact that he was on his way back to the living room.

"Little piss-ant," Peter swore under his breath.

Feeling my way around, and with Hannah next to me, I finally reached the attic. By now I knew the way a little bit, but in the darkness it was near-impossible to see where I was going. Fortunately, Daisy's shrieks and Luca's barking – who was probably standing next to her now – steered us in the right direction.

I pushed the door open and saw Daisy lying on her back in the corner, her knees pulled up. Next to her were her mother Joanna and her sister Jill. They'd covered her up with a sheet from the waist down. The two men in the corner were too injured to move, but were both telling her that everything would be okay. Which was nonsense, of course. How in all the hell would this ever be okay?

The candles flickered, giving the room an eerie glow.

As soon as Daisy's mother spotted me, she jumped up. "We have to get her to a hospital."

Luca just kept barking.

One look at Daisy was enough for me.

Shit, shit, shit.

"There's no time. Her water broke."

"Don't you think I know that?" Joanna said bluntly. "I had two children myself. But come on, this is no place for her to give birth?"

Behind me, Victor entered the room. "I'm afraid we have no other choice."

Luca squeaked, then barked again, before running in circles next to Daisy.

I rushed over to her and sat down on my knees in front of her. "Hannah, can you make sure Luca keeps quiet?" I asked, annoyed. "He's driving me nuts."

"Luca, come here," Hannah ordered. She went over to another corner of the room and slightly bent her knees. The dog did what he was asked, but kept barking.

I cast a look underneath the sheet. What I saw, convinced me I'd never start a family myself.

Is that the head?

My stomach turned.

How the hell am I supposed to do this?

"Okay, Daisy. Keep breathing evenly. Deep breaths. In, and out."

She looked at me with fear in her eyes. Tears shone on her cheeks. Her voice was hoarse from all the shrieking. "Help me."

I'll try.

Everyone had gathered in the attic by now. Towels scissors, a jug of water, washcloths, and some clothing were put on the floor next to us.

Julia's baby kept crying.

Luca was barking incessantly.

"Julia, could you take your little one and the dog downstairs?" I pleaded. "The noise is distracting me too much."

But Julia stood rooted to the spot. I could imagine why: downstairs, she'd be all alone. After what just happened, that'd be the last thing I'd want too. I thought about asking Hannah to accompany her, but that was ridiculous. I didn't want to let my sister out of my sight. If I lost her too…

Daisy huffed and puffed. Jill took her hand, squeezing it lightly while she joined in. "You're going to do this, sis. You are."

"Oh God, oh God." Carla repeated the words like it

was a mantra, anxiously digging around in a few boxes to find more candles. She found four of them and lighted them before placing them around us in a circle. This enabled me to see the look of pure fear on the faces of everybody present for the first time – and Daisy's face in particular. A shiver ran through my body.

An intense contraction made Daisy cry out. "Jesus, make it stop!"

"Hang in there, girl." I shouted to no one in particular: "Put a wet washcloth on her forehead." I glanced under the sheet again.

Jesus. The baby's really coming!

Something told me I had to get a hold of the head and pull it out, but was that really the right thing to do?

Think! What did they teach you about this at school?

I couldn't remember. I was having a total, utter blackout.

Please. Come on, come on, come on!

Voices. Shouts, coming from outside.

"What's happening out there?" Julia screamed, which made the baby in her arms wail even more loudly.

Max ran toward the window.

Peter did the same and pointed to something outside. "What is *that*?"

A car alarm went off, the noise mingling with the racket that was already there. The cacophony of sounds was driving me crazy.

"Someone's out there," Carla whispered, who was standing near the window too. Her voice trembled.

"Those shooters again?" Hannah's voice rose an octave. As if frozen she was standing in the far corner of the room, holding Luca by his collar. Her body was almost completely obscured by dancing shadows. Just

103

her hands and head were clearly visible, giving her the appearance of a human *Cheshire Cat*.

"I can't see. It's too dark out. But *something* is moving out there," Peter replied.

More screaming from the street.

"Nooooo!"

"Stay away from us!"

"Fuck. What *is* that?" Max exclaimed, almost in tears.

I wanted to get up and see what was happening outside, but Daisy – or actually, her baby – kept me here.

"Get it the fuck out of me!"

"I…" I stuttered, my heart in my throat and my palms were sweaty.

"I can't take this much longer!" Her facial expression was contorted into an agonized grimace. She was puffing. "Get it out."

"Keep pushing, honey," her sister encouraged her.

"I can't!"

"You must!"

Daisy shrieked.

"Get out of my way!" Joanna yelled at me. "I'll do it."

Before I could react, my vision was blurred and my hands started to shake. I felt like throwing up.

As though someone had turned the volume down, the voices around me faded away. The head slowly emerged, tortuously slowly…

My hands shot forward as if I was hypnotized. Carefully, my fingers curled around the slick little shoulders. They were covered in blood and slime.

The moment I started to pull, all sounds came rushing back and the world started to turn again.

Crying. My arms were wet and warm. In surprise, I glanced down and saw the tiny, naked body. It was a boy. The child screeched shrilly.

The few seconds after that were wiped from my memory. I momentarily blacked out. The next thing I remember, was a hand on my shoulder. "Anna?"

Dizzily, I looked up. Victor was next to me, his face white as a sheet. His hands were holding a pair of scissors. "She wants you to cut the umbilical cord." He had to repeat his request up to three times.

In an attempt to not faint and see sharply again, I blinked my eyelids. "Sure…"

Just then, I heard Peter scream. "Crapshoot, they're headed this way."

"What? Who?" Hannah asked.

"They?" Joanna cried. "As in, more than one?"

Luca barked again.

Only now did I register that it had become dead silent outside.

"Looks like it," Peter responded. "I don't know. Shadows. I can't make them out. But they were at the door just now."

"*Our* front door?"

"Shh," I hissed.

Everyone fell silent, apart from Julia's baby and Luca.

I pricked up my ears. Creaking footsteps on the stairs, hardly audible due to the barks and the cries, but nevertheless: clearly present.

"Shit. They're inside," Max whispered.

Who?

I held my breath and stared at the door, my heart skipping a beat.

With a creaking sound, it opened.

Carla shrieked.

Frozen, I stared into the darkness.

Feet, hands. It was the first thing I saw of them, before their heads followed. Children – six of them, ranging in age from six to twelve. No, they weren't children. They looked like kids, but the unnatural, gruesome grin on their faces betrayed their true nature. They were something else altogether, something *more*. They were covered in blood and they queued up in one straight line while looking around curiously.

Only now did I see the bloodied butcher knives their little hands were clutching.

Luca barked and growled, but didn't attack. With his tail between his legs, he took a few steps backward, like he knew how bad this whole situation was.

Just for a beat, the children looked at one another, then they scattered off into various directions, into the darkness. What followed was permanently etched into my retinas.

There were screams, curses, fights.

Peter yelled: "Get the fuck away from me!"

"You sick motherfuckers..." Max started, before launching off into a blood-curdling scream. I whipped around and saw the child that was standing behind him. He pulled Max backward by the hairs, tripped him on purpose, and slit his throat with one fluid movement. Blood bubbled up from the cut. Max gurgled, casting one final panicked look around before tumbling down to his death.

"No, not my baby!" Julia implored before her head banged into the wall. A knife was protruding from her lower back. One of the children had seized her baby. He studied it impassively for a second before twisting its neck and casting it to the side.

Luca's barks morphed into whines of agony.

Shocked, I turned toward him.

Jesus. They broke his leg.

Whimpering, the animal curled up in the corner.

More shrieking. It was now all around me.

Victor was wrestling with two children on the blood-stained floor. He cursed, fought bravely, but lost. Joanna, Jill, and the two wounded men in the corner didn't stand a shimmer of a chance.

"Anna!" A begging voice in the corner of the room.

Hannah.

Crap, crap, crap.

At last, I forced my limbs to move. As fast as I could – and still clutching the crying newborn to my chest – I ran toward the sound. Before I could reach my sister in the corner, however, I was tackled to the floor. With a bang I smacked against the planks, only managing to turn around at the last second so I wouldn't crush the baby. My elbows hurt. The baby started to cry even more loudly, but I couldn't hear anything else anymore.

Hannah?

I flipped around onto my back. In the flickering light of the candles, I saw six pairs of shoes in a circle around me. Anxiously, I glanced up.

Those faces! Those eyes.

They were nothing more than black holes. They weren't human!

So what the holy hell are they?

Fear tugged at me like strings on a marionette.

Their gazes had been full of rage, but now I saw surprise in their dead eyes. They looked at each other with a question in their eyes.

"You're one of us," one of the boys said wonderingly.

I shot him a look of incomprehension through my

tears. "Leave us alone."

"What's your purpose?" one of the girls inquired.

Please, please, please, please.

I turned my head and looked around me. Bodies – they were all around me. Still, dead.

Hannah?

Please, please, please, please.

"What have you done?"

The children looked at each other again. "Kill the baby," I heard one of them whisper.

Jesus, was he talking to me?

That revolting grin appeared on their faces again. They turned around and bounded down the attic stairs. The echo of their footsteps on the wooden floor will remain with me forever. Before they left the attic, they blew out the candles, trapping me in the dark.

A few minutes later, the front door was shut with a bang and I heard them giggle as they ran back onto the street.

I gasped for breath and felt the adrenaline surging through my body. It shook uncontrollably. The baby in my arms wailed without pause. In one corner, I heard Luca whimper again.

"Hannah?" I stammered.

No reply. I knew what that meant. A shiver of sheer sadness and intense loneliness shook my body.

Please, please, please, please.

I cried.

And fainted.

-14-

Cries of agony made me open my eyes again. The world had turned back to its colorful self again. Or actually, no – that wasn't true. The world would *never* be its colorful self again after what happened, not in the way I once knew it. No, what I meant to say was that the sun, so indifferent to whatever transpired on the insignificant planet millions of miles away from its burning core, was coming up. Its rays shone in through the window and cast lines of light onto the dirty, wooden floor. Dust motes were dancing in the glow.

I moaned.

A pungent smell made me sick to my stomach. It wasn't just sweat, it was something stronger, something more definitive.

Oh, sweet Jesus.

Realization kicked in and caused adrenaline to surge through my veins, enhancing my vision. I looked around me and saw the bodies.

The dead bodies.

Victor was slumped against the wall underneath the window. Max and Carla were stretched out on the floor. Julia and Peter were lying a bit further away, their skin as pale as ice. Their glassy eyes were fixed on me as though they were waiting for me to get up.

I shivered, swallowing to fight back the vomit in the

back of my throat. It burned, working its way up to mingle with a strange metallic taste. From what it felt like, I must have bitten my tongue pretty hard. The wound stung as I ran the tip of my tongue over my teeth.

There was clotted blood everywhere.

My fingers tightened around a lump of moving flesh which was lying on my chest. It was sticky, just like my shirt, and slippery, and it was crying its lungs out.

The baby!

Startled, I sat up while supporting the baby with one hand. Big mistake – that was way too fast. The attic started to spin around me, and that sensation combined with the horrible image of the dead bodies around me made me lose control. As fast as I could, I turned my head away from the baby before I threw up all over the floor. The stuff mixed with the blood there. I moaned again, wiping my mouth on my shoulder.

My heart was beating like crazy. A dull headache started to pound and grew worse with each passing second. I swallowed. The sour taste of my vomit was awful. I looked down. My hands were covered in blood.

Deep breaths, Anna. In, out, in, out…

It didn't help much.

Panicky, I looked from the child in my arms to the dead bodies on the attic floor and back.

At that moment, I saw Hannah.

Oh, fuck.

No, no, no!

As fast as I could, I pushed myself off the slippery floor with my free hand. The baby pressed against my chest, I shuffled toward my little sister. For a second, I was afraid I'd pass out again, but I strongly resisted the impulse.

"Hannah. Oh, God. No!" Every syllable hurt my throat.

She was lying in the corner in a puddle of blood. *Her own blood!* Her left hand rested on a gaping wound in her side, and her right hand touched Luca's ear. From the looks of it, the dog had used his nose to lift her hand, so he could slide underneath with his head. The animal whimpered softly, defeatedly. His right front paw was bent in a weird angle and his black eyes looked at me pleadingly, as though to say: "Help me. Help *us!*"

I grabbed her wrist but didn't feel a pulse.

"No!" I screamed my lungs out and kicked the empty cabinet close to Hannah. With a loud bang, the piece of furniture tumbled to the floor. After that, all energy seemed to seep from my limbs and I dropped to my knees, crying. I almost let go of the baby and desperately clung to the newborn. With one trembling hand, I caressed my sister's cold face. Her head was sagging to the side, her mouth hanging open and her eyes partly closed.

Not you, Hannah. I can't deal with this if you're gone, too. What am I supposed to do now?

I looked around searchingly, half-wishing for one of those kids to still be in the corner, sporting that creepy grin and brandishing a knife to finish the job and put me out of my misery. What was the point of living now that I had no one left and the world was filled with bat-shit crazy maniacs?

On the other hand, I hoped one of those snotty children – or actually, all of them – were in this room right now so I could do to them what they'd done to Hannah and the others, but slowly. Much more slowly. God, I'd make them all suffer. It was either that or die trying, which would probably be the better solution.

Why did they spare me?

In my mind's eye, I saw the children around me again, surrounding me in the dark.

"You're one of us." The voice resonated in my skull and made me cower with fear.

What the hell had that kid meant when he said that?

My heart contracted. I had difficulty breathing and could do nothing else but rocking back and forth like some patient in a psych ward. Maybe that was it – I was in an asylum because I'd lost my marbles. God, I hoped that was true. Because that meant the world out there, outside my head, was still normal. Mark would still be there, and so would my family.

My family…

The realization hit me. I had no one left. No one except Steph, and I hadn't seen him in years. And who was to say he was even alive after all of this?

Snot dripped from my nose onto the floor. I was sobbing, the sound blending with the cries of the baby.

As though it didn't really register with me, I looked at the child in my arms. And just for a split second, I was honestly surprised to find him there. Eyes closed tight and fully naked, he was screaming his lungs out, a tiny fist punching the air. His other hand moved toward his mouth. He smacked his lips, then shivered violently.

It only hit me just then.

Crap, crap, crap.

I hastily jumped to my feet, my eyes darting through the attic room. Something inside of me wanted to run over to Daisy, give her the child, shake her.

Wake up. You're his mother. He needs you!

But Daisy was nothing more than an empty, human

husk.

I was on my own.

Crap, crap, crap.

I flinched with fear. On my own, the situation was dire enough, but with this baby...

What am I supposed to do, for God's sake? I don't know the first thing about babies!

I needed help.

Goddammit.

The baby boy just kept crying and shivering. Quickly, I took a few steps to the side and rummaged around in one of the plastic bags filled with clothes. I took out a long scarf, which I wrapped around the tiny body three times. That was slightly better, but the real problem was harder to tackle. He was hungry!

Where am I going to get formula?

"Shh, calm down," I said soothingly, but in a trembling voice. I was pacing the room, thinking fast while looking around me.

Outside, a bird cawed. I looked up, went over to the window and cast a desperate look down into the street. Now, at the break of day, the spectacle was even more terrifying. The bodies, the cars parked haphazardly, all the front doors fully open. It was like I was stuck in a damn zombie flick. The most alarming thing of all, though, was the fact that it was so quiet out there. So deserted. Not a thing was moving, not even a stray cat. In the distance, the city was no longer burning, but just smoldering.

This isn't really happening!

But that was just it – it was. It *was* happening.

What's that?

I squinted my eyes to see it more clearly. Was that a

baby stroller in front of one of the houses?

Of course. Formula, somewhere inside that house. There has to be! And if not, you have to go to a store.

I hesitated for a beat. I was right, but this meant I had to go outside and I wasn't sure I was ready for that.

You have no choice. If you don't, you'll be responsible for that poor baby's death.

The child kept crying. Just a few steps away, Luca moaned.

I sighed, took a deep breath and made a decision. With the baby still pressed close to my chest, I limped over to Hannah to stroke her face one last time. "I'm sorry," I whispered.

Luca barked, begging me not to leave – or at least that's what it sounded like. He got up, whining when his broken paw was lifted up into the air, but he followed me nevertheless.

"No, stay here, boy," I told him. "I'll come back, I promise. With help."

If I didn't even believe those words, why would this animal? I once read somewhere that they listen to your intonation, and mine was clearly punched with fear. He kept yipping. To make sure he didn't hurt himself even more by following me out the door, I closed it behind me. As I limped downstairs with the baby in my arms, I heard his whines and him scratching the door with his paws. It broke my heart.

Miraculously, the baby had stopped bawling. He was now just letting out tiny sobs, completely wrecked from his first few hours living on this planet.

"You'll be all right, buddy. I promise." Children were being brainwashed all the time by telling them lies. Santa, the Easter Bunny... who was I to break that tradition?

It was bizarre to walk down the street. I made a conscious effort to avoid my parents' car so I wouldn't see them. I knew that would shatter the tiny bit of courage this little baby had given me. I did furtively keep an eye on my surroundings, though, since I was expecting those kids to pop up again, or the men with guns. My heartbeat violently in my throat.

You can do this, Anna. Step by step.

The thunderclouds of the day before had dissolved. The sky was bright blue with a few fluffy clouds here and there. The sun caressed my skin and felt hot. It made me feel so small. I mean, here we were, the human race pretending for decades that we were superior to all the other species, that everything evolved around us, but the truth was: life went on just fine without us.

I skirted around the stationary cars, dead bodies, abandoned suitcases, and the baby stroller I'd seen from the window. Only now did I see that it was actually a doll carriage. Which made me decide to go for the next house, which had the front door wide open.

"Hello?" I didn't know why I even bothered. Did I really expect to find someone inside? Of course, those kids could have skipped a few houses, but I doubted they'd have left anyone else alive. I couldn't hold out hope. Ultimately that would destroy me.

Complete silence.

Once inside the living room, I halted. I felt like I was trespassing. Like I didn't belong. A family with two little girls had lived here. The photos on the mantelpiece made it clear that they'd been twins, about seven years old. Their youthful smiles and heads full of hair reminded me of Hannah and Joey at that age. Didn't I just see these kids out on the street, unmoving beside one of the cars..?

Stop thinking about it.

I stopped right in front of a well-stocked bookcase, filled with literature that would never be read. A few games were on the floor. The thing that stood out to me most was the absence of people.

I swallowed.

The baby started crying again.

"Yeah, I know, honey." I hurried on to the kitchen. Against my better judgment, I yanked open every cabinet and drawer in my search for milk powder and a baby bottle. Those twins had long since passed the age of being bottle-fed.

I rushed outside again, heading for the neighboring houses. But after searching through six more houses and not finding anything, I felt my courage falter. I toyed with the idea of running to the supermarket, but the fact was that I didn't dare leave this street right now. I was too afraid to run into those children again, or the shooters.

Someone's bound to have at least some formula in this neighborhood, right? The street's littered with dolls and dead – oh Jesus, kids and babies.

The crying child in my arms was the only thing that kept me going, reminding me that I couldn't give up.

The seventh house I tried was locked, but I saw one of the windows had been shattered. There were shards of glass everywhere. As carefully as I could, I stepped onto the ledge and pulled myself up and inside – which wasn't easy with a baby in my arms. The glass crunched under my feet when I landed in the room. There was an upholstered couch, two guitars, a piano, and a table on top of which two cats were feasting on dinner leftovers.

Whoever had lived here, they'd left in a hurry.

A framed photo on the wall showed me a family of four, one of which was a baby. My heart made a little jump.

Please let that photo be recent.

I couldn't get to the kitchen fast enough to open all the cabinets, indifferently hauling out all the stuff that was still in there. A bag of rice, canned vegetables, bottles of soda. I almost cried out in ecstasy when I finally found what I was looking for. The box of powdered milk was half-empty, but it gave me renewed hope.

"Look at that, little one," I babbled excitedly, holding the box up in front of his eyes. "And now, a bottle."

I had to scour the entire house, but finally I found what I needed in a nursery on the third floor. Now I had to tackle the next problem: the tap water was allegedly poisoned, if the news on TV was to believed. This meant I had to find bottled water, which wasn't anywhere in this house but turned out to be present in a house three doors down. Quest completed.

Tucked away inside the pantry of the next-to-last house on the street, I read the instructions on the milk powder box out loud. "One level scoop of powder to one fluid ounce of water." Fortunately, the bottle had markings for the ounces. As fast as I could, I mixed the two ingredients and gently shook the bottle up and down. I knew the water was supposed to be lukewarm, but how should I heat up the bottle? Without electricity, I wouldn't get a peep out of Mr. Microwave. While cooing at the baby, I cast a doubtful look around. It took me a few seconds to think of turning on the hot tap and holding the bottle underneath the water.

No dice, you idiot. A boiler needs electricity too.

So I kept looking until my eyes settled on the gas stove. *Okay, the ignitor also uses electricity, but they must have a lighter in this kitchen somewhere.* Hastily I pulled open a few drawers. I didn't find a lighter, but I did find matches, which was just fine. I quickly switched on the cooker, put a pan onto the ring, and tossed the contents of the bottle into the pan to heat it up a bit before pouring it back into the bottle. I tested the temperature of the milk on the inside of my wrist.

"There we are." I sat down on one of the kitchen chairs and finally fed the baby. I'd never seen a human being gulp up milk more eagerly.

After my mad rush to feed the baby, it was suddenly so very quiet. The only sound I heard was the baby drinking. Fretfully, I glanced around me. The walls seemed to cave in on me. I stared outside. Was something moving out there?

It's those children. They've come back.

I jumped to my feet and peered outside again.

You're imagining things, Anna. Don't give in to your fear, or you'll go off the deep end.

This time, I didn't see anything move, but of course, that didn't mean anything.

We have to get out of here.

Great plan. But where to go? Where was it safe?

No, you can't leave. Your parents, Hannah, Luca... they don't deserve to be left behind, especially not like this.

The walls were closing in, seemingly crushing me. I started to hyperventilate. The silence was becoming too oppressive. I hurriedly yanked the bottle from the little baby boy's mouth. Immediately he started to cry again, which, in a strange way, was the best weapon against the loneliness and the sheer madness that were nestling deeper and deeper in my brain with every passing second. At the same time, his cries were heartbreaking.

Jesus, Anna. Since when are you such a hardass?

I quickly slipped the nipple back into his little mouth.

One thing was for sure: I had to leave here and find a place where I felt secure that no one would barge in to kill us. I needed time to think and sort things out – make plans.

Carrying the newborn baby and the bottle in my arms, I started up the stairs. Midway, I froze when I heard something outside – a trashcan falling over? A cat was hissing. But that's not what had stopped me in my tracks. I heard voices – whispering and very close by.

It's not real. Get this – it's your imagination!

But what if it wasn't? What if someone was in this house?

Are those footsteps?

"Who's there?" I cried out, my voice catching. My mouth was suddenly dry. No one answered, but my eyes, pricked up to hear every little thing, heard a faint thumping noise on the other side of the front door.

It's a dog!

No, it was something else, I was sure of it.

Keeping an eye on the front door, I backed up the stairs with shaking knees.

Shit, you were right. They're here!

The smell of cold sweat crept up my nostrils. Man, I was jealous of the child in my arms, blissfully ignorant of everything. The only thing he worried about was the next meal. In a way, I was even jealous of the people who got killed, no matter how crude the thought. After all, they didn't have to go through this.

At the top of the stairs, I turned around. I had to run,

flee the scene, but where should I go? I searchingly looked around, checking out the other closed doors. Because they were closed, hardly any light entered the second-floor landing, and everything was plunged in gray shadows. What if someone was hiding behind *those* doors, waiting for me to open them?

Stop, Anna – stop! You shouldn't think like that.

Too late.

From the corner of my eye, I clocked the bathroom. It was the only door that was ajar, and I could see no one waiting for me inside.

I swallowed and made my decision, running into the tiled room as fast as I could. My heart beating frantically, I pulled aside the shower curtain, a part of me expecting to see a dead body in the bathtub. Thank God that wasn't the case. I slammed the door shut as fast as I could, and locked it from the inside. Through force of habit, I reached for the light switch before realizing that the electricity was out. Whatever – the sun shone into the room through a tiny window just below the ceiling, and that was enough for me. The most important thing right now was that I felt safe. I know – naïve, right? If someone really wanted to break and enter, they'd make it work somehow. Besides, I had to get out of this house at some point – and that point wouldn't be far off. The baby was bound to get hungry again soon.

"How am I ever gonna pucker up the courage to open this door again?" I whispered to myself.

I put the baby bottle on the floor and lowered myself onto the edge of the bathtub, the little baby boy precariously balancing on my left hand. I was panting from the exertion. Somewhere in the distance, a dog barked and I could have sworn I heard someone shouting. I closed my eyes, shaking my pounding head before I broke down crying.

Through my tears, I looked at the little boy attentively. I felt sorry for him. He'd never know his mother. The fact that he had to have a father somewhere came to mind, but I wouldn't be able to find him. No – this child was stuck with me as much as I was stuck with him. And yet, I could feel his presence giving me strength. I wondered what I'd have done if I had been all by myself.

Bullshit. You don't have the balls to off yourself.

Maybe not, but loneliness can change a person beyond recognition. It can crush your soul; your selfness.

With squinty eyes and a facial expression that looked like he smelled something bad, the baby stretched. His little legs kicked against my stomach. I'd never seen a cuter thing in my life, and against all odds, a smile erupted on my face. I put the bottle down and moved the child to rest against my chest, which made his head just pop out above my shoulder. Gently, I patted his back, which made him burp three times in a row.

"Well done," I whispered, wiping away my tears. I held him out in front of me, supporting his neck. "What's your name, little man?"

By way of response, the baby punched the air in front of him with his little fists.

I thought about it. The first child to be born after the so-called end of the world – or at least, the first child I knew. How to baptize such a child? The answer came to me immediately.

"How about Adam?"

The boy opened his mouth and clasped his hands together. He couldn't smile yet, but this looked a lot like it, in my opinion.

"Yeah? You think that'll work?"

The baby boy opened his mouth, then closed it again. A warm glow pervaded my body. "All righty." I held him close. It took another second for my body to register a different kind of warm feeling on my skin, and a few more seconds for me to realize that Adam was peeing. Hastily, I held him out, causing the trickle of urine to splatter onto the floor, but the damage had already been done. *I have to find some diapers and fast.*

Sunbeams landed on Adam, showing me not just how dirty he was, but me just as much. My clothes were sticking to my body. I couldn't remember ever having felt this dirty before. Carefully, I got up to pull open the two drawers underneath the washbasin. To my relief, I found three towels. No fresh clothes – I'd have to open the door…

Yeah, right. Forget it!

… and in all likelihood, I'd have to search the bedrooms. I was hoping to find some diapers there, too, but didn't think I would.

I put two towels into the washbasin, building a sort of nest for the baby before I lay Adam down. As soon as he felt the cotton against his skin, he pinched his eyes shut as though giving his seal of approval. I winked at him, caressing his left cheek with one finger. Then, I headed for the tub and switched on the shower. While the water poured from the showerhead with an almost wheezing sound, I peeled off my filthy clothes. No steam was coming off the water, which made sense – there was no electricity, so no hot water. Something told me that I'd be crazy to rinse off under the shower under these circumstances, but my sticky skin and dirty clothes were driving me nuts. I picked up the baby from the washbasin, took off his scarf, and stepped underneath the cold water. He was already shivering before the water hit him.

A bang. Downstairs, something must have toppled over in the living room. Or was I just imagining things? My first reaction was to switch off the shower again and listen carefully, but I didn't have the guts. Drowning out other sounds was the only defense I had. It enabled me to feel safe, even though the shower curtain didn't fully close and I continuously kept one eye on the door.

Water had never felt more liberating, even if it was ice cold. It washed away the sweat and blood and made me alert. It also made me relive the memories of the past few days, which was strangely therapeutic. Of course it frightened me, but it also gave me strength. I felt hate flooding my body – hate for the ones who'd done this to me and the rest of the world. That emotion was exactly what I needed to survive this. I had to block out the rest for the time being. No time to mourn – I'd take my time later. If I let it in now, I'd crumble and I had no idea whether I would ever get back up again.

I kept Adam away from the cold water, but washed him by wetting the tip of a towel and gently rubbing it over his body. I expected him to start crying, but he just silently stared ahead at nothing in particular. His body curled up in fetus position, and it melted my heart. It was in that moment that I made him a promise – as long as he was around to fight for, I'd do everything in my power to conquer my fears and keep him alive. The thought terrified me just as much as it gave me hope, especially whenever I glanced at the bathroom door thinking I'd have to open it again sooner or later.

By me, or by someone else.

-15-

After half an hour, I was sitting on the edge of the tub, shaking with fear and wrapped in a towel. It had suddenly dawned on me that I may have made a fatal mistake.

What if the water isn't just poisonous when you drink it?

I was ready to kick myself. Why hadn't I thought of that before?

Don't go there. Maybe there's nothing wrong. Do I feel any different?

No, but of course that didn't have to mean anything.

With my ears perked up, I stared at the bathroom door. As though it would enable me to see through the wood and make out someone waiting for me at the other side, I narrowed my eyes and squinted at it. I didn't hear any sound coming from the hallway, so maybe I'd imagined things before. Silence roamed the room like a ghost, even more so now that the tap had stopped dripping into the bathtub. Adam was in the washbasin, wrapped in towels. He was asleep, his little legs playfully kicking at the air in his dreams.

For the past few minutes, I'd tried to put all the pieces of the puzzle together and take stock. Several events from the moment I'd woken up naked in that terrible room had crossed my mind. Something told me that they were all connected – that they were the reason I was still alive. It was a ridiculous notion that I filed away as best as I could.

I had a plan – or actually, it was more like a goal I'd set myself. The simple fact was: I had no one left. Sure, Steph might still be alive, but I couldn't allow myself to put too much hope in that. The idea did give me courage and a reason to not stay here forever. I had to keep going – not just in order to find Steph, but also in order to take better care of Adam. A baby needs a lot of food, and I had to find it ASAP.

So the first step would be to open that bathroom door.

I sighed, balling my hand into a fist before casting a look at Adam. Then, I stood up and nodded to myself. If someone was indeed waiting for me at the other side of that door, they'd better be fast, because I'd throw the first punch and fight dirty. Still, I didn't want to just head out unprepared, so I busied myself by looking around for an object I could use as a weapon. At last I had to settle for the shower curtain rail. I pulled it off the wall and clenched it in my left hand so tightly that my knuckles turned white. In an attempt to slow down my heartbeat, I took a deep breath. One last time, I put my ear to the door.

I listened.

Nothing.

It's all in your head, Anna. There's no one there!

I'd find out soon enough.

I opened the door to a crack and peered out into the hallway.

Nobody.

It gave me courage. My heart skipped a beat from sheer euphoria.

I pushed the door open wider and stepped onto the

landing. The wooden floor creaked under my weight. Holding my breath, I looked around. I didn't see anybody, didn't hear a soul.

My gaze fell on the closed bedroom door next to me. I tiptoed toward it, opening it as carefully as I could while brandishing the plastic curtain rail like a club.

The room contained nothing more than a double bed with bedside tables on either side, a painting on the wall, and a wardrobe in the corner. I rushed toward it and quickly slipped into some clean clothes. After that, I tiptoed back to the bathroom, carefully lifted Adam, and snatched the baby bottle off the floor before heading for the stairs. I stood at the top for a moment.

The front door was right there in my line of vision. Just a few steps down, but a world away at the same time. Again, I listened for intruders.

Nothing.

In an apparent attempt to calm me down, rays of sunlight shone through the little window above the front door. They made me aware of the fact that the sun would set in just a few hours. Darkness would be master and commander of the world once more, and I'd have to face it with just Adam in tow. The thought paralyzed me with fear. I knew one thing for sure, though – I didn't want to wait around on my own for the darkness to descend. I had to get out.

God, I hope I'll find a different group of people by then.

Looking around furtively, cradling Adam against my chest and holding up the plastic rail, I descended the stairs step by step, until I was at the door.

No one's here. If anyone were here, surely they'd killed me by now. I mean, why wait?

I had a point, but still…

I opened the front door and gingerly stepped outside. The wind knocked me back a bit, but other than that, the street was quiet. Too quiet, almost. This time, I forced myself to truly look at the dead bodies and the havoc that had been wreaked. I realized I needed to toughen up. I had to if I wanted to live – and keep Adam alive. It wasn't easy. I bit my lip, fighting the tears that welled up as I came to terms with the fact that I had to leave all the dead behind – including my parents and sister. What I wished for the most was the chance to give them a proper burial because they deserved it, but I'd never manage that on my own. The street might have seemed peaceful right now, but at any moment new groups of armed children could round the bend. What if they didn't spare me this time, or worse: what if they took Adam from me? No – I had to get out of here and get help.

Once you find people to help you, you'll probably be able to ask a few strong men to help you dig graves.

I sure hoped so.

Death was a stomach-turning visitor in these parts. Its stench, its presence. I hated it like it was evil incarnate, an actual creature. A creature that had taken away everything and drained me like young kittens suck their mother dry before she collapses onto her side because she can't go on anymore. That's how I felt: drained and exhausted. But I had to keep going, for Adam.

My gaze landed on the parked Jeep on the driveway, surrounded by a few scattered dead bodies. The trunk was open and was crammed full of overnight bags. I had no time to check out the contents – I didn't need to. These people had made a run for it and so they packed all the bare essentials. Clothes, foods, mementos. There was bound to be some useful stuff in those bags – things that would help me tough it out until I found a place where the whole world hadn't gone to shit. Provided there was such a place.

There has to be!

One thing I needed for sure were supplies for the baby. Diapers, wipes, formula. I heaved a sigh and looked back at the house. A shiver ran through me. I didn't want to go back in there. What if there was somebody after all – someone who was waiting for me, looking for me?

You don't have a choice. Come on, chin up.

With a grunt, I tossed the baby bottle in the trunk and forced myself to run back to the nursery. For a second I contemplated leaving Adam behind in the car. If I didn't carry him, I could take more stuff from the house – if I *could* find more stuff. But I quickly dismissed the idea. I'd never leave him on his own.

As fast as I could, still clutching the shower curtain rail in one hand and staring straight ahead, I stormed up the stairs and into the nursery where I stood gasping for breath. I looked around me – I didn't want to spend one second longer than necessary in this place.

I didn't find much – a half pack of diapers, a few rompers, socks and a jacket – but it would have to do. It could have been worse; I could have returned empty-handed.

Balancing the baby and the curtain rail in one hand, I wedged the diapers and the clothes underneath my other arm and I ran downstairs. On my way out, I also grabbed the pack of milk powder from the kitchen top and hurried outside. I made a beeline for the Jeep, dumped the baby stuff in the trunk before slamming it shut and sliding into the driver's seat. A sleeping Adam and my 'weapon' were beside me in the passenger's seat. In order to get the key, I had to get out again and walk over to the dead man who was stretched out next to the car, his hand half open.

"I'm sorry," I said as I pried the keys out of his stiff fingers. I sat down behind the wheel quickly.

After the silence that had been my companion for the past few minutes, the humming of the engine shattered my eardrums like a steel pan clattering onto a tiled floor. The sound seized me by the throat and prompted me to do a quick scan of my surroundings, afraid someone up to no good might have heard us. Adam jolted awake and began to wail. The difference between the silence of before and the present noise around me was so surreal it almost made me lose all courage I'd mustered up so carefully.

I yelped when something emerged from behind one of the houses, running my way. The animal strutted forward in my direction as fast as his three functional legs could carry him.

"Luca?" I asked, partly dazed and partly relieved.

I opened the door, stepped outside and sank to my knees. The dog buried his head in my stomach, causing me to lose balance and fall backward on my behind. Luca barked, licking my face and hands while giving me a searching look.

"How did you get out of the attic, huh?"

Luca barked in response.

Maybe someone set him loose, someone who is now observing you.

The thought made me scramble up fast and cast an anxious look around. I didn't see anyone.

Doesn't mean a thing.

That was absolutely true, so I opened the back door, lifting Luca to put him on the back seat. He immediately shifted into a position that stopped his broken leg from bumping into anything.

"Don't worry, boy. Once we're safe, I'll set the bone for you."

I slammed the door shut and sat down behind the wheel again. For one final time, I looked from Adam and Luca to the empty street ahead. For a split second, my mind wandered back to my life as it had been before, the way you think of something that might either be a dream or a long-lost reality. Thinking of the past meant being there in a way, which was good. Still, I realized the past could never catch up with the present anymore. What had once been, would never come back, and that included my family.

With a lump in my throat and trembling knees, I hit the gas pedal and left my street behind. In the rearview mirror, I saw some translucent, ghostly figures staring after me with pain in their eyes. They were the now-dead inhabitants of this street, and my parents and sister were at the front of the group. I knew it wasn't real – that my mind was playing tricks on me. And yet, I kept seeing the people like the ghosts that they'd turned into. I swallowed, shaking my head and wiping the tears from my eyes before whispering: "I'm sorry."

-16-

Present time – three months later

I'm on the floor inside a gray emptiness, where time has been banished, fog curls in wisps around me, and sound can hardly penetrate the air to reach my ears. My body is shaking with fear, my mouth dry. In the real world, sweat is pouring down my body – I can smell it from here.

I know that this shadow world isn't real. I've been here before – in fact, I visit this place at least three times a week. It's like my brain only has a scant selection of videos available to show me in my sleep, and it's completely disinterested in which one it picks before I go to bed.

They're coming. Already, I can hear their eerie laughter, their footfalls. I curl up into a ball, looking in vain for a way out to get to Adam, but I know I'm here all alone. Maybe that's the most frightening part of all.

The six children step out of the foggy haze. The dream worlds have colored their features with even more terrifying traits. Their red eyes light up in the fog, and the grins around their mouths are too big for their faces. Those grins are too broad, like the corners of the mouths are stretched too wide. The children stand around me in a circle, surrounding me, fencing me in.

"You're one of us."

The words echo around me, coming toward me from

all sides, apparently repeated by the emptiness surrounding me, because the children haven't spoken – they just stare at me with those creepy grins.

One of them takes a step into my direction. I want to scream but lie there as if frozen.

"Kill the baby! Kill the baby! *Kill the baby!*"

The words envelop me like some sort of mantra. I squeeze my eyes shut, hoping to wake myself up. For a split second, I think it worked, because the voices fall away. But the temperature steadily drops to the freezing point, telling me that I'm still a prisoner of my own imagination.

A shudder runs through me, this time caused by the cold. I open my eyes, staring ahead into nothingness, where I can see my warm breath in the cold air like puffs of smoke. I look down at my hands. All warmth had seeped out from them. They look gray and dead to the touch.

Voices – behind me, pleading with me.

"Why didn't you come back for us? Why did you leave us?"

I turn around and see a car rise up from the low-hanging fog. The windshield is shattered. My mom and dad look at me disapprovingly.

A girl steps out from behind the car. I instantly recognize my sister. She's dragging her left leg and she's covered in blood. "I'm so alone. Come back for me."

I cry and scream, crawling backwards. I don't make it far. The floor turns to quicksand, slowly sucking me down. I fight it, all the while knowing that it's useless. My feet are gobbled up, just like my hands and my behind.

My sister keeps advancing, stretching out her hands

in a helpless gesture. She's so close now that I can see the blue veins in her white arms and face, just like the dark rings under her eyes.

My chest goes under next, and then my shoulders and my neck.

Hannah is standing next to me, her legs only inches away.

"Help me," I beg her.

She shakes her head. "You had this coming."

"I had no choice but to leave you behind!"

In response, she puts her foot on the crown of my head and speeds the process along, shoving me into the ground, where darkness reigns and a shrill sound finally heralds my release.

With a shriek, I jolt awake. The smell of cold sweat drifts into my nostrils and makes me gag. My heart is racing painfully. My eyes are wide open, but can't yet shake the haze of my nightmare – my vision's still blurred.

What the hell was that sound?

I lift my head an inch off the overnight bag that has been my pillow for the past two nights. With my common sense still entangled in a cluster of thoughts, I make a sheer Herculean effort to separate reality from illusion. Putting my hands on the rug that separates my body from the earth, roots, and leaves on the forest floor, I push myself up, my body taut and my ears perked. I look around me. The early sun filters through the treetops that stretch out over my head like protective hands. Spring has only been here for a few weeks, and the mornings are still quite chilly.

Adam's lying next to me. He's wrapped inside a thick sweater and he's wearing a warm hat, pulled down all the way past his ears. The now three-month-old baby clearly didn't hear anything, because he sleeps soundly on. I wonder whether the noise was part of my nightmare. Still, I slip my hand underneath my bag and clasp my hand around the gun that's there, pulling it out. I can't allow myself to speculate whether it was a dream or not – I have to be sure.

Rustling in the undergrowth not far away from me. Now I know for certain that it wasn't just a lingering part of my dream. Luca, who is lying at my feet, looks up and starts to growl. It's not out of fear; it sounds like a warning. I put my hand on his back. With glistening eyes, he looks up at me and softly whines.

Maybe spending the night in the forest wasn't such a good idea. We should have kept going last night. But honestly, I couldn't go on anymore after twenty hours of non-stop walking with a bag on my back, a gun in my left hand, and Adam in a baby carrier against my chest. But right now, I curse myself for it.

We're being hunted. This is why I avoid big cities and traveling by car. Much too noisy. No, we have to keep a low profile, move from place to place as quietly as we can.

We can't trust anybody.

I get up. Tightening both hands around the gun, I take a few steps toward the sound while staying low. A branch snaps underneath my foot. All my senses are on high alert, poised to register the slightest disturbance of silence.

Birds twitter away above my head. From the corner of my eye, I see a rabbit flitting away. It's one of the few live animals I've seen in a long time, save Luca, of course. I did see a lot of dead animals in the past few days, though. Deer, cats, birds, squirrels.

It was probably just one of the few rabbits still hopping around in these woods.

I have to know for sure.

Luca growls again. He gets up, making his way toward me.

"No," I say sternly. "Stay with Adam."

Luca stops, cocking his head slightly to the left to give me a questioning look, then turns around to stay with Adam like he's told. Hannah was right – he's the most faithful dog anyone could wish for. And he's smart. Sometimes, I get the feeling that he understands everything I tell him.

Voices. Still faint and far away, but they're getting louder by the second. Men – and they're coming this way.

"How much further?" The voice sounds old.

"No idea," a second person replies, sighing with exhaustion.

"Well, I hope you're satisfied."

"Excuse me?"

"*You* were the one insisting on a shortcut. If only we'd have stuck to our normal route back to camp, we'd have been there by now."

"Oh, so now it's *my* fault that the car broke down half a mile before 7-Eleven." The voice grows louder. "Besides, *you* agreed with me."

"And look where it got us…"

"At least we got two bags of food. This will feed the camp for a week, if not more."

"If we ever get there."

"We'll get there."

I press my back against a tree and listen carefully

while my heart leaps in my chest. A camp! This means that Adam and I are *not* the only civilized people left in this region – or even the world. Of course, I shouldn't have resigned myself to that thought. They can't possibly have killed *everyone*, right? I mean, I'm aware that the disaster – or whatever you prefer to call the event – was a global thing. And if Hunters roam these parts, they must be everywhere around the world, but surely there are *some* survivors?

Hunters don't need camps. They roam the countryside with a single goal: to track down and kill people. I can't allow myself too much hope. After all, how am I to know if these men speak the truth? Maybe they've already made me, and this is some sick game for them.

No. Hunters don't play games. They just kill you.

Something urges me to approach the men, ask them where they set up camp. God, what I wouldn't do to be among people once more. But I don't move. In my mind's eye, I once again see images of the men with guns who roamed the streets on D-Day – that's what I dubbed that fateful day – killing off every living thing. I see the six children who instigated the bloodshed up in the attic and still haunt my dreams to this day. Images of creatures that seem human at first glance, but don't live up to that impression when you look closer. Because they're something else altogether – and it's too late to get away.

Like I said: I can't trust anybody.

Besides, the two men have probably arrived at the same conclusion. The guns slung across their shoulders are clear evidence of that. They'd probably shoot me before I can even open my mouth to address them. And who could blame them? I'll do the same if they come any closer than this.

The old voice speaks up again. "Let's turn left here. There's clouds drifting in and I don't want to be stuck out here when the rain starts to fall."

More rustling. Footsteps. I hold the gun even tighter and see both men walking away from me. Only after they disappear from sight do I exhale, allowing myself to relax a little bit.

Looks like I won't have to kill anyone this morning after all.

-17-

The past

Three days after I'd left my parents' and sister's bodies behind, we crossed eastwards in the direction of a veritable wall of thunderclouds rising up on the horizon, like a stampede of buffalos. In the rearview mirror, the sun sank below the horizon, as though even she was running away from what lay ahead.

We had to pull over soon. Traveling in the dark didn't just give me the heebie-jeebies, it was also dangerous. The Jeep was comfortably warm and fast, but it was also loud and it stood out. In the mornings and afternoons, the odds were evened out – I could see danger coming just as well as that danger could see me. But I lost that advantage once it turned dark, which wasn't true for my possible attackers – they only had to follow the sound of the roaring engine and the intermittent shrieks of the baby. The fact that this Jeep stood out was also the reason why I decided to take a huge detour and drive through the forest. After all, the odds of serial killers roaming these woods were a lot slimmer.

For the past few days we'd pretty much stayed inside the car to go about our business. We ate here – from the horn of plenty that the original car owners had fortunately left in the trunk – as well as slept and traveled inside the vehicle. Luca and I only got out when nature called, and even then I always kept an eye on the car. Adam peed and pooped inside the car in a diaper, one of the few I still had left. Of course, I cleaned him up afterward, but the foul stench was hard to get rid of.

According to a road sign, we were only seven miles away from a gas station. Which was a good thing, because the Jeep had nearly run out of fuel. We still had another 1300 miles to go to get to Keystone, Colorado, where Steph lived according to the latest reports. I knew the trip was probably doomed. I knew which city to go to, but beyond that I had nothing – no street name or house number. How was I supposed to find my brother like this?

I thought back to the last time me and Steph spoke. We kept in touch through the secure server provided by the protection program. My emails never went straight to him – they had to be read by a third party first, to make sure we wouldn't blab about our location in any way. It always made my emails sound a bit like status reports. I grimaced. The witness protection program… I thought my life had been a mess back then. But it couldn't hold a candle to the mess I was in right now.

It felt like a hand was squeezing my heart. Steph had wanted to get married and was about to get a promotion – that's what he'd told me in his last email to me. The next two years were a big gap in my life. I'd missed it all – the wedding, the party, the look on my parents' faces when their son had walked up to the altar.

Had the protection program made an exception so they could have a wedding party? After all, a party like that would have been an ideal occasion for the Colombians to strike.

I pushed the thought away. It wasn't getting me

anywhere anyway. In all likelihood, I'd never find out.

Adam had woken up but luckily kept quiet, just like Luca. That was equal parts positive and negative. It meant he wasn't presently hungry and he didn't need a diaper change, but the silence allowed my inner demons to rear their ugly heads, their voices whispering in my ears. My parents, Hannah, Carla, Peter, Julia, Max, Victor, Daisy… they were all in the back seat. Yup, the back seat was seriously overcrowded, filled with ghosts staring me down the way only ghosts could – I assume – and shaking their heads at me.

Victor: "Might as well give up. You're never gonna find him."

Max: "And what will you do if you *do* find him? What's the point?"

I wouldn't be alone anymore. I don't know how much longer I can bear this isolation.

Hannah: "None of this is even real."

Daisy, in a hysterical voice: "My baby! You took my baby. Bring him back."

Hannah: "Turn this car around and come back to us."

It was hard to resist the voices, especially when driving through lonely forests, where the barren road meandered past miles and miles of trees and undergrowth. It was a place where you could get away from reality and be lulled into a trance. Here, there were no bodies, no demolished houses. Just a serene silence, interrupted by the hum of the engine and the wind playing with the tree branches. It almost made me change my mind. *What if the voices were right? What if it wasn't the world that had gone mad – what if it was me?*

I gave Adam a sideward glance.

What if I did snatch that child?

141

I shook my head, mentally picking up that thought to put it under lock and key in the back of my mind. I had to stay strong and make sure that these random thoughts and emotions running through my mind wouldn't drown out my sanity.

Your 'sanity'? You're hearing voices. Reddest flag ever.

The other me had a point.

The road curved to the left and took me further and further into the darkness.

A flash of light split the sky in two. It was followed by raindrops, announcing a rainstorm by splattering onto the windshield. It didn't take long for the thunderous serenade to come into full swing and the Jeep was doused in thunder and lightning. It drowned out the hum of the engine and made me flinch. In the back seat, Luca growled. Strangely enough, Adam kept quiet. He attentively looked up at the windshield and reached out with his hands.

"Mmpf," he laughed.

"Oh, so you like this, huh?"

"Mmpf," the baby replied, his hands waving around.

"Well, I don't." With a sigh, I switched on the radio, hoping for something more than just static this time. No luck, though. I changed the frequency, but that just gave me more static, so I gave up.

I turned around for a second. "Can't you sing us a song, Luca?"

Despite his broken leg, the dog wagged his tail.

"Didn't think so."

The sign said that the gas station was three miles away from Woodstone, a small town which I could only hope had some form of civilization left.

Surely they must? It makes sense for the enemy to destroy

large cities, but all the towns and villages?

The thought made me feel marginally better, as much as that was possible. It would mean I'd get to speak to people again, could ask them for help, and maybe even ask some volunteers to come back to and bury the bodies of my family.

Fill her up first, or you won't even make it to Woodstone.

The windshield wipers bravely battled against the pouring rain, but it was coming down in buckets now and I had to slow down considerably. The gas station sign had withstood the fall of mankind, though, and it beckoned me closer. By some miracle, the red LED-light of the electronic signage was still working. Either they had a backup generator, or they hadn't been struck by electricity failure here – not yet, anyway. I pulled up into the forecourt next to the only pump in the station, covered by a canopy fitted with functioning strip lights. I lowered the windows by an inch to let some fresh air in, and got out.

"Keep an eye on Adam for me, Luca. I'll be right back." I slammed the car door shut with a bang.

The wind battered my body and made my shirt flap around me. Some raindrops managed to touch me, but overall the canopy stopped the storm from reaching me.

I cast a look around. The forest was hardly visible anymore. Apart from the darkness that had drifted in due to the bad weather, the dusk had turned into the dark of night in the past few minutes. Around the gas station, everything was now pitch black.

While I operated the pump, I glanced at the tiny store, hoping to see someone in there. Nobody. In this case, I reasoned the owner was out of luck. I'd seen enough horror movies in my life to know that I shouldn't, under any circumstance, enter the deserted store. No way – as soon as the tank was full, I'd get the hell out of here and drive to Woodstone next.

But when I was about to screw the cap back on, a man appeared behind the counter. I saw him through the glass, and he saw me too. His first reaction was seemingly one of anger – of outrage, even. He narrowed his eyes and started to come out from behind the counter. Once he was there, though, he froze, his face a mask of genuine surprise.

I stood rooted to the spot.

Luca barked. Adam started and began to wail. The closed car doors and the rain pummeling the canopy muffled the noise.

The man stepped out. With his white Einstein hairdo, a mustache to match, and a simple outfit on, he looked haggard. "What are you doing here?" He had to repeat the question twice before I could understand him. Each time he did, he took a step closer until he was only a few yards away from me.

"I'm getting gas," I replied.

"You on your way to Woodstone?"

I nodded.

"But that's *my* area."

I shot him an uncomprehending look. "Excuse me?"

"The orders were changed? They think we can't handle it on our own, or what?" His hair was dancing in the wind like a sea anemone.

"Orders?"

The man frowned, nodding at the car. "Why do you have a baby and a dog with you?"

I didn't respond and took a step back. There was something fishy about this guy.

The man took a menacing step forward. "Soldier, what's your objective?"

Dear God – is he talking to me?

"Ex-excuse me," I stammered.

"Your objective, soldier. What is it?"

"I don't know…"

He looked me up and down at length. "You no longer remember, do you?" he said at last.

I kept quiet, trying to find a way out of this situation, but failing.

Just great, girl. Good job! You got yourself some quality time with the village idiot – or worse. Now what?

A damned good question.

The man crossed his arms in front of his chest and flashed me the same sardonic smile as the children did, back in the attic. "You don't remember you're an angel, do you? How God wants to wipe the slate clean and sent his Hunters to do His work." He shook his head disbelievingly. "Your human identity has taken over. I can sense it. They told us this might happen from time to time." He clenched a fist and took another step in my direction. "They also told us what to do if we encountered an Aberration." And with those words, he went straight for me.

I gasped for breath. With a shriek, I jumped sideways and broke into a run. As I dashed off, I glanced over my shoulder. The man hesitated for a fraction of a second, then I heard him call out: "First you, then the baby, then Woodstone." After which he started to chase me.

Shit, shit, shit.

Fighting for air, I ran away from the building. Once I was away from the shelter of the canopy, I was soon soaked to the bone by the downpour. Einstein was in pursuit and was gaining on me. I wasn't going to outrun him.

Quickly, I thought about my options.

What options?

The dark was beckoning me like a witch from a fairytale.

Come into my arms, my child. Already I have gobbled up the trees and the rest of the world, and now it's your turn. With us, you will be safe. He will not follow you here. In here, nothing will follow you ever again.

Which was exactly my problem. Fleeing into the woods might get me out of this predicament – although it was just a temporary stay of execution since I had no dry clothes, food, or even a source of light on me – but I'd sign the death warrants of both Adam and Luca if I did this.

So I went around the building instead, doubling back to the store.

Right, because that's the smart thing to do – going in there? Those horror movies, remember?!

But when the heat closes in…

The man was still yelling at me. He burst through the door and into the store on his way after me. "Give it up. If you forgot about your assignment, you have just as little right to live as those humans out there."

"You stay away from me!" My voice trembled with fear, much like all my limbs. I ran through the store room screaming, shoving all the display racks I passed so as to make them fall over. The man dodged most of them, but the one-to-last one tripped him up. He face-planted on the floor, cursing loudly, which gave me the opportunity to fly through the door next to the counter to seek refuge in the little office behind it.

146

There were two bodies in the corner. Motionless. Fresh blood on the floor.

That man had been on his way to Woodstone to rain death and destruction down on the townspeople, and he made a stop here.

I looked around me in a panic. I needed a weapon, something to protect myself. But what kind of useful weapon could be lying around in some back office at a gas station?

Think, think, think!

My heart beating in my throat, I gasped for breath as I heard the man scrambling to his feet while still cursing.

At that moment, my gaze landed on the fire extinguisher. Knees trembling, I rushed over to the thing, yanking it off the wall before I lined up next to the door. I knew the man was about to burst through it any second now.

If I'd been just a few seconds slower, I probably wouldn't have made it. The door flew open, which made me push down the handle on the extinguisher with a scream.

Nothing happened.

The safety pin!

The man was already inside by the time I had a second try. This time, a hiss of hydrogen and foam squirted out of the nozzle. It hit him in the face and filled the room with white smoke. He screamed, swinging his fists around in an attempt to localize me. I only saw his hands coming toward me. I ducked down and away, running into the other direction. Apparently, he'd been counting on that, because the next thing I knew, his face filled with rage emerged from the smoke.

I raised the extinguisher in the air and slammed it

down onto his forehead.

Uttering a cry of agony, the man slumped to the ground.

My stomach contracted, my shoulders slumped, and I lost my hold on the fire extinguisher. With a dull, metal thud it landed on the floor. I was panting. Adrenalin scorched my veins. The smoke disappeared and showed me the man, lying motionlessly on the floor.

Somewhere in the distance, I could hear Luca barking. I was ready to leave this place behind and I whipped around to get out. But just as I was about to move, I felt a cold hand clasping itself around my ankle. In slow motion, I looked down. The man showed me an almost maniacal grin while grunting. Blood trickled down his cheek from a cut in his temple. It didn't seem to cause him any pain.

"I was sent by Him to rain down His wrath upon Woodstone. Do you really think I'm that easy to defeat?"

His touch made my skin crawl. My stomach twisted itself into a knot and I felt like throwing up. A shudder ran through me like electric current. All my muscles contracted. I slumped to the floor and squeezed my eyes shut, shrieking with agony.

From afar, I could hear the man's voice. "See…"

Suddenly, all sensation was gone, just like all the noise.

In surprise, I opened my eyes.

I was standing in the middle of a blank canvas, an utterly white nothingness. The space was filled with a kind of mist that seemed thick but didn't obscure my vision completely. It was emitting a glow that made it seem alive, filled with its own intensity, its own respiration.

Out of nowhere, a few entities emerged – faint lines in this milky world, but I could *sense* I was connected to thousands of them at once. One of them was stronger than the others, though. Like a humongous shepherd, it towered over all of us as though he was about to address his flock. And I was one of his sheep. This was life – *his* life before he had been reborn, inside my naked body, strapped to a chair. I knew it, *understood* it, because right now I *was* him – the entity trapped inside me. The Shepherd spoke to us, explained His plans and goals. And I understood. We were all pawns in His grand scheme. It didn't matter, because we were all happy to serve Him. It was why we were created. Not a single one among us questioned His motives. After all, we all knew He moved in mysterious ways.

We would become one with human bodies. Use their mortal coils in order to do our work on earth. We'd be scattered all over the planet, among people from all walks of life, from beggars to presidents. We'd be people with the terrible might to effect terrible things – people who had access to nuclear codes, who were able to 'press the button', so to speak.

This is a memory! Not my memory, but his!

All of a sudden, the white started to fade away. The world trembled. White noise interfered with the images. A few seconds later, I fell to my knees, completely drained and back at the gas station.

"Now you remember?" Einstein cackled demonically, his voice barely rising above the din of the storm outside – the howling wind, the rain pummeling the roof.

I shivered.

My stomach heaved and I threw up at last.

Don't believe this. It's not real. It can't be. God, angels,

149

none of that is real. And even if God was real, he wouldn't act out like Satan.

But what if He was one and the same? Judge and offender, water and fire, sun and light.

And there was the rub – I *knew* it was all true. I could feel it in every fiber of my being. It was exactly the reason why I curled up like a fetus and trembled with fear.

I'm not human – not fully human, anyway. On the outside I may look like a human being, but there's something hiding inside, someone *else. Someone has possessed my body.*

But how could that be? I had memories from before I was *reborn.*

A different idea floated to the surface. I wasn't raised a Christian. My parents were both atheists, and I never bothered to ponder the possibility of there being a deity. Now, I was experiencing with all my senses that the stories were true. I wasn't a believer, because 'believing' meant there was room for doubt. And I didn't doubt this for one second. It made me cry like a little child. God wanted to cleanse the earth. What would he do with the souls of the dearly departed? My family's souls, for instance.

A shadow towered over me. Einstein looked down at me, his fists clenched. Only now did I see how soulless his eyes were.

"Why are you going along with this?" Tears rolled down my cheeks and blurred my vision. "Can't you see that it is wrong?"

The man shook his head. "That is a human opinion. There is no right or wrong, but you won't be able to understand unless you come back as *you* and accept your angelic essence."

"No, that doesn't make sense. I have memories!"

The man sighed. "A body is human, and so is the soul. That's the basis. A celestial soul blends with the basic makeup of a body – a process that may take months. Which means the person in question can feel what's happening and struggles against it accordingly. From time to time it happens that the angel in question seizes control over the body in question, then loses it because the soul hasn't been completely vanquished yet. It fights back and seizes control of the body once more."

Those weapons in my home, I thought, baffled. *Joey. The angel inside of me killed him. I killed him before my soul fought its way back and made me flee the scene. Apparently, I didn't get far before they found me again.*

"When that happens," Einstein continued, "a team is dispatched to track down those Aberrations to bring them to a secluded spot, tie them down and keep them away from any human impulse that the soul can latch onto, so the angelic soul can battle the human soul again. Usually, the human soul is no match for the celestial one, but on very few occasions, the human survives and the angel is a prisoner inside the body." He sighed. "These days, we just kill Aberrations. Less messy." He fixed me with a threatening look. "I'll give you one more chance. Accept who you are, kill the soul within you, and join me when I go to Woodstone. We have work to do."

"I can't," I sobbed.

"Yes you can, you just have to fight."

My eyes were looking for a way out, but there was none. I was trapped. This was it. He was going to kill me and there wasn't a damn thing I could do about it. I cursed myself for allowing this to happen. If I hadn't decided to take a detour, I wouldn't have been in this position. I wouldn't have known the truth, and I'd still have driven around in blissful ignorance.

In my mind's eye, I saw Adam and Luca.

I'm sorry, guys.

"Hello?" A voice. It resonated in my brain and it was coming from the store. "Anyone there?"

When Einstein and I looked up in surprise, the door opened and a young, muscular man stepped inside. He was wearing a checkered plaid shirt and a baseball cap.

A second voice piped up. "Who in all the hell would leave a baby and a dog unattended inside a car, in times like these?"

"Maybe it's someone on the run. If all the stories are true..." The muscular man abruptly fell silent when he saw us. He wanted to open his mouth and react to what he was seeing, but Einstein didn't let him. Before the beefcake knew what was happening to him, the angel had twisted around to face him. He grabbed him by the neck and lifted him an inch off the floor like it was nothing.

"Hmmpf," the muscular man managed to choke out. The fear in his eyes made it clear to me what this meant for my situation. As fast as I could, I scrambled up and away, dashing past him and into the store.

A loud thud was coming from the office, and I imagined Einstein snapping the guy's neck before casting him away like a piece of garbage.

"Jesus Christ, what's happening, John?" The second man was standing on the threshold. He was just as muscular as his buddy and his outfit was just as woodchopper-fashionable. "Who are you?" he asked as soon as he caught sight of me.

"Get out *now*. He's strong, inhumanly so..."

Stammering, I darted past him on my way out, passing the Honda that was probably their ride. Without looking back, I yanked open the Jeep door and jumped behind the wheel. Luca was barking, Adam was crying. With jittery hands, I turned the key in the ignition. "Come on, come *on*." I'd never stepped on the gas like this. With skidding tires, I peeled out of the gas station.

It was only when the rain slid down the windshield once more and we were on route again that I risked glancing in the rearview mirror. A part of me expected to see Einstein chasing the car. A shiver snaked its way down my spine. He'd lifted that man like it was nothing – like he was stronger than was humanly possible. And if he was stronger than any human, maybe he was faster, too.

Angels on the warpath. With creatures like that, who needs demons?

I was just able to catch Einstein leisurely sauntering outside with Lumberjack Two's lifeless body dangling from his hand. He was holding him by his plaid shirt and he grinned as he amicably waved me goodbye.

I let out a cry, pressed the pedal to the metal, and tore past the sign that proclaimed: Woodstone, 7 miles.

We all had one thing in common: me, that town, and the whole damn world.

We were all royally screwed.

-18-

Present time

A branch snaps under my feet. Birds are singing in the trees. Luca is darting ahead in front of me. It is no longer evident that his leg was once broken, although it was a heavy battle to set the bone without him biting my arm off in defense. He stops at a bush and sniffs it before lifting a leg in approval. Urine splatters against the small leaves and marks this part of the forest as his territory. I chuckle when it occurs to me that Luca has claimed more territory by now than most kings of old.

Adam is asleep in the baby carrier resting against my chest. *His* weight isn't the problem right now. Despite the fact that we've only walked for a few miles at most, the bag on my back is getting heavier by the minute. Which is strange, because it's practically empty. I've become too weak. This way of traveling – anonymously and away from places you'd expect to be most dangerous – is beginning to take its toll. I'm beginning to think I made the wrong choice. It's cold, tiring, and not that much safer than I expected beforehand.

I push aside a branch and catch sight of the 7-Eleven – a lone tower of strength along a deserted highway. It has just been three months since all hell broke loose on earth, and yet this place looks like it all happened years ago. Because the lights aren't working, the building seems to have an eerie glow about it. It doesn't bother me. We're dealing with mercenary angels here, so why would ghosts bother me? Although... Images of my parents' dead bodies in the car and Hannah in the attic creep into my mind. Okay, I take that back. Some ghosts *do* bother me – a lot. I shake my head to erase the images from my mind like it's an *Etch-a-Sketch*. I can't dwell on the past too much. All it will cause is misery and despair. Not that the future is any rosier, but at least I still have Adam and Luca.

I feel for my gun and walk over to the entrance of the store, all the while casting furtive looks around. Luca is already there, sticking his nose in the air and turning toward me with a question in his eyes. I know what he means, but I have no choice. Our supplies have been more or less depleted. I have to stock up.

Please, let me find some leftover food here.

I don't have to open the door – the glass has already been shattered into a thousand pieces. It crunches under my feet when I walk over it and step inside the store.

The smell here is atrocious. I try to sniff out what kind of odor it is – rotting fish? Spoiled fruit? No, something different. In all probability, there's a dead body in here. No electricity, no AC. My stomach turns at the thought of what might happen to a dead body in all that heat. It may still be chilly in here now, but I don't doubt that this building has been in the scorching sun many times in the past few months.

The place is trashed. Apart from the glass shards, the floor is covered with torn-down display racks, glass jars, and empty soda cans. Clearly we're not the first people to loot the place. The walls are lined with beverage coolers, all the glass doors smashed, but to my surprise, I still see some stray bottles of soda inside. When I scour the premises for more, I also find some forgotten chocolate bars, bags of chips, and other candies. I'm satisfied with my find. Had this been a store closer to town, I'd have had to make do with scraps left by others, so me venturing out into the woods has been good for something, at least. Fine, it's just junk food, but I can't be picky. Unfortunately, I don't find any baby food, formula, or diapers – my lucky stars aren't *that* bright. No dog food either, but I don't think Luca minds. He eats what I eat, even though we haven't found the kind of food he can eat too, these past few days. It worries me more and more.

With a sigh, I lower the backpack onto the floor, making the glass crunch. Luca is near the counter. He softly whines and looks back at me.

I understand his signal and walk over to him, gun drawn just in case.

Oh yes, we have a winner. It's a dead body. A dead woman's body, from the looks of it, although there's hardly anything left. It's just bones with a thin layer of leathery skin. Her left eye is missing. A crow probably picked it out. I shove my upper arm under my nose and turn around in an attempt to block out the smell. I barely manage. In the past few weeks I have seen a lot of death and destruction. On the one hand it toughens you up, and on the other hand it never gets any better.

I make sure no one else is here before I do the round to grab as much stuff as I can. I know the backpack won't get any lighter like this, but what choice do I have? It might take days for us to run into another store. And who's to say the next one won't be completely robbed of all things useful? In that respect, my decision to stay off the main roads has been wise.

I sink down next to the backpack, my back against some shelves, before I take off the baby carrier with Adam still in it. I rest him against the backpack and shoot Luca a dubious look. "Maybe we should travel by car anyway, old boy. That way I won't have to lug this stuff with me. Besides, it'll be nice and dry."

Luca slightly cocks his head, a question in his eyes. My inner voice repeats what he would have told me if he could speak. Although the term 'inner voice' takes on a rather sinister – not to mention *creepy* – meaning when you consider I truly have a separate entity trapped inside me. *Sure, yeah. By all means, take the car. Keep a 'low profile'. Seriously, are you* gunning *for them to track you down?*

I shrug. "Who are we kidding? It's only a momentary reprieve. Sooner or later, the Hunters will find us."

Luca barks in protest.

"It's true, though." I shoot the Labrador a questioning look. "But hey, maybe you're right. A car wouldn't be exactly practical either."

I've seen them from the edge of the forest – rows and rows of cars on the road, plus scores of dead bodies. All belonging to people who were fleeing the cities that hadn't been destroyed by nuclear weapons yet. The angels had committed a veritable massacre there. It'd be impossible to even get through, driving a car. A motorcycle isn't an option either, although I saw two parked outside a roadhouse only three days ago. Type: Harley Davidson. Gray with a lot of chrome accents. Not that bikes were ever my thing – I wouldn't even know how to start one – but it would enable me to sail right past those cars blocking the freeway. The real problem is that bikes have only limited space – where the hell would I leave Luca?

Nope, there's nothing for it. We have to keep walking. If the last road sign I encountered three days ago was right, then Keystone shouldn't be much further. But to be frank, I'm mostly just walking for the sake of walking, not because I'm so eager to get to the Colorado ski resort. What's more, I could have been there by now. The idea that the whole resort plus village will have been destroyed and Steph might be just as dead as the rest of my family… it terrifies me. It's keeping me from really wanting to get there. But what else should I do? Stay here – in this stench? Forget it.

I sink to my knees, empty the backpack, carefully put aside the notebook I use to write down my story every day – who knows, someone might actually read it someday – and start to stack the newly-scavenged food into the bag. From the corner of my eye, I see that Adam's now awake. He stares at me with his beautiful, blue eyes. He seems to want to ask me something – he stretches out his hand, seemingly waving at me before he yawns and pulls a disgusted face.

"Well, well, sleepyhead. Decided to join us at last?" Stupid habit: asking questions to which you know the answer already.

Adam gurgles.

"Hungry?" I take one of the four remaining Gerber fruit purees – my loot from one week ago – and twist off the cap so I can feed Adam. I know at this point he should probably still be on formula, but my stash is gone and I haven't been able to find any new powdered milk yet. I bet this will upset his gut flora and result in cramps, but there's no way around it. Another reason to get to Keystone ASAP – assuming they still have stores and there are still people alive up there.

There have to be!

Also, it's obvious he needs a diaper change.

Fifteen minutes later, Adam is sitting up and leaning against me. We should actually get a move-on. This is not the right place for a child to be in and the stench is all-consuming, but I simply have to catch a breather.

I look around me and see the photo I've taken out of my backpack. I pick it up and caress it affectionately. It's a picture I found in one of the abandoned cars a few weeks ago, while I was looking for food and shelter for the night. I don't even know the couple in the photo, who are smiling lovingly at each other. Why did I take it? Well, the answer is because that couple reminds me of me and Mark. Not because they look like us – not at all, in fact – but it's the *love*, frozen in time, that touches my heart every time I look at it.

I wasn't exactly an easy person to live with, especially during the first few months I got to know Mark. He was very clingy because he didn't have that many friends, and he adored spending all his evenings with me watching movies on his couch. It drove me crazy, resulting in me treating him to the infamous 'it's not you, it's me' routine three times.

I can still remember the moment I last gave him that line – so well that it plays out like a movie in front of my eyes sometimes.

I surprised even myself with the matter-of-fact way I spoke those words. Was I really such a cold-hearted bitch? Our relationship was probably the best thing that had ever happened to him – or am I being overly self-congratulatory here? – so how could I tear out his heart and take it apart so easily? Had he really been such a nuisance? No, he hadn't. Didn't I love him? Yes, of course I did. So didn't I want him to change? God, *yes*. On the other hand: no. After all, didn't I fall for him because of the man he was, with all his flaws, much like the other way around?

What the hell was wrong with me?

Even knowing I'd done this to him twice already – and me having backed out of my decision afterward – he still looked panic-stricken for a moment. But only for a split second, because it was replaced by that calm confidence of his.

We were sitting next to each other at the bar in some café, our hands entwined. Mark addressed me in a surprisingly calm voice.

"Are you really sure?"

"Yes." *No.*

"That's what you said last time."

"But this time I mean it." I squeezed his hands. "Come on, Mark. This is the third time I'm having doubts. Why do you still believe in us like this?"

"Because I choose to." No detectable tone of anger or whisper of sadness in his voice. He was just stating a fact. "Because I love you, *because* of your volatility."

"But this is not a healthy relationship. It's not *normal*."

"Is any relationship normal?"

"We can't keep doing this…" I nervously picked at the hem of my shirt.

"Why not?" He gently wiped a tear away from my eye with his thumb. "How about telling me what's really bothering you?"

And that was my problem, right there. I couldn't. I think I knew, deep down, that this thing that annoyed me in him was actually very dear to me – that I should cherish it.

A few months later, he asked me to move in with him, and frankly, by then I often caught *myself* being the clingy one in our relationship. Maybe my insecurity had something to do with the fact I'd lived with my parents up till that point, and I'd felt trapped at home, what with the lie we were living and the thing that happened to my father.

Anyway – let's just say I've always been struggling with my inner demon, even before it turned out to be an angel of death.

End of movie. I bring my thoughts back to the present.

You stubborn cow. Don't think about the past – it's no use. It'll only make you sad.

But this is only partly true. Memories can give you strength. A memory may be the only place where your loved ones live on. Isn't it a good thing, then, to think of them?

Not in today's world. It makes you weak, and you can't afford to be weak.

That's probably true, so I flick away the photo of the couple with a sigh of frustration. It tumbles against a fallen display rack, sliding across the floor for a moment before it lands face-down underneath an empty pack of cookies.

I get to my feet. I stuff food into the bag up till a point where I'm still confident I can carry it, then slip Adam back in the baby carrier on my chest, and start to make my way out of the store.

"Come on, boy."

I'm already outside when I notice the Labrador hasn't followed me out.

"Luca?"

Cursing inwardly, I go back inside. Luca's sitting next to the empty cookie pack and looks up at me plaintively.

"What?"

Luca barks.

I sigh. "I don't even know them."

Again, he barks.

Tears well up and I repeat to myself aloud what my inner voice told me. "It makes me weak, and I can't afford…"

Luca's eyes silence me.

"Fuck it." I walk over to Luca in a flash, stooping down to push aside the cookie pack. I pick up the photo and give it one more attentive look before shoving it in the carrier, between Adam and my heart. "You happy now?" My voice trembles.

Luca barks again, wags his tail and runs ahead as we go outside again.

-19-

Abel

The landscape flashes by me in shades of green, yellow, and gray, as though a painter is using his brushes to paint colorful streaks in the corners of my eyes. The fields of corn on either side of the road that seems to go on and on, and the sun lighting them up – it's a magnificent picture, one which I am glad to be able to see with my very own eyes. Although 'my own eyes' is a relative term in this case. The body I've taken possession of is that of an eighteen-year-old guy who goes by the name of Matthew Parsons. A good-for-nothing who had no clue what to do with his life, so he wasted it away hitting the bottle or breaking into homes, just like his dad. He'd only been in and out of juvie for short periods of time. Well, say hello to an extended prison sentence, Matthew – though this is a prison that must be a thousand times worse than the places you've done time in. More lonely, and much darker. Not my problem. He deserves it, just like the rest of humanity. The first few hours I possessed his body I could still sense his soul's presence. He fought but didn't stand a chance. Now I no longer feel anything.

I'm stretched out on the backseat of a Buick Enclave and cross my booted legs. The hum of the engine is the only thing disturbing the silence. The scorching heat of today's sun penetrates the windshield. "You gotta admit these humans have a knack for making pretty things. Just check this *ride*. So big and comfy." I run the palm of my hand down the headrest of the backseat. "So soft…"

The car veers to the left and my body is pressed into the backrest. An unfamiliar sensation in my stomach makes me temporarily close my eyes, cursing inwardly. I haven't gotten used yet to this phenomenon called centrifugal force. It's one of the things that make me long for home. Because despite the fact that I've always dreamed of seeing earth with 'my very own eyes' – since angels are only dispatched to this place on special errands for the prevention unit – I have to admit I hadn't taken the downside of an earthly existence into consideration enough. The putrid smell that surrounds you, the clammy air outside, the light, the sounds… it's all sickening, really. But the landscape, fortunately, makes up for it.

Muriel's grotesque fingers are around the wheel, almost squeezing it to a pulp. She doesn't turn in her seat to face me, just grunts out an unintelligible reply. She hasn't done much else ever since we took off. She's almost six-and-a-half feet tall, with a waistline half that size, and she's been curiously quiet. She's not going to win any awards for Best Travel Companion. Maybe she's ticked off that she got stuck in a body belonging to a woman who must weigh at least four hundred pounds and looks like she eats babies for lunch. She only has five teeth left, a wart on her cheek, and a pointy nose. I already knew her as an angel from before the time of the Retribution. Honest, lethal, but definitely vain.

I chuckle inwardly. "It's just so sad that they don't understand technology and money aren't the truly important things in life. Love, charity... not just for each other, but for the rest of the planet, too." I shrug. "Oh well. Not my problem." I shoot a look outside, through the windshield, and continue: "Still, I don't understand why He thinks this is necessary."

Muriel shoots me a reprimanding look in the rearview mirror.

"I mean it. Sure, humanity has fucked up in not getting that God didn't just create them but also the rest of the planet – that His love isn't just meant for them, but meant for all things living, great and small. Humanity has become the weakest link in the struggle for survival. But really, why would He send us? There are easier ways to dispose of a species, aren't there?"

Muriel gives me another exasperated look.

"I know, God moves in mysterious ways. He forced Moses to inscribe those commandments into the Tables of the Law, and He even sacrificed His own son. But still..."

My travel companion steps on the brake so suddenly that I jolt forward, rolling off the backseat with a scream. The brakes squeak demonstratively. The engine gives a roar. The car shudders to a halt.

Rubbing my painful head with one hand, I scramble up. "Was that really necessary?"

But Muriel has already gotten out. Now that the car is emptied of her body weight, it springs up a bit. After slamming the door shut, she walks over to the corn field on her side. I only spot the car parked there when I decide to follow her.

The black Bentley looks like it was transported there from a different time – from a world of faded glory where peace was on everyone's mind, just like hippy music and… flowers, funnily enough. The butt of the car is facing us while the front is parked in between plants and withered weeds, climbing up on either side of the car. The country road that leads away from it is completely blocked by the vehicle. It's like the spare wheel – which is attached to the tailgate and adds to the allure of the classic car – is watching us like an eye. The chrome bumpers glint in the light of the sun, which is at its highest. The gearstick and dashboard inside are also cast in chrome. Okay, I take back my words about the Buick. Now, *this* is what I call a ride. We'll take this baby for a spin later, I promise myself.

The sun burns my skin, but the light breeze cools me down enough to stop the beading sweat on my brow from pouring down my face. Insects buzz around me.

I follow Muriel as she forcibly shoves the plants aside and wriggles past the car. Her bulging ass skims the surface of the metalwork. The plants crackle under her feet. She leaves a path of destruction in her wake once she's managed to get past the car and continues her trek down the cracked pavement at a brisk pace.

A second vehicle is standing in the middle of the road, but nothing remains of this one save a rusty carcass. No tires and no interior. It completely blocks the narrow road, which explains why the owner of the Bentley pulled over where he did. But why he left the car there is a mystery to me.

Silently, we go past the rusty car and a Georgian colonial mansion of times past, lit up by the gold-colored sun, slides into view. A little ways away from the mansion is an old church, which has been boarded up. Both buildings look as though they've fallen out of use years ago. The woodwork is weathered and full of holes.

The mansion is in the worst state – there's hardly any roof left and a large hole is gaping on one side, which has caused the former living room to be overrun with weeds. Here and there, the planks look scorched and blackened. Maybe this house once belonged to an old plantation owner with slaves, who'd sit on his porch in his rocking chair to oversee his cotton fields. I shake my head. Men ruling other men with an iron fist to make their own lives better? Maybe it isn't that strange that God has had enough of humanity.

Muriel casts a look around before fixing her eyes on me, a question showing in her gaze.

I shrug. "Maybe that Bentley's been out there for a long time. Doesn't look like anybody's here. Besides, we don't have time for this. This is no longer our objective. We got new orders, remember? We have to track down the Aberrations."

Without reply, Muriel storms off in a huff in the direction of the church. I shake my head and follow her. The porch planks squeak under my feet in protest.

How can they even support the weight of Muriel's body?

The church looks run-down too, her former glory gone, although it has stood the test of time a lot better than the neighboring building. It even has a roof! Inside, it's dark. Church pews are lined up in an orderly fashion. They're moldy and give off a strong odor of fungi and rot. Rays of light somehow manage to break through cracks in the boarded-up windows. The altar is nothing more than a slightly elevated, empty stage with a large cross nailed to the back wall. Once, this room must have contained a congregation of men and women who were singing their hearts out about the Lord's mercy. Now, the altar only features a lone worshipper – an elderly man with dark skin, kneeling down on it. He doesn't rise, doesn't turn – he just sits there, staring unresponsively up at the cross.

"Have you come here to pray or to kill?"

Muriel and I shoot each other a look.

The man gets to his feet with the movement of a vise that's gotten stuck. He turns to face us and I realize he is one of the oldest people I have ever laid eyes on. His back has a hump and he's leaning on a cane. Wrinkles grace his dark skin, and in the half-darkness of this place, his eye sockets are nothing more than a black blur. "Oh, I see," he whispers. Softly moaning, he shuffles toward the front pew in order to sit down, his back to us. He sighs. "I've been stuck here for two months already, can you believe it? A cotton farm, that's what it used to be, though that's hard to imagine these days. This is where pickers got whipped, worked to the bone, humiliated, and all the other things they can conjure up to break a man's soul. But that was years before I traveled these parts with my wife and unborn child." He stops talking for a minute, and I see him raising a hand to his eyes. I think I hear a quiet sob. "This is the first time I dared come back to this place. I couldn't do it before – didn't have the strength. This is where they were murdered... my wife and unborn child." He turns his sad face toward us, and in his gaze lingers an unspoken agony. "Leo – that's what I was going to name my son. Oh, I knew it was going to be a boy, I could sense it. Don't you think that would've made a charming name?" He nods as though we've confirmed it. "Yes, quite charming, and a powerful name at that. I'd have named him after my father – if we'd just kept going on that fateful day, that is." Shaking his head, he turns away once more. "The year was 1960. We were on vacation and we were just passing by here when all of a sudden, a man came running for the road, straight through those cornfields. I almost hit him with my car. Hit the brakes and swerved just in time to avoid him. He didn't even notice. When I got out to scold him for being such a fool and ask him whether he'd lost his mind, the look in his eyes was telling enough. His face was pallid, his eyes devoid of feeling and red-rimmed with tears. 'She left me,' he kept stammering, dazed and confused. 'Now I have nothing and no one to live for.' The next moment, Sarah stepped out of the car and the man completely flipped. His eyes widened like he'd just seen a devil. He started to yell at her, drawing a gun. 'You! It's all your fault,' he said. I only found out later that Sarah looked a bit like the woman who had caused his wife to leave him. The next thing I knew was that he shot her in the head first, then himself. Seconds later, I was all by myself with two dead bodies on either side of me." He shakes his head. "I'll never forget the image, just like I will never forget the sound of those bullets fired." He sighs. "One minute we were on the road, the sun guiding us to our destination, and the next I was all alone." He laughs cynically. "Yeah, that's life for you." The man looks around him wistfully. "I can sense their energy here – my wife and son, I mean. You feel it too?"

I don't feel a thing.

"They were buried somewhere else, but they were killed here. So I want to die here too, you see? I just never thought I'd have to drive myself down here, least of all in that old Bentley. I've been tinkering away at it for years, as a hobby, but I'd never driven more than two miles with it. It's a miracle I even made it." Then, he repeats his question of before. "So, are you here to pray or to kill?"

"I'm afraid prayers go unanswered these days," I say.

The man nods. "That's what I fear, too. It's time to pay for our sins."

I know Muriel expects me to approach the man now and do my job, but somehow his behavior perplexes me – makes me feel rooted to the spot. "Why aren't you trying to run?"

The old man barks out a short laugh. "Like I'd stand a chance, with these old bones of mine. Besides, life is fleeting, and my time has come. If you don't kill me today, then old age will do it. And to be quite frank, I don't even want to live in a world filled with sadness, death and murder. No, I prefer the hereafter, where I'll be reunited with my loved ones."

"No one is waiting for you on the other side, old man," I say. "Heaven's gates have been closed, and I doubt they'll ever reopen. Nothing but eternal darkness is waiting for you there."

"That's not what I believe."

I notice this guy is putting my back up. The blood running through my veins seems to burn them up. Why? What's wrong with me? "How on earth can you hold on to your faith in these circumstances?"

The answer is simple. "It's all I have left."

I can sense Muriel's gaze boring into my back. She roughly shoves my shoulder, causing me to step forward. The message is clear, and she's right. I understand the emotions flooding my system – sympathy, compassion – but what I don't understand is *why* I'm feeling them. I do know I have to get rid of them, though. It's not fitting for an angel – it'll make me weak. I nod and head straight for the old man, still standing there and staring up at the cross.

He doesn't move. "I can sense their energy," he mumbles. And then: "They're here."

I stand next to him, towering over him, his head just coming up to my belly button. "There's no one here, I can guarantee it. No one but us." I put one hand onto the crown of his head, the other one on his shoulder, and then I break his neck with a single twist of my hand.

-20-

The past

Woodstone was basically a main road lined by rows of houses on either side. The road was blocked by three parked cars, but that wouldn't stop Einstein. The forest surrounding this village couldn't be fenced off, after all.

I parked the car just in front of the blockade, next to the sign proclaiming 'Welcome to Woodstone' and ironically enough, I was welcomed by two armed men popping up behind the cars. They were headed my way. Both of them were wearing yellow raincoats with hoods to match and they were aiming their guns at the Jeep. The only reason I could see them was that they were caught in my headlights. Everything outside that beam of light was obscured from view, trapped in the dark of night.

Luca growled.

Adam kept quiet. During the short drive from the gas station to here, he'd fallen asleep, miraculously enough.

"Down, boy," I whispered to Luca, as I got out of the car. "Stay here."

The heavy rain had stopped and turned into a slight drizzle. Not that it mattered much – I was already soaked to the bone – but it did make for a more serene silence out in the open, only interrupted by the wind, the slamming of my car door, and the voice addressing me.

"Stay back."

I did as I was told and raised my hands into the air.

The men edged closer, raindrops glistening on their raincoats and their eyes shining with the kind of aggression that was obvious even in this darkness.

"You're not welcome here." The man on the left, a bearded guy with a pockmarked face, aimed his gun at me. "Turn around."

"You gotta listen to me. This man… he's coming for you…" I fell silent, realizing that my story was way too incoherent for them to make sense of it. My heart was still beating in my throat, making me gasp for breath and struggling to get the right words out.

By now, my showing up here had attracted an audience. From behind the blockade, more armed men and women came out, about seven of them. Although I wouldn't exactly call them 'armed' – they were carrying pitchforks and clubs, holding the makeshift weapons so tightly that their hands seemed fused with them. *Which was basically a good sign, just not for me in this instant.*

During my disjoined monologue, the two guards hadn't lowered their guns for even a second. What's more, it looked like they were about to pull the trigger.

"Jesus, Patrick, lower the gun." One of the women had stepped forward to take a look inside the Jeep. "Barry, you too. She's got a baby and a dog with her."

The men didn't comply.

"You heard what's going on in the rest of the world," the bearded man shouted. "Killers are on the loose. Men, sure, but women and children too. We can't trust anyone."

"What do you suggest we do?" the woman snapped. "Shoot her?" She angrily stepped forward to push down their guns. "You guys are teachers, goddammit, not soldiers."

"Yeah, so? Someone's gotta help the sheriff to patrol our borders."

The woman laughed. "Patrol? You can't even tell the difference between maniacal lunatics and a woman on the run."

"You don't know that..."

"Please," I sobbed, my voice shaking from the cold and blind panic. "Please, listen..."

"Lower your weapons, guys." One of the men stepping out was apparently the sheriff. He was wearing a green uniform with a star to match. He nodded at the two men, who complied straight after. "If she showed up here with evil intentions, she'd have tried to kill us by now. It's not like she needs our help to break into our version of Fort Knox or something." He beckoned me forward. "Come on, get your kid and the dog from the car and I'll take you to the office to get you some dry clothes."

"Thank you." I sighed with relief. "But I do need some help with my dog. He's broken his leg."

"I'll carry him." The sheriff walked over to the car.

"You're too trusting, Rick," Barry warned him.

"And you're too suspicious." Rick opened the car door. He shot an uncertain look at the growling dog, then proceeded by lifting him up and out. "Not everyone's a potential killer."

"But that's the problem, right there," Patrick chimed in to back up his colleague. "You can't tell by looking at someone."

Rick ignored them as he waited for me to get Adam out of the Jeep, Then, he steered me around the parked cars into the village, heading in the direction of the sheriff's office. Inside, a man and two women were discussing the state of the world. I shivered from the cold, but part of it was also fear, I realized. My mind was still reeling from the shock of everything that had happened in the past few days, and now that I was finally sort of safe, my state of shock came back with a vengeance.

"Jesus, what happened to you?" one of the two women asked me when I stepped into the office. She was a bit chubby and she was wearing a hideous, flowered dress.

With my knees knocking together and my arms wrapped around Adam, I sat down on a chair. The sheriff lowered Luca onto the floor, right beside me. The dog looked around with alarm in his eyes, his gaze lingering on the woman in the flowery dress. He pulled up his lips and bared his teeth.

Though I was there physically, my mind was elsewhere. I had difficulty staying focused on the present. All the memories of the past few days piled on top of each other, fighting for precedence in the movie reel that was playing inside my mind. It made me flinch. The only thing keeping me grounded was the crying baby in my arms. Adam made me not lose my mind and be here, now.

"The gas station…" I stammered. "A killer there. You have to get out… he's coming…"

"Rick, do you really think this is wise?" An elderly man in his sixties shot me a suspicious look. His white, scraggly beard, the hard lines in his face, and the scar under his right eye made him look like an ex-criminal who'd decided to walk the straight path for the remaining years of his life.

"Not now, Pete," the sheriff cut him off. "Could you see to it that she gets a towel and dry clothes on her back? She'll get sick like this." He grabbed a chair and sat across from me. Luca whined for a moment, then let out a low growl. "And get Dave to have a look at the dog's leg, will you."

Pete eyed us doubtfully before finally strutting off, shaking his head as he left the building.

"He must be hungry." The other woman – thin and lean, but with a soft face – pointed at Adam. "I'll make him a bottle." And she was gone, exiting through the same door as Pete had done.

"Can you tell me what happened?" The sheriff tried his best to sound calm, but it was hard to miss the undercurrent of fear in his voice. No surprise there, really. From what I'd seen of Woodstone so far, hardly anything had happened here because of the remote location, but I suspected the sheriff knew all too well that hell on earth wouldn't pass by his town – fire and brimstone were bound to rain down on this place soon enough. Which explained the barricaded road.

The chubby woman sidled up to me and asked me dozens of questions in a trembling voice. It sounded heavy – and slow, like she'd almost run out of batteries. The high notes were muted and I could mostly just make out the bass notes, which made it seem as though she was shouting the questions at me from inside a neighboring building. I ignored her. All I did was look down at Adam, rocking him in my arms and humming a tune. I was teetering on the edge here – if I fell to the wrong side, I'd lose my sanity. I would go crazy if I fell, but keeping my balance felt like an impossibility, even with Adam to hold onto. The tightrope was wobbling

176

under my feet.

A wet tongue licked my trembling hand. Luca looked up at me with a whine. The sound was clearly meant as a warning to me, but at the same time he seemed unsure of himself and his senses. Luca's black eyes were like a deep water well. I had the sensation of falling, falling as though in a dream. The well beckoned me, pulling me down into the deep until I ended up in the black dung at the bottom. A voice- echoing off the stone walls. Hannah? *Don't give up. Stay with the program. Adam and Luca need you.*

A hand on my shoulder, gently squeezing. It guided my spirit back to the present moment. It was the sheriff. "Ma'am?"

"Hmm?" I mumbled.

"What's your name?"

"Anna," I stammered. "Paula."

He shot me a puzzled look. "Which of the two is it?"

I shook my head, looking at Adam in surprise before inspecting the room I was in. It took me a while to reconnect with where I was, and what had happened to me...

And what was coming for us.

"The man!" I screamed, suddenly jerked back to the present moment. "He's a killer... he's not human... he's coming..."

"Easy," the sheriff tried to calm me. "Who are you talking about?"

"Is this about what happened in the big cities?" The chubby woman took an anxious step back.

"Give her a moment, Geraldine," the sheriff said. "She looks like she went through hell. Give her time."

Time! This town doesn't have time. He's coming – he could

177

be here any minute now.

For a split second, it occurred to me that Einstein was coming all by himself. Surely he couldn't take out an entire town on his own?

Uhm, hello? Not human, remember?

I swallowed hard.

I have to make it clear to them.

Then another man – Pete, if I remembered correctly – stepped back inside with dry clothes and a towel for me. He looked at me questioningly, and my gaze bounded from him to the chubby woman to the sheriff and back again. I could see the fear and confusion in their eyes.

"Look, I don't know which news reports have been able to reach you here," I sighed. "Probably you know a lot already, but I can tell you from my own experience: it's pretty horrific out there."

"But do you know what's going on *exactly*?" Pete asked. He'd put one hand in his side and used the other one to stroke his beard. He looked old and wise, and somehow less panicky than the rest of them. "There have been reports that we found hard to believe."

"Why?" I said. Adam started to cry. I slipped my little finger into his mouth by means of a pacifier, which kept him quiet for now.

"According to the person telling us, it's not just the big cities that were bombed – it's the countryside, too. Towns and villages. Billions are dead."

Billions? Jesus Christ!

And I understood what the man was trying to say. It *was* kind of hard to believe – too surrealistic to conceive of it, even more so because everything had happened within the span of a few days, even hours, while up here in Woodstone, Colorado everything seemed to be

178

normal. Nothing had happened here.

Not yet.

"Well, I believe all those reports, and so should you." I swallowed down the lump in my throat. "You should count yourselves lucky the electricity up here hasn't gone out yet. In Manhattan, the power was cut within a few hours. I've seen the city burn, but from a distance... The other things I know I've seen in news broadcast before the power went out. But I did see, with my very own eyes, how killers were roaming the streets to take out everyone crossing their path."

"That's what we heard," the sheriff admitted. "Which is why we took precautions. But all of this has got to *mean* something, surely?"

"Oh, don't go all conspiracy-theory on us, Rick." Pete sought my gaze, then nodded at the sheriff. "Been reading too many books, that one. He seriously thinks it's some experiment gone wrong – chemtrails, but worse. Something airborne, spreading so rapidly that it's covering the entire globe. That's what the news reports said, anyway – that it was a global problem. Something's turning innocent people into murdering machines. It's like we're stuck in The Walking Dead, except the murderers aren't dead yet."

No, they're angels, I thought to myself.

"That's ridiculous. I mean, clearly, *we're* not affected." Geraldine nodded at me. "And neither is she."

"Maybe we're immune?" the sheriff suggested.

"Yeah, right," the woman shot back. "Are you even listening to yourself?" She shot Luca a hesitant gaze. The dog started to growl at once.

"Do you have any idea what's happening?" Pete asked me.

179

I started to open my mouth, then shut it again. I couldn't possibly tell him the truth, right? My story was just as implausible as the sheriff's chemtrail theory. Telling them the truth wasn't really important right now, anyway. What *was* important was that this town should get into a state of high alert. People needed to be prepared or there wouldn't be any Woodstone left to listen to my story, if I could ever bring myself to telling these people.

"I just got off the 55 and pulled over at that gas station to get fuel. The man who was there killed the two attendants as well as two customers who came into the store later on. He tried to kill me too." I gave the sheriff an almost pleading look. "He's one of the guys who you think got infected with something. He's headed this way. We gotta come up with a strategy. Maybe, if we all pulled together..." I swallowed. "He's strong. Didn't take him any effort to lift up one of his victims by the neck."

Silence. Disbelief reflecting in their eyes.

Pete pinned me with his gaze. "Why am I getting the distinct feeling you're keeping something from us?"

I shrugged. "That's not important right now."

"Why don't you tell us and let *us* be the judge of that?" Geraldine hissed.

I shook my head. "Even if I did, you wouldn't believe me. Plus, we don't have time for this. Maybe later..."

"She's right," the sheriff said. "That guy could be close already. The gas station's only a couple miles down the road." He looked at me. "As you can see, we put up a barricade. We split up into groups that patrol the street so others can get some rest, although I doubt anybody's getting much sleep in these circumstances. I'm not saying

180

we're ready to ward off an attack – I don't think we will ever be. I'm the only one with a military background, and I have no clue as to how we could do any better than that to protect our town."

"We're too vulnerable, Rick," Pete claimed. "I tried telling you that this very morning. If that guy she's talking about – or anybody else, for that matter – sees the barricaded road and simply goes around it, he or she can use the forest as cover and strike from there before we can do anything. He could take us out, one by one."

"I'm open to other suggestions, Pete," the sheriff snapped.

"What the hell are you guys talking about?" Geraldine interrupted. "She's talking about one man, not an entire army!"

"One man acting like a sniper is all it takes to kill a few people before we can kick into action," Pete said, giving the sheriff a pointed look. "We have to gather them all in one place. It's easier to safeguard one building than an entire community."

"Let me guess," the sheriff mocked him. "The church?"

"It's the only building big enough to host us all."

Rick clucked his tongue. "How can you still be a believer after everything that's happened?"

"My faith's got nothing to do with it. It's a purely practical matter. But if you really want to know: God didn't do this – *we* did. Humanity caused this, just like all the other misery in the history of this planet."

If only you knew, I pondered. "Sticking everyone inside one building isn't very smart, though. If he barricades the door and sets fire to the church, we're toast."

"I'm afraid we're out of options," Pete commented.

"It's the best idea yet to make sure we can keep everyone together in a safe place. Isn't that obvious, Rick?"

"This is all a load of bull." Geraldine's hands shot up in the air in a panicked gesture, her gaze darting to the window as though she expected someone to jump in at any moment. "This can't be really happening. Right?"

"Rick?" Pete insisted.

The sheriff stared ahead pensively.

"Come on. For all we know that man may already be here. You said it yourself."

The sheriff got to his feet. "Fine. All right." He turned toward Pete. "Start gathering everyone." He clenched his fist and punched the wall with it. "Goddammit."

Geraldine sighed. "I'll pray to God that he won't come our way." Her voice trembled.

I shook my head at her comment. *God is exactly the problem we're dealing with here, woman.*

-21-

A sudden shriek outside made us all look up, through the windows and into the night.

We're too late. He's here!

Gunshots, alarmed voices. The two lampposts across the street were the only direct source of light that we had out on the street. Once they'd been shot to pieces, the street blacked out and we were even blinded by the glare of the overhead strip lights reflecting in the glass.

Luca jumped up, barking loudly before erupting in an agonized whine. His leg was still broken, of course.

Another cry in the dark pierced my heart like a dagger. "No, not my childr..." The voice was cut off mid-sentence.

"Shit, shit, shit..." Pete pressed his back against the side wall before grabbing his gun and casting a searching look outside. "Can't see a damn thing."

The sheriff followed suit, using the wall on the other side. "Geraldine, turn out the light."

The chubby woman stood like frozen near the desk. She was pale as a sheet and her mouth was hanging open in horror.

"Geraldine!" Rick yelled at her.

No response. Or wait – was the color seeping back into her cheeks, or was I imagining things?

Cradling Adam to my chest, I got up and went for the

light switch. Moments later, the darkness cast its black cover over all of us, turning the people inside into mere silhouettes. I looked outside and saw running shadows in between the houses. The ones who were carrying flashlights lit up like dancing stars.

Luca's barking was so loud it was driving me crazy, and Adam joined him with his shrieking.

"Keep those two quiet or I'll do it for you," Rick told me firmly, but his voice skipped with panic. For the first time, I wondered whether it had been wise to make him sheriff of this town.

I pulled Luca back by his collar and led him over to a secluded corner while desperately trying to quiet down both the dog and the baby.

"Rick, what's our plan?" Pete shouted above the barking.

"Plan?"

"My God, man. We gotta help them, don't we?"

The sheriff seemed petrified.

"You gotta be kidding me, Rick. You're the *only* one with military experience. I'm just an old fart spending too many of my days in the bar."

"We... we can't go outside. We'll be even more vulnerable there."

"Well, we can't stay here. We're sitting ducks in this office, and besides, we can't just allow this guy to murder the entire town. Don't you think we should do something?"

"I'm – I'm not sure..."

Pete slapped the wall with his hand. "You asshole. I *knew* you were a coward, deep down. You and your tall tales, but now that the shit has hit the fan, you're staying low to wait out the storm? Well, wake up and smell the coffee, because this storm ain't gonna blow over. It'll only get worse from here on in."

With a snarl on his face, Rick went for Pete, grabbing him by the collar of his shirt and shoving the barrel of the gun against his jaw. "Don't you *dare* call me a coward. I've seen things in Iraq, man, things that would make your worst nightmares pale in comparison."

"Maybe that's where you went off the rails, Rick," Pete went on unperturbed, as though the gun pointed at him didn't bother him in the least. "Maybe you having seen those things means you're mentally broken. Maybe the sound of gunfire makes you so terror-stricken that you can't move when it matters. That's it, am I right? You were invalidated out of the army. Why else would you become the sheriff of a small town like this one?"

"You know jack *shit* about my past."

"That's true," Pete agreed. "But I know something about your present. In the present, you're a yellow-belly son of a bitch."

Rick pressed the barrel up into Pete's neck. "Say that again if you dare."

"Pull that trigger and prove me wrong."

Meanwhile, I was trying to silence both Adam and Luca, but it was no use. I couldn't keep my heart rate down. Adrenaline was surging through my body. Luca pulled away, but instead of heading for the door or the two bickering men, he tottered over to Geraldine of all people. In total surprise, I looked at the woman but recoiled when I saw the sick grin on her face.

My brain was too slow to register the extent of what was happening. "Watch out!" I screamed, but by then it was too late.

A gunshot rang out, making me flinch as my

eardrums seemed to shatter. The sound was followed by a loud thud when Pete's lifeless body slumped to the floor, blood pouring out of the hole in his head.

"If you can't, I'll be only too happy to assist you, Rick," Geraldine said cheerfully, pointing the gun at Rick next. Before the sheriff even had time to respond, the bullet dug its way into his forehead. The man stood there waveringly for a moment before also crumpling to the floor.

My breath faltered when I stared at Geraldine.

And then a memory of that conversation at the gas station came back to me. *"The orders were changed? They think we can't handle it on our own, or what?"*

The angel wasn't working alone!

It was in that moment that the bleak situation we were in hit me full force – God's treacherous plan for mankind, and how lost we all were. Had He sent repugnant creatures, demons that would be easy to recognize, we might have still stood a chance, but God's helpers were hiding inside human bodies. It was impossible to tell who was friend and who was foe. Your former best friend could be out for your blood. How was I ever supposed to trust anyone again?

I was alone, trapped in a room with an armed maniac who was pointing her gun at me and Adam this time. This was how I was going to die.

Strangely enough, I didn't feel fear. In fact, I felt myself being enveloped in a peculiar serenity. Maybe it was for the best. No more fear, no more pain. Maybe I'd see my family again. I closed my eyes.

"You don't want to know how long I've waited for this day to come around." No pain, no eternal darkness – only Geraldine's voice. "I'll even tell you: more than a year. Fourteen months, to be precise. Months during which I still had to pretend this body was inhabited by a human soul. It wasn't easy. I hope my colleagues in other towns and cities were having an equally hard time with it. I mean, seeing through a human's eyes, living her life – surely that's beneath an angel like me? It's too boring, too colorless, too *deprived*."

Puzzled, I opened my eyes. Geraldine was perched on the desk, waving her gun back and forth with a dreamy look in her eyes. Outside, more gunshots and cries rang out.

"It's just that one angel for an entire town is too little. Besides, we had our orders. We had to wait for the Day of Retribution, and I had to sit this one out until reinforcements would show up, but oh my Lord, did it take long!" Geraldine shook her head, taking in me, Adam and Luca with her eyes. "To be honest I should kill you. You're an Aberration – that much is obvious. I can sense an angel's presence inside you. However, I don't enjoy killing one of my own kind. Enough killing's going on in the world already."

"So why take part in it?" I held Adam so close that it was a miracle he wasn't squished in my arms. Luca was protectively lined up between me and Geraldine, letting out a bark in alarm.

Geraldine didn't pay him any attention. She shrugged. "Not my decision, dear." She slid off the desk and kept a few steps away from me, her eyes boring into mine. She looked worried – her eyes were empty and sad. It was like I was in direct contact with the human soul trapped in there. It gripped me like a vise and chilled me to the core – even more so because I realized it was the exact other way around for me. Deep inside me, a strange entity lingered, a soul that undoubtedly fought hard to win dominion over my body – an entity that my soul had been able to valiantly resist up until this point. I felt dirty. I felt used.

"Who's inside you?" Geraldine squinted at me. "Let me help him out." Before I could fathom what her words entailed, she grabbed my arm and stars erupted in my vision. I felt like someone was turning my stomach inside out. Feelings of deep sadness crashed over me in waves. A bang – then darkness. For a moment there was nothing.

The next thing I remember seeing were the gray walls. I was lying on a cold, concrete floor in a space I immediately recognized. Strip lights flickered above my head. Off. On. Light. Dark. The temperature was hovering around the freezing point. I was sitting on a wooden chair, stark naked. The four walls didn't have any exit points – they were absolute, like four lifeless guards. Indirectly, I understood where I was. A mental prison. The angel inside of me and I had swapped positions. This was the place in which the angel was trapped. And something else became apparent to me, too.

Inspector Rogers told me that the room I was found in was empty, apart from me. No lifeless body looking exactly like me, no gun, no blood. What if it had all been in my head? What if the room had indeed been empty? What if it had been my soul, telling me that she was engaged in a fight she'd have to give up sooner or later?

Had that moment come at last?

Next to the strip lights, two small lights shone inside. With trembling knees, I made my way to the two holes in the wall, not much bigger than marbles. I realized that the body I was currently forcing to move was, in fact, an astral one. I was like a ghost, and the thought gave me the creeps. With every step I took, a sound was growing in the background. I stepped up, peered through the holes, and looked out through the eyes of my own body.

It was no longer night – I could see that. The sun had just come up and was casting her orange light over the small town. The streets were littered with dead bodies, bits of glass, and blood. Practically all the windows in the townhouses had been shattered. Doors were wide open.

The angel looked down at his – *mine* – bloodied hands, and the gun he was clutching.

No! Did he kill these people? Did I kill these people?

The sound of barking drew my attention. Four dogs ran around the corner, and Luca was among them. Actually, he was limping, not running, but it looked like he'd gone for help and brought in the cavalry to risk an attack. As soon as the gun in my hand shot one of the animals – a terrier – the dogs scattered while whimpering, leaving a barking Luca to fend on his own.

Being so powerless was excruciating. I'd lost control over my limbs. I could only stand by and watch.

My left hand was raised in the air to aim the gun at Luca.

"No!" I screamed, banging the walls with my astral hands as hard as I could. "Run, Luca. Run!"

"Dean, stop. We're not here to kill animals."

The gun hovered in the air for a moment before my hand slowly lowered it. My line of vision moved to one of the houses, where Geraldine – or actually, the angel who had seized control of her body, with Geraldine trapped inside as a helpless witness just like me – just came out the door. "Those are not our orders."

"No one's going to miss them." My voice sounded strangely distorted.

Geraldine came to stand next to my body. "That's not the point."

The angel who presently controlled my body, going by the name of Dean, let out a sigh. "Fine, whatever." He flung the gun away. It clattered onto the asphalt. "Thanks for liberating me. I was going berserk in there."

Geraldine's nose curled up with disgust. "How could you have allowed yourself to be subdued by a human soul? Are you really that weak?"

"She was strong."

"Sure. I can't wrap my head around the fact that He chose to send all of his servants down here, even the noobs. I mean, how old are you, exactly? You can't be a day over thirty-thousand. You're just a child."

Dean shrugged noncommittally. "Guess He just needed more soldiers. Besides, look around you. I can take care of business – and myself."

"Get out of here. You don't even know how to destroy one human soul."

Dean clenched his fist. "I just told you…"

"Hey, you want to kill this one?"

The eyes turned toward the sheriff's office, from which the man who had clued me in to the truth back at the gas station now emerged. He was holding up a crying Adam with one hand.

No!

My breath faltered.

The gas station murderer went on: "Personally, I'd have chosen to kill you. Come on – how can you be of use to the great cause if you can't even subdue a simple human soul? Anyway, Eva here has given you the benefit of the doubt, so for God's sake make yourself useful." He threw Adam toward me when he was still more than a yard away. Dean caught him and stared down at the baby.

Adam was crying, punching the air with his little fists and kicking his feet.

Luca barked. He stepped forward, then edged back before trying it again.

"You think I won't do it?"

Einstein taunted him with his eyes. "That's exactly what I'm thinking, you weakling."

Dean took a menacing step forward. "Say that again, and I'll show you something after I'm done with this child."

"Show me what? That you're a wimp?"

It was the strangest thing. The space I was in bled to red. I could feel the adrenaline coursing through my astral body, but I could also feel the hate mounting in my human one.

Through the peepholes, I saw how my eyes were turned to Adam, how a hand was slipped onto his head to twist his little neck.

My vision blurred. I got so mad I couldn't see straight, and something bubbled up within me. I clenched my fists so hard I hurt myself. Like an animal, I bared my teeth and sucked in the cold air.

I opened my mouth and screamed more loudly than I'd ever done before in my life.

"Noooooooooooooooooooo!"

An earthquake shook the floor. The walls and ceiling started to crumble, big lumps of stone crashing down next to me. The darkness beyond then was an even lonelier prison, but it wouldn't be mine. A bright flash of light blinded me.

The trembling stopped. Color seeped back into my field of vision.

Baffled, I stared at the baby on my left arm. Adam was crying, but unharmed. Luca was barking. I looked up and saw him a few steps away from me, wagging his tail cheerfully. Like he could feel I'd once more seized control of my own body, and that I cast Dean back into the gray dungeon deep within my mind.

Only now did I realize I'd kneeled down on the pavement. Einstein was lying still next to me, his face so battered that I hardly recognized him anymore. His bloody nose was bashed in, his left eye purple and swollen. He was dead.

Did I do this?

Moaning.

I looked up in a rush.

Geraldine was there, a few yards away from me, lying in between five dead bodies. Her head was resting on top of someone's pelvis. She stared at me incredulously. "How..?" It was the last word she spoke. Gasping out one final breath, she dropped dead.

Still shaken, I crawled away from the bodies, holding Adam very close. Tears rolled down my cheeks. I gasped for breath, but the oxygen had a hard time making its way to my lungs.

Black spots danced in front of my eyes. I tried to grasp what had just happened here, but I was missing a few vital parts. For now, I just knew I had won the battle with my inner angel again. Dean was still inside of me, though. The thought made me so sick that I had to throw up. Sobbing, I crawled backward, away from the steaming vomit, with a foul taste in my mouth. For a second I imagined his presence within me, like a hand closing around my heart to slowly squeeze it to death. But I decided it was just an illusion. I had to stop thinking about it or I'd go mad, and that would make me lose the battle once and for all.

I looked at the baby in my hands and the dog at my side. I was oblivious to the rest of the town, as though I was suffering from tunnel vision. Something told me I had to find someone who could take care of them, so I could leave them behind. They weren't safe with me. If Dean ever clawed his way back up and took my soul hostage, they'd be doomed. But I also knew I couldn't find it in my heart to leave them behind. Besides, what would I turn into without them? They were giving me strength and hope. I needed them just as much as they needed me.

I looked up and took in the now lifeless town – the deserted streets, the houses, cars, and bodies.

First the big cities, and now the insignificant town of Woodstone. In the span of just a few days. If they continue like this, pretty soon there'll be no one left on the planet.

That thought freaked me out even more than all the dead people around me. I rocked Adam gently in my arms, humming a lullaby. It seemed to calm him.

No one except you and me, buddy. Soon we'll be the only members of the human race left on earth.

It wouldn't come to that, I hoped. There had to be more survivors out there.

Sooner or later, new angels would appear to take us out, though – it was a fact of life. What the hell was I supposed to do?

193

-22-

Present time / Abel

We were the hunters and they the prey. Simple as that. They run, we follow. We kill until we get assigned a different task. We don't doubt our mission. The faithful follow blindly, the ones who have encountered His wrath even more so. I'm one of His soldiers. He has devised a new purpose for this world, and we are the tools in His hands to make it happen. That's what we were told.

So why does this feel so wrong?

Four parallel streets with houses lined up on either side – that's all there is to the village we're now traveling through. Other hunters have been here before us, that's obvious. Cars parked crisscross on the streets, doors wide open, dead bodies, but most of all: a tell-tale silence. The sky above is dark gray and charged with a storm that is about to erupt any minute now. It's still dry now, fortunately. I hate water.

We're not here to hunt – that is no longer our purpose. No, we're here to look for Aberrations. There's one quite close. I can sense it just like Muriel can. She parked the Bentley somewhere ten minutes ago and is now calmly walking through the empty streets. A crow is circling above our heads, uttering a hoarse cry.

Unlike my colleague, I move about carefully, ducking away behind cars, trees, or the corner of a house. The

Aberration knows we're here and that we're looking for him. I can almost sniff out his fear, feel his eyes on us. "Get off the road, you idiot," I hiss at Muriel. "If he's got a gun, you're a dead woman."

She ignores me and doggedly walks on, searchingly looking around. Why is she being so negligent? Sure, we can't really be harmed, being angels and all, but our astral bodies are trapped in human ones. We can heal these bodies if we wish – fight the radiation sickness and make them stronger. But these bodies can get injured. They can die. Maybe that's what she wants. It would mean she can return to the place we came from, back to Heaven. But if that's the case, why doesn't she just kill herself?

Suicide is a cardinal sin, even for an angel. She'd have a lot of explaining to do up there. Anyway, that won't be any different if she turns herself into a human target.

A trashcan crashes to the ground, a hissing cat emerging from a side street and darting across the main road. It sees us, sits perfectly still for a moment with its back up, then makes a run for it. Muriel stops to look at me. I melt into the back of a Volkswagen and demonstratively put a finger to my lips, signaling for her to keep quiet. With my other hand, I beckon her closer. *Take fucking cover, you idiot.*

Instead of heeding my warning, she slowly edges toward the side street. I sigh, pricking up my ears and scanning the street before carefully making my way to the alleyway too. I hide behind a low wall and cast a look around the corner. It's just shy of a yard wide, I'm estimating, and tall brick walls line the alley on either side. I guess it's a miracle Muriel didn't get stuck in between them. Two toppled-over trashcans on the pavement, that's all. Apart from a few leaves scattered by the wind, I don't see anything moving.

Where are you hiding?

My gaze lands on the corner at the end of the alley. Is that a head sticking out? In an attempt to see more clearly, I squint my eyes. Whoever it is, he's made me – the head disappears. I hear running footsteps and soft cursing.

"There!"

My cry is redundant – Muriel's already in pursuit. It's the first time I witness her running, and it's so comical that I almost forget to follow her. The ground literally shakes every time she sets a foot down. And yet I have to hand it to her: for a ten-ton semi, she's pretty damn fast.

I round the corner and almost miss the front door of a townhouse being slammed shut. Muriel cries out before jumping onto the porch and ramming the door with her shoulder like she's a rhino on the loose. The wood shatters and the door flies open. I rush after her and take in the destroyed living room. There are obvious signs of a struggle having happened before we barged in here, most likely between members of my species and the original owners of this place. Windows have been blown out of their frames. The sofa, dinner table and chairs are upside down. Paintings hang crookedly on the wall or have fallen down. The walls are covered in blood and the floor is littered with junk. Papers, bags, pens, books…

Three anxious figures are huddled in the far corner. The one in front is pointing a gun at us.

I freeze midstride and see Muriel doing the same from the corner of my eye.

The group of three consists of an elderly man, a little girl, and a boy who looks to be about twelve. He's the one training the gun on us. It's a chubby kid, with greasy, black hair that's stuck to his forehead in strands. "Stay away from us!" he screamed.

"I'm afraid we can't do that, boy," I say calmly while cursing myself for my carelessness. That guy only needs to pull the trigger and we'll be over. Sure, others will come for him, but that doesn't mean anything to us. On the other hand – maybe it'd be better to be taken out of the game. The task He has given us is too confusing, too much of a burden. I have to agree with Muriel on that. I'd be lying if I said I wasn't looking forward to returning to our Creator soon. The question is, will He welcome us with open arms?

Tears roll down the boy's cheeks. How is it possible that the angel within isn't equipped to force his soul into a dark corner of his mind? Just look at him! He's nothing more than a crybaby who'd give anything to be able to curl up like a fetus or shit his pants. Slowly, the boy gets up.

"Shoot them, Harold." The elderly man pulls the little girl close. She's crying and pressing her head into his shoulder. The man's eyes aren't tear-stained, though – they're burning with hatred.

Harold doesn't pull the trigger. "Why are you doing this?"

I shrug. "We were sent here. You've got someone inside you who isn't strong enough. We've come here to send him back to the place where he belongs, where he will be met with His wrath."

Harold's beady eyes widen. "Someone inside me?"

I nod. "I bet you've felt his presence every now and then. A certain pressure within your skull, a voice addressing you…"

197

I see in his eyes that I'm hitting a nerve. His mouth twists as though he's just eaten a sour plum. He lowers the gun, aiming the muzzle at the ground now.

"Watch out!" the elderly man screams, but it's already too late. Muriel seizes her chance by jumping the boy. She's tackled him to the ground before he even has time to utter a cry of surprise. She yanks the gun from his hand and fires off three bullets, hitting him in the stomach. The sound is deafening and seems to shatter my eardrums. On each impact, the boy incredulously gasps for breath. He coughs, retches up blood, then takes another baffled look at his stomach as red fluid bubbles up and leaks out, just like his life that's draining away. It covers the floor as he sags down on it, lifeless, unmoving.

I'm rooted to the spot. Sounds come to me as if muffled, and my line of sight is trapped in a tunnel vision with blurry walls on each side. As if in slow motion, Muriel stands up and heads toward the old man and the girl.

"Take me," I vaguely hear the man beg. "Please, let my granddaughter live."

Why can't I move? Why don't I rush over to kill the man myself, like I've done to so many people in the past weeks? What's happening to me? The blood in my veins feels frozen, but at the same time it's like my brain was doused in kerosene then set on fire.

Lord, I beg of you – help me. Is it the human soul gaining in power? No, I don't feel him at all. It's me, isn't it? Tell me. I'm listening, Lord.

No reply.

Please, Lord.

Nothing.

My anger flares up. We are His tools. Why won't He

even take the time to respond to my plea? The possible answer to that question makes me cower in fear.

Have I offended You in some way – done something wrong? Or is this what it feels like to be an Aberration… feeling all this fear, this incomprehension, these crippling doubts? No, in Aberrations the human soul has taken over. And Matthew Parsons is long gone.

Muriel's grunt snaps me out of my trance. I look at her and see how she shoves the man toward me. He trips and falls to the floor at my feet. Trembling, he glances up at me, teary-eyed. "Please," he begs. "Don't harm my granddaughter."

Puzzled, I look down at him. I notice the lump in my throat, just like the adrenaline flooding my body, and it makes me sick. I'm stronger than this – I shouldn't think too much. I'm here with one goal only: to serve Him. What could be more important than that? By doing what He desires me to do I might be able to win back His love, hear His voice once more.

The thought gives me strength. My hands close around the old man's neck. As I squeeze, he struggles to breathe. Tears roll down his cheeks and his face turns red. It doesn't take me long.

"You brought this upon yourselves!" I squeeze harder and harder. Pointless, since the man is already dead and lifelessly slumps to the floor. With a burning anger that permeates every fiber of my being, I look over to Muriel. She is standing a few feet away from me, keeping a close eye on me as she gestures at the little girl trembling in the corner.

She's testing me. She doesn't trust me! She knows something's up with me. I have to prove her wrong!

I stalk over to the girl and tower over her. She shrieks

and buries her head between her pulled-up knees just to avoid looking at me. I lift her by her neck. She's light as a feather, I establish. Which makes sense – she's stick-thin. Her clothes are dirty and her face is sunken. With tear-stained, wide eyes, she gapes at me. The fear reflecting in her eyes paralyzes me yet again.

"Please, please, please..." She repeats the words like it's a mantra, her voice barely above a whisper. I want to crush her windpipe like I did with her grandpa's, but my limbs aren't cooperating. A warm feeling seeps into me invades my chest. No, I can't give in to this. A little voice inside my head – not Matthew's but mine. The voice of my conscience. *She's just a child. How can she be punished for something the previous generations have done to the earth?*

She can't, obviously. But children grow up, and they'd be capable of making the same mistakes.

You can't punish her for something she hasn't yet done. That's like killing a cub for growing into a lion that will one day hunt down a zebra.

That's different. That's the law of nature.

But she is nature. Made in His image, and gifted with the same ire. She's innocent, just like all those other kids we've killed by now. Even most adults have nothing to do with the destruction of this planet. They just had the damn luck of being born into a society in which the wheel of destruction had already been set in motion. They didn't know any better. All you can blame them for is standing idly by while they could have known.

Exactly.

But that doesn't mean they're bad people, does it?

The voice is a pain in the ass. I shouldn't listen to it. My head is about to explode.

Like a statue, I just stand there. At long last, I lower

my arm and put the girl down before my legs collapsed under me, making me sink to the floor. "I can't." I rock back and forth like an upset child and see the girl hastily scurrying away from me. I close my eyes, knowing full well what the consequences of my action will be.

Muriel's footsteps, heavy and hulking. A grunt, followed by a gunshot. And then: silence.

I open my eyes. The girl is two yards away from me, a bullet hole in her temple. The blood that runs out of it makes me nauseous. I want to crawl over to her, comfort her, no matter how futile the gesture. But all I can do is watch her and mumble while sobbing. "I'm sorry."

-23-

Present time - Anna

The mountain track I stumble along is narrow. The pavement is interspersed with potholes. In some places, rocks have dropped down from the mountainside overgrown with pine trees. They partially obstruct the path. I pause to take a breather while setting down the backpack and taking Adam off my chest. My clothes are drenched in sweat. Even the sun is siding with the angels to kill us – it has to be at least ninety degrees out here, if not more. The wind tousles my hair like Mark's ghost is running a hand through it in a sweet caress. It's a relief, both mentally and physically. It makes me feel less alone. Of course, Adam and Luca are with me, but by now I'm craving a conversation with a grown-up, so in the past few days I've started to talk to Mark and to my family, as though they're here with me undertaking this journey. And who knows – now that God and His angels turn out to be real, ghosts might be just as real.

I can hardly feel my legs anymore. My feet seem to have a will of their own. In the past few hours they just kept going forward and forward, as if they were even more hell-bent on reaching our goal than I am myself.

A little bit further up the road is a sign. It's askew and is teetering on the precipice stretching out on my right side. Below me is the forest in which I've dwelled in the last few days. The sign is a welcome friend in troubled times that have almost made me lose courage.

Keystone Valley, 2 miles
Keystone River Run Village, 10 miles

"Guys, we're almost there," I whisper. None of the ghosts answer me, but Luca does. He's sat down next to me and he's barking in jubilation while licking my hand. I pet him on the head while digging around for my water flask in my backpack. I take a few greedy gulps before letting Luca drink by pouring some water into my cupped hand. Then, I pour some into Adam's bottle and slip it into his mouth. He pushes the bottle away in protest, but I don't let him and force him to drink something. It's the only kind of fluid I can currently offer him, even though water is not necessarily good for a baby. Food has become scarce too. Two more fruit purees, that's it. I hope we'll stumble upon a few abandoned houses once we get to the valley, because the village is ten more miles of trekking. Maybe I can replenish my supplies before that. I can only hope that River Run Village hasn't been completely plundered already.

The Keystone area is a small community and not nearly big enough to be deserving of a nuclear bomb being dropped on it. Which is a good thing, because otherwise the radiation would still be all around us and take us out slowly, like a covert assassin taking his time to kill us from the inside or even mutate our genes. I look at Adam and swallow. God forbid that would happen. However, I'll only know the state of things in Keystone

Village once I get there, and by the time I can witness it with my own eyes and see whether it's a site of impact, it'll be too late to retrace my steps. For all I know we may have trotted around on radiation-poisoned land already. On the East coast we were never far away from big cities, after all. Besides, so many bombs were dropped that I wouldn't be surprised if the planet is blanketed by an eternal cover of black clouds in some places. If that's true, I might as well enjoy the sunshine while it lasts, because even that could be taken away from me eventually.

Don't think about that.

I pack up all my stuff, haul the backpack onto my shoulders, then strap Adam to my chest again and pray to whoever's listening that my legs won't give up.

Only a few more miles.

But what if nothing's left of this valley and its inhabitants? The thought – or rather, the ridiculous idea – that I would find my brother here is what kept me going for so long. What if he isn't here? Or worse – what if he *is* here, but dead? I don't know if I can deal with that. What'll be left for us if that happens? Where will we go?

The roads curves to the left in the distance, which gives me a view of the ravine stretching out below the road and the sun in the sky. Only two puffy clouds have dared to venture out and invade the territory of the clear, blue sky. I follow the road but stop midstride when I encounter five parked cars around the bend. They're abandoned and parked crisscross alongside the road, covered in dust. The doors are wide open and two of them have the trunks popped open. The windows are grimy. Some of them have holes in them… caused by bullets, perhaps?

Just beyond the last car in line is the entrance to a tunnel which leads to the valley and the Keystone village. Or it used to: now it's partially blocked by a huge rock as well as a diagonally parked truck.

"I'm afraid we're gonna have to climb over," I whisper.

Luca looks at me incomprehensibly.

I shift the weight of the backpack slightly to the right and head for the tunnel.

A gunshot echoes off the rocks, the bullet missing me narrowly before it ricochets off the bumper of the car next to me. With a yelp, I duck down. I lose my balance, fall forward and scrape my knees on the gravel on top of the pavement. Adam starts to cry because of the sudden movement. I crawl around the car as quickly as I can to find cover, in case they'll shoot at me again. I shrug off the backpack hastily and cradle Adam's head in my hands. His wailing makes my head hurt, my temples pounding in agony. I cover his mouth with my hand and try to shush him. "Hush, baby. Sshh." My voice is trembling so badly that it doesn't sound very convincing. It doesn't help – Adam keeps crying. A fresh bullet bores into the asphalt right next to the car and drowns out the sound of Luca's barks. I cast a quick glance over the open trunk and see the Labrador looking around searchingly. The fact that the sound echoes makes it hard for even him to locate the location of the shooter. "Luca, come over here," I whisper. My hand slips into my backpack to take out the gun. "Now!" *Please. I can't deal with this world anymore if they shoot you too.*

Luca stops barking and hesitantly glances my way.

"Come here!" I repeat adamantly.

The words have barely left my mouth when the dog comes running my way. I pull him in and whisper in his ear to stay put. He obeys, but still growls to warn me when another shot rings out.

It's followed by silence.

Gasping for breath and trying to slow down my heart rate, I look around me, half-expecting to see the shooter coming at me from somewhere. Two minutes pass, then five, then ten. I take a deep breath and gather courage before slowly standing up straight to look over the opened tailgate. To my left, there's the ravine next to the deserted road. To my right, there's the other cars and the blocked tunnel.

Nothing moves.

I try to gauge where the shots were coming from and am about to crouch down to crawl around the car again when I hear a gun being cocked. A voice addresses me. "Drop the gun and turn around. Slowly."

The barrel bumps against the back of my head and I hear the shuffling of feet. My heart beats erratically in my chest. "Please. I'm not dangerous…" I've already established that my assailant isn't a Hunter, or I'd be dead already. In all likelihood, he's just as freaked out as I am. I have to use this to my advantage. I do as I'm asked and put the gun down. With both hands raised in the air, I turn halfway so my shoulder is pointed at him and I can take a look at him, but Adam stays out of his firing range.

What I see makes my knees buckle. The man isn't that old yet. He's wearing a long rain slicker caked in dust with faded jeans and biker boots underneath. A baseball cap is shielding his face from the sun. He's definitely in need of a good shave and his eyes radiate a certain toughness, but I immediately recognize him.

"Steph?"

His hard stance wavers. His left eyebrow quirks up questioningly.

"Steph. It's me, Anna." Tears start rolling down my cheeks and hit the crown of Adam's head. My throat feels dry all of a sudden, and the lump stuck in there throbs painfully. I suddenly realize that he's never used that name for me. He always addressed me as 'hey, sis' after we got our new identities, refusing to use my new name. "Paula," I add quickly.

He's not real, he's a mirage. You want *him to be here, so here he is.*

No – the barrel of the gun pressed against my head was real enough. This is not just my hopeful imagination. But it's too good to be true. Of all the people I could have bumped into, I run into the very person I set out to find here? That only happens in books or movies. It's too much of a coincidence.

And I don't believe in coincidences.

Why, then, do I stand there with my mouth hanging open? The answer is simple: I've been touched by hope. Inspired by the thought that good things might still happen to me in this world. What if it *is* true?

"Paula?" His voice sounds older than I remember – jaded by life experience. How long has it been? Five years… seven? Too long.

I nod. "It's me."

Clearly debating with himself, he stares at me, the baby, and Luca. He lowers the gun somewhat, but the weapon's still aimed at me.

Adam, meanwhile, is screaming at the top of his tiny lungs.

Another voice – low, threatening. "Drop it."

Startled, I look over Steph's shoulder. An old man of about seventy is standing right behind him. He must have come out of the tunnel. He looks like a weathered and especially confident, retired soldier. A cigarette is dangling from the corner of his mouth. His back is slightly bent and his clothes simple. And yet, the look in his eyes tells me that this guy is not to be messed with. But of course, the rifle in his hands already clued me in to that.

To my surprise, a faint smile tugs at Steph's lips. He raises the gun and both his hands in the air before turning around.

"Steady," the man warns him. "I really don't mind pumping you full of lead."

"You're really willing to kill reunited siblings in cold blood? With that baby watching you?"

The old man cocks his head and looks at me. It makes me shiver, especially since the gun's still trained on us. Apparently, he's only seen Adam strapped to my chest just now. He quickly recovers, though. "I will if you leave me no choice. So, put down the damn gun."

Steph doesn't comply. Instead, he slowly lowers his gun again, aiming it at the old man. "How do I know you're not one of *them*?"

"You'd be dead by now, son."

"Same goes for you. We're on the same side here."

"I'll be the judge of that. Lower your gun!"

It doesn't look like Steph is going to obey that order.

I feel it in every fiber of my being: this is going to spiral out of control. Well, I'm not about to lose Steph – not now that fate has handed him to me on a silver plate. "We're not here to harm anyone," I quickly cut in.

"We're just on our way to Keystone." I shoot Steph an unresolved look. "Or we were, at least."

"Why?" The man spits on the ground like it's the most disgusting thing he's ever heard. "Nothing's left of River Run Village."

I nod at Steph and raise my voice to make myself heard over Adam's wailing. "I was looking for him."

Baffled, Steph turns toward me. "For me?"

I look at him disbelievingly. "Yes, of course!"

"So you didn't travel here together," the old man points out cynically.

That seems to be the breaking point for Steph. With a deep sigh, he says: "Look, grandad. You're outnumbered, even if you're the one armed."

The man bursts out laughing. "Ah, is that what you think? Well, look around you, buddy."

And that's what I do. At first glance, I see nothing that stands out to me, but upon closer inspection, I can make out more armed people huddled between the trees on the mountainside.

We're surrounded.

"So, brother and sister, huh?" the man continues with a sly grin. "I really don't know what bothers me more – the fact that you're lying, or the ease with which you're doing it."

"But he *is* my brother!" I stammer.

"Sure he is."

"She's right." Steph looks around and also spots the guns pointed at us from everywhere. It makes him realize how much *he* is outnumbered – how violence won't get him out of this. So he does as he's told: he sinks to his knees with his hands in the air, then puts the gun down on the pavement. "I'm not looking for trouble."

"And that's why you were holding your so-called sister at gunpoint?" The man spits on the ground once more and squints his eyes at us. "Not very convincing, is it?"

"I didn't know it was her. Besides, I wasn't really trying to hit her. But you can't trust anybody. I just wanted to…"

"I'm glad we're agreed about one thing, at least," the man interrupts him.

"I had to know for sure that she wasn't one of *them*. The fact that she's got a live child with her convinced me that she isn't. But I only saw him when I came closer." He takes me in with an intense look. "Though I have to admit it would be the perfect decoy."

"Excuse me?" I stare at him, completely baffled.

Adam keeps on crying.

Luca's right next to me and lets out a few barks when more men emerge from the tunnel – five of them, all armed. They climb over the car blocking their way and come to stand around the old man. Only now do I see that one of them isn't a man at all – it's a woman with short, black hair. She takes a step forward and puts her hand on the old man's shoulder, who hasn't moved an inch ever since they came and seems to be debating whether he should shoot us now or three seconds later. "Lower your gun, Howard," she commands him, her voice cold as ice.

"They know our location. We can't allow them to leave."

"I agree."

"Good. So you won't mind if I…"

"And that's why they're joining us in our camp."

Shocked, Howard gapes at her. "What's that?"

210

"You heard me."

"Are you insane?"

"They have a baby with them."

"The guy just told us: it's the perfect cover."

The woman takes us in one by one – me, Adam, Luca, and Steph. In the sky above, an eagle screeches out in the charged silence surrounding us. Well, him and Adam, of course. At long last, she simply states: "That's a bit far-fetched. I refuse to believe that."

The man's eyes grow wide. "You *refuse* to believe it?"

"Listen. I'm the last one to claim we shouldn't be careful. And believe me, it's not like I'm bringing out the welcome wagon and give them food and a tent. They'll be put in prison for the time being, and they'll be monitored round the clock until the council has decided whether they're to be trusted or not. But what we *aren't* going to do here is shoot innocent people on a hunch, just because you believe they *might* be dangerous. Not here, not now. Besides, I seem to remember giving *you* the benefit of the doubt not too long ago."

"But…" the old man tries again. He turns to the other four men for support. "What do *you* think of this?"

"She's right, Howard," one of them replies.

"Enough blood's been shed," another one adds.

"To be honest, I'm with Howard on this one," a third man calls out. "Besides, think of all the extra mouths we have to feed. It's not like we're drowning in supplies as it is."

The woman puts her hand on Howard's shoulder again and squeezes it while she fixes the third speaker with her stare. "We can always kill them later. Bringing someone back to life is a lot harder."

Howard yanks his shoulder out of her reach. "You'll

211

regret this, Elaine. I can feel it in my bones."

The woman shrugs noncommittally. "I guess we'll see. But by now we are with so many that even one or two Hunters wouldn't be able to fight us off."

I doubt that.

Slowly, the woman approaches us. I hastily cover as much of Adam's body as I can and turn away from her. "What a cutie." She smiles at me. "You must be tired. Don't worry about us locking you up, that's just out of precaution. As soon as we're sure you guys pose no threat to us, you're free to go wherever you want." Her voice drops a notch, and she gives me and Steph a pointed look. "But don't get any funny ideas. The minute I feel you've been lying to us, I won't hesitate to kill you myself."

At that moment, a cry bounces off the rock face, making us all look up anxiously. "Steph? Oh, Jesus." Followed by: "Wait, don't shoot!"

One of the sentinels on the mountainside slides down as quickly yet carefully as she can. Her voice is the only thing clueing me in to the fact that she's a woman. She's wearing jeans and a flannel shirt that's way too big for her. A bandana keeps her long hair away from her eyes and her face is half-covered by a scarf serving as a face mask, which she is now pulling down. Out of breath, she stops in front of us, her rifle dangling against her side. "Is it really you?" Open-mouthed, she stares at my brother.

"Sasha?" Steph squints his eyes as he looks at the woman disbelievingly.

Hearing her name, Sasha begins to cry. With a sob, she wraps her arms around him. "Thank God. I thought you were dead."

Steph hugs her back – gingerly at first, but then his arms really pull her in and he holds her close. "Sasha, is it really you?"

"You better believe it, babe."

Cocking an eyebrow, I look at the scene in front of me. "Uhm, Steph..?"

Apparently, I'm not the only one puzzled by what's happening. "You know these people, Sasha?" Elaine asks doubtfully.

The young woman wriggles out of Steph's grasp and turns around. "Steph's my boyfriend." She then turns toward me. "And you are…"

"His sister."

Sasha nods in agreement. "Yeah, of course. We had a photo of you up in our living room. Steph told me all about you and your family. So terrible. Are your parents and sister, ehm…"

I nod with tears in my eyes, not brave enough to look Steph in the eye. My gaze lingers on Adam. Absently I stroke his little head, which finally calms him down a bit.

"That's what I suspected," Steph says dejectedly. "It's a miracle I've found the two of you back already, actually."

"I'm so sorry," Sasha says with compassion. Then, turning to Elaine: "You're not going to hurt them, are you?"

"She wants to throw them in jail," Howard replies cynically.

"You want to do *what*?" Sasha gives Elaine a wide-eyed look.

"Hey, at least I'm taking them to camp," Elaine defends herself. "That's risky enough as it is. I'm only locking them up until we find out for sure they're good

213

people."

"I just told you I know them?"

"You haven't seen your boyfriend in months," one of the men behind Elaine comments.

"What's that supposed to mean?" Sasha snaps.

"A lot could have happened in those few months, girl."

"You fucking..." Sasha clenches her fists, then pleadingly addresses the obvious leader of this troupe. "Come on, Elaine."

"I'm afraid we don't have a choice," Elaine says. "It's either this or shooting them on the spot, because letting them go is just not an option. If Hunters take them prisoner and torture them for information about our hideout, we're dead."

"And if they *are* Hunters, you're leading them right to us," Howard points out, still in a huff.

Sasha puts her hands in her sides demonstratively. "Well, if you're going to lock up Steph, I'll be in the same cell with him."

Elaine shrugs it off. "Your choice, dear. It's a free country." To the men behind her, she says: "Tie their hands and bring them to camp."

-24-

Abel

A stone wall doesn't usually give, especially not when it comes into contact with something much softer like the back of someone's head. The back of *my* head, that is. Pain flashes through me and I can see stars.

My feet kick the air as Muriel's greasy left hand clamps down on my windpipe. Her other hand is bunching up my shirt in her fingers.

"Aberration," she fumes.

How I even manage to respond to her allegation with just the little air I can suck in through my clenched teeth, I don't know. "No, I'm not. I'm… *oomph*." Her fist hitting my stomach makes me double over, knocking all the air from my lungs. Livid, she hoists me into the air even higher. The room is spinning around me. The next moment, my back hits the floor with a painful thud and I see Muriel towering over me.

"You're a disgrace." Her voice is low, like a man's voice. She balls her fist.

"I'm not an Aberration." I protectively raise my hand in the air to ward her off before she can hit me again. "The soul within me is dead, I swear."

"You're lying! An angel who is in full control over his body would never hesitate to carry out His orders."

"Is that a fact?" I cough and roll onto my side to draw a deep breath. From the corner of my eye, I see the girl's dead body. She's just a few feet away from me. My stomach convulses.

"What are you trying to say?"

"We're *angels*."

Muriel gives me a puzzled look.

"Aren't we supposed to protect humans from evil?"

"In his infinite wisdom, *He* has decided that they no longer deserve that protection."

"Would a shepherd kill his sheep when they're lost, or would he try to guide them home? Isn't *that* supposed to be our task?"

"Our job is to kill them so He can start anew."

I shake my head. It's all so very clear to me now, all of a sudden. "What if *we* are the misguided sheep?"

Muriel barks out a cynical laugh. "Misguided? By who – by *Him*?"

I spit on the floor and crawl backward, away from her, until I feel something sharp stabbing into the palm of my hand. It must be a shard of glass. I hope it goes unnoticed when I edge my right hand toward it. Yes, I was right – it's glass. I grab it and wait for an opportunity. My gaze darts to the window, where more shards of glass remain in the frame. Two pieces point upward like glass stakes. "Maybe."

"Who else?"

I shrug. "The black man, maybe? He who rules the dark."

"Say his name, you pussy."

"Lucifer."

"Have you ever considered the possibility that light and dark are one and the same thing, Abel? One can't exist without the other, so God exists by the grace of the devil."

216

"But He is omniscient. Surely he must have seen this coming – what humanity was going to do to the earth? Why step in now? Why not root out the problem where it started, thousands of years ago? I'm telling you, His plan must be bigger than He has made it seem to us. What if all of this is a mere test? Not for humanity, but for his most faithful servants, the angels? For *us*?"

"Nonsense."

"You really think so? Admit it, Muriel. It's eating away at you too. I can see it in your eyes. You don't care whether your body lives or dies. Deep down, you want to have nothing to do with this."

She considers my words for a moment. Then, she shrugs. "It doesn't change the fact that we have our direct orders, which you decided to ignore." Taking two firm steps toward me and lifting me up again, she continues: "You're weak and you're doubting His intentions. Faithful servants of the light don't do that. It makes you as much of a traitor as Lucifer. Or have you forgotten that he was once one of us?" She seizes me by the neck and her thumbs start to crush my windpipe. "And traitors won't be tolerated."

We're killing in God's name. Does that make us any better than all those human killers?

My hand clenches around the shard of glass that's lying behind my back. The sharp edge digs into my flesh. I ignore the pain because I know I'll have one chance only. I have to do this now. I take a deep breath. Colors drain away from the world around me and I feel as if I'm suffocating.

With a mighty haymaker punch, I ram the glass shard into Muriel's upper leg. Her grip on me immediately slips as she reaches for her bleeding leg. Her eyes shoot daggers at me. "You filthy little…"

I don't give her a chance to finish expressing the sentiment. I pull her toward me and stick out my leg so she trips. Her eyes widen. In an attempt to keep her balance, she wildly mills her arms about, but she's still not used to the mortal body she's stuck in during her time on earth. With a smack, she lands onto the windowsill, her throat hitting the protruding glass spikes full-force. Her body twitches and blood gurgles up from her mouth before she collapses like a sack of potatoes. Before her eyes close for good and she draws her final breath, though, I swear I can see a faint smile – of gratitude? – around her lips.

Struggling for breath, I rest one hand on my knees while rubbing my sore throat with the other. I remain like this for interminable seconds.

Lord, what am I supposed to do next?

Of course, there's no response. For all I know my questions will never warrant a reply anymore – this action may very well have sealed my fate for good. What if I was wrong?

No, I say, giving myself a mental pep talk. *There has to be a bigger plan. I have to believe that. God created* everything, *including my fears and doubts. He has a plan for this world yet. All I need to do is find out what it is.*

Exhausted, I stagger outside into the lonely, cold world. Without a purpose, without any clue as to where I should head next… let alone what my final destination will be.

-25-

Anna

The tunnel is too long and winding to see the end of it from the entrance, and it's dark inside. In other words, I'm glad when Elaine pulls out a flashlight.

I feel the muzzle of a gun being shoved into my back. I can take a hint, so I gather all my courage and start to shuffle forward in between the car parked across the road and the boulders to enter the tunnel. The others climb over them. Adam coughs quietly a few times, but other than that he fortunately keeps quiet. Luca hesitantly walks beside me, tail between his legs.

The footfalls sound heavy trapped in between the cracked walls. This tunnel was clearly manmade, but must be from an era during which they didn't bother to finish the walls. We are surrounded by roughly-hewn stone on all sides. A little ways further down is a ventilation system that's out of order, barely visible in the fading light coming from outside.

Even though Elaine walks ahead with three men – literally acting as a beacon in the darkness – Sasha and Steph walk alongside me, and Howard is situated at my rear, I can't shake the feeling that a Hunter might jump out from the darkness at any moment. It lunges at my throat and makes me look around furtively. I keep an extra close eye on the darkness to my right, because no one's walking there. Nothing but a rocky wall, and yet

I'm certain that red eyes and demonic grins are lurking in the dark. I know it's just my imagination fueled by the trauma I've experienced in the past few months, but that doesn't change the situation. When we reach the end of the tunnel and see the sunlight again, I couldn't be happier. The light after that darkness is so bright at first that it feels like it's burning my retinas.

I haven't even properly left the tunnel behind before the next one pops up, about three hundred yards further up the road. It's cutting through another mountainside and seems to taunt me with its darkness.

The red eyes! Can you see them? Dozens of them. They're hovering...

A shiver runs through me.

This tunnel is barricaded too, this time by two trucks. I was hoping to at least get a glimpse of Keystone Valley, so I'd know for sure that Elaine had spoken the truth about the village still being there, but the mountain's blocking my view. It doesn't really matter at this point, though – I have already found Steph. Or rather, he has found me.

Only now do I see the smaller road that's branching off this one, winding its way down to a village at the foot of the mountain. It looks peaceful from afar, as though it hasn't been touched by the apocalypse at all.

Slowly, we trudge down the road. I look back at the tunnel one more time, taking in the darkness it contains.

The red eyes. They're hovering...

I quickly shake off the thought.

Within the relative safety of the human caravan I'm a part of, I can feel the prying eyes of armed sentinels keeping a close watch on the mountainside. I'm beginning to understand why they decided to block both tunnels for traffic. If this is the only way to get into the valley, that village is a safer place right now than most of the cities and towns in the US.

I'm impressed. Looks like these people have managed to build a stable community within a short time span. It's obvious that Elaine has quite some authority, though it's hard to tell just how far her decision-making power stretches. Plus, the fact they have guards posted on every corner gives me hope. There might be a place in this world where we can be safe after all. And then it occurs to me that we're basically prisoners here and I don't know these people at all.

Our weapons were taken from us, of course, but one of the men was also kind enough to carry my backpack.

"Are you sure you don't want me to carry him for a while?" Sasha, who's walking in between me and Steph, gestures at Adam.

I shake my head and put a protective hand on his little head. "No, thank you."

Sasha just shrugs.

Steph takes her hand and shoots her an inquiring look. "How is it that you're still alive?"

Sasha laughs bitterly. "I could ask you the same thing."

"Were you not in the valley when River Run Village was attacked?"

"It wasn't bombed, then?" I ask quietly. I follow the people in front of me further down. My heels ache from the descent on the steep road, and it gets worse when we leave the paved road behind and take a mountain track that seems to lead straight to the village.

Elaine shakes her head. "No. Everyone was simply killed within the span of ten days. They came in waves –

I think in total they were about forty. Heavily armed men, women, and even children. They didn't back down for anything and combed street by street like a bunch of lunatics. They were cunning, you know. I bet if they'd stormed the village all at once we'd have had a lot of casualties too, but at least we'd have stood a chance to arm ourselves against these attacks. The way they operated was that they'd come after dark, all alone, sometimes in groups of two or three. They came likes thieves in the night, killing us one by one in our sleep. The people who did wake up and tried to run, were caught and killed too. The ones still standing after three weeks just had a lot of damn luck."

"People like you?" I asked, baffled by her story. It sent a shiver through my body just listening to it.

Elaine didn't reply, but I saw tears well up before she hastily turned her head away.

"I wasn't in town when it happened," Sasha continued for her. "I had to travel to New York for an assignment, so I'd left two days before it all happened. I was on my way back when I heard all the news reports on my car radio. At first I really couldn't believe it, but when I saw all these Youtube notifications on my phone, I knew it had to be true. That was just hours before the world blacked out. Cellphone networks, electricity, it all just went away. When that happened I was *really* at my wits' end. Just before midnight, I pulled into a motel. Apparently the owners had been living under a rock up till that point, because they had no clue what was happening and of course they didn't believe me. Sure, the electricity was down, but that happened all the time, according to the woman who owned the place. I couldn't show them any proof – not that I tried very hard to prove my point, anyway. I reckoned they'd find out soon enough. After a short night's sleep, I finally puckered up the courage to drive the last stretch back to Keystone Valley. I encountered nothing but death and corpses. I must have spent at least five hours combing through the houses of River Run looking for you, Steph... but very quickly that turned into a search for survivors, for anybody at all. I clearly remember thinking at some point: *Please, God, don't let them all be dead. If I have to walk around here all by myself much longer, I'll lose it.* That's when Elaine found me."

Sasha's story is impressive and bleak, but the way she tells it sounds almost cheerful. In fact, nothing seems to be able to wipe the grin off her face – I'm seriously considering it – and she's practically skipping. She's holding Steph's hand the way six-year-old years do: swinging it wildly back and forth. *That girl's bat-shit crazy. Was she always like this, or did the circumstances make her take a trip to La-La-Land?* The insecure look in Steph's eyes is telling me enough – he doesn't know how to handle her. This isn't the same girl he fell in love with not so long ago. I wonder how long they were together before the apocalypse happened. What happened to Kim, the girl he chose above his family? I get too distracted to think about it when Sasha starts on an entire saga about something they did before – Steph and she were apparently on a picnic together somewhere in these mountains.

I cast an irritated look over my shoulder, partly to distract myself and partly to keep an eye on Howard. He may be suspicious of us, but I'm even more suspicious of him. He's been training his stupid gun on me the whole way down this path. The lanky guy presently walking next to him sees me rolling my eyes, and he laughs. "Yup. Give Sasha a dime and she'll run her mouth the whole afternoon."

Sasha pauses mid-sentence. She laughs, then sticks out her middle finger while staring ahead. "Fuck you, Thomas."

We reach the bottom of the valley and head for the village. It surprises me how little evidence there is of the world having ended. Admittedly some buildings are missing glass in the windows or front door, and some walls even sport bullet holes, but the place looks pretty tidy and well-kept. The dead have been buried.

We go in the direction of a courtyard, where most people are gathered. I count about thirty of them – men, women, and children who gape at me and Steph with distrust in their eyes. I don't get much time to properly look around, because our next stop is the prison.

The narrow building is right next to a candy store. Two armed men are flanking the front door, and a bit further down are more guards watching our every move. More armed men are positioned on the mountainside. If I took the slightest misstep or committed the most minor infraction, I'd be riddled with so many bullets I could make a colander jealous.

"Who are these people?" one of the guards asks Elaine.

He's just a kid – no more than sixteen years old.

"Open the door, Roy."

"Elaine – are you sure this is wise?" Howard pipes up again behind me.

"Like I said: we lock them up and keep an eye on them 24/7. Meanwhile, the council can convene and decide what should be done with them. A meeting is scheduled for tomorrow."

Roy shoots me and Steph an anxious look but does as he is told. He walks us inside.

Jail is nothing more than a simple, square space with three cells on the right side. There's a desk on the left, piled high with paperwork, as well as a chair and a computer. That's all. The cells are pretty bare-bones, too. A plywood foundation without as much as a mattress on top of it and a small toilet in the corner. The gray cement of the ceiling is cracked. Tubes wrapped with insulation material run from left to right. The walls are covered with weird scribblings like: *Hilly Billy 2010. Boot camp 2.0. I spread my wings 4 U, if U get my drift. Love U, Susan.* Of course, there are also generous helpings of porn graffiti: sketches of penises, tits and vaginas. Light penetrates the small cracks between the wooden planks and shines in through the window right next to the door. There is a lightbulb on the ceiling, but the fact that it's not on tells the story of this community lacking electricity. As a result, the corners of the cramped space are shrouded in shadows.

"Faded glory, I'm afraid," Elaine comments as she shoves me and Adam into the cell on the left. Luca runs ahead and starts to sniff every corner. Steph is locked in the cell next to mine, with nothing but bars between us. They take the ties off our hands. Before I even have the chance to turn around, the door squeaks on its hinges as Roy pulls it shut and turns the key. "Like most things around here," Elaine adds. "Let me get you both a mattress or something. Maybe something to eat and drink? How does that sound?"

"You could just set us free, of course," Steph suggests.

"You'd like that, wouldn't you?" Howard hisses.

Elaine shoots Howard a withering look, but her voice still sounds gentle and compassionate as she replies: "I'm afraid we can't do that just yet."

I sigh. "We're not dangerous, I swear."

"I believe you, honey. But I hope you can understand why we need to be careful. That's life, these days."

I slowly nod "I do understand."

Steph's cynical laughter bubbles up in the cell next to me. "Oh, you *understand*, do you?"

I nod again and look at him sideways. There's something in his eyes that I've never seen there before, although I can't quite place what it is. "Wouldn't we do the exact same thing if the tables were turned?"

"Glad to hear you feel that way." Addressing the men who brought us in, she continues: "You can leave now. They're not going anywhere." The sudden change in her tone of voice makes me shiver. To us, she sounded compassionate, but now she seems quite cold. Her voice clearly states that she's not to be messed with. All the men comply save Howard. Sasha doesn't move either – she's eyeing the cell hesitantly.

"You're free to be locked in with him, you know," Elaine calmly states as she nods at Steph.

Resolutely, Sasha shakes her head. It makes me dislike her even more. "I'll make sure they're fed, okay? And I'll have a look around for two spare mattresses. There should be enough." She's looking at Steph rather than Elaine.

"Naturally!" Howard has lowered his gun by now, but he's still holding on to it as though he expects one of us to yank it out of his hands. "Why don't we just give them the key to the town gates while we're at it?"

Elaine ignores his quip and cocks her head as if in

doubt. In the end she agrees to Sasha's plan, though. "As long as you show Justin what you're taking from the storeroom. He needs to keep track of all the goods."

"Of course."

Howard shakes his head incredulously, as though he's giving up in the face of so much stupidity. "I truly hope that this decision won't turn itself against you, Elaine. Because if it does, I'll be here before you can blink, be sure of that." And with those words, he turns on his heels and struts out the door, slamming it shut with a reverberating thud on his way out.

"Don't mind him." Elaine shakes her head. "He wasn't selected to be a member of the council and he couldn't accept that. He's been on my case ever since."

"Why would he deserve to be on the council?" Sasha says. "Why would anyone leave decision-making in the hands of that numbskull? *You're* the one who found us this place. *You're* the one who made sure we're all safe here."

"That's all very well," Steph suddenly bursts out, "but how on earth are you going to test us and make sure we can be trusted?"

Elaine pulled a face. "Yeah, that's exactly our problem: I'm not sure we can."

"So we're screwed no matter what?" Steph approaches the bars in front of his cell and wraps his hand around one of them. He tries to pry it loose, but the cell's not quite that decrepit yet. The bar stays put.

Elaine shakes her head. "I hope not."

"Do you happen to have any baby food for Adam?" I nod at the child in my arms.

"Not a lot, I'm afraid," Elaine says. "We don't have a lot of food left in general. About one week ago we sent three teams of two out to scavenge for supplies, but so far they haven't returned."

I suddenly remember the two men I encountered in the forest, and I nod understandingly.

"We have some bananas, though. I could mash them and bring that in a bowl?" Sasha proposes.

I nod gratefully and sit down on my bunk. Luca immediately follows suit and drops his head down onto my upper legs with a groan.

Steph refuses to sit down and glares at Elaine through the bars. "If we were indeed Hunters, these bars wouldn't be able to stop us. Don't you know that?"

"Which is the reason why you're under round-the-clock surveillance." And with those words, Elaine leaves the room. As soon as she's out of sight, the two guards come in.

Sasha lingers for a bit. "I'm sorry, Steph, but after everything that happened I can't be locked up. I hope you understand."

"Do whatever you think is best, love," my brother replies. He doesn't seem to care much.

"I'll be back soon with some food and drinks, okay?" She looks at me. "And something to eat for your little man."

"Thanks," I reply.

Sasha smiles. She nods at the two guards before exiting the building, leaving me behind with the only living relative I still have.

-26-

The wall I'm leaning against with my back feels like ice. It's in sharp contrast with the warmth of Luca's head on my legs and a sleeping Adam in my arms. I groggily stare past the bars of the room I'm in. How did I end up here? It all feels so unreal. A part of me still hopes that Mark will kiss me awake soon – that it will turn out to be a lazy Sunday morning, one day away from an ordinary workweek. Oh, what I wouldn't do for *that* to become a reality. But of course, holding out hope is pointless. This is life in all its hideous glory. This is what I'll have to settle for.

The two guards are on either side of the door and keep a close eye on all our movements, guns cradled in their laps. The rays of the sun shining into the prison room are receding with each passing second. Dusk is setting in. It won't be long before I'll be subjected to utter darkness once again, like a long-lost friend waiting in the corner to embrace me. A shiver runs down my spine. I can't say I'm looking forward to meeting him again, fenced in behind bars like this.

I turn my head and carefully observe Steph. The bars between us divide my brother into separate pieces of him, but the cut-up version of Steph is still clearly smiling to himself.

"Why the hell are you smiling?" I snap.

Like me, Steph is sitting on his prison bunk, his legs pulled up. Sasha brought us some pillows an hour ago, as well as some food and drink. She also brought mashed banana for Adam. She said she had to pop out and get something else, but she hasn't been back since. If I were in Steph's shoes, I'd feel betrayed and question her motives – not just as a girlfriend, but as a human being in general. Steph, on the other hand, doesn't seem to care one way or another.

My brother shakes his head, still smiling. "This situation makes me smile."

"You think this is *funny*?" I ask incredulously.

"Totally. You don't?"

"How can you possibly…" I swallow the rest of my retort. Instead, I ball my hands into fists and clench my jaw. What the hell is wrong with him? It's obvious that Sasha's a few fries short of a Happy Meal – could Steph have lost his mind, too? I stop myself from saying it out loud, though. I don't want to pick a fight with him. He's the only family I've got left, and even though I imagined our reunion very differently, I can't be picky. I should be thankful I even got to find him again at all – that we're both still alive. And yet… I sigh, nervously biting my nails as I whisper: "Steph. They're all dead."

"Who?" The smile remains, though it falters slightly.

"Mom, Dad, Joey, Hannah." I quickly swallow the lump in my throat.

My statement is followed by silence, which he breaks by saying: "Yeah, I figured."

Yeah, I figured? What the fuck?!

"That's all you have to say?"

"What else do you want me to say?"

"I don't know!" I fume. "But just saying *that* makes it sound like you don't give a shit."

Steph doggedly stares ahead, devoid of emotion. "Well, I could break down and cry, but it won't bring them back, will it?"

"No, but..." Disbelievingly, I shake my head and decide to try a different angle. "What happened to Kim?"

"Kim?"

"Yeah, you know, the love of your life. The one you professed your undying love to."

"Ah." Steph shrugs carelessly. "Haven't seen her in years."

"I thought you guys were planning to get married. That didn't happen, then?"

Steph's eyes bore into mine. He squints at me before slightly baring his teeth like a dog that's growling at me. "I don't want to talk about it, okay?"

"But isn't it..." I say, still confused.

"You really don't get it, do you?" He flies off the handle, jumping up and gripping the bars between us in his fingers so tensely that his entire body shakes. Of course, the bars don't budge at all. "Nothing from our past matters anymore. The past is dead and gone – all of it. There's no point talking about it or reminiscing about things. It's *gone!*"

Adam jolts awake due to my brother's rant and he looks frantically around him, just like Luca. Fortunately, he doesn't start to cry.

Like this is the final straw for them, the two guards jump up and rush forward, pointing their rifles at Steph.

"Get away from those bars, my friend," the guard who introduced himself as Harvey an hour ago says. The rifle in Roy's hands is shaking, but he holds on to it

231

intently.

My heart beats in my throat.

Steph lets go of the bars, grinning again and sticking his hands up in a gesture of surrender. "Calm down, boys. My bark's worse than my bite."

Luca growls at Steph like the words made sense to him.

Steph sits down on his bunk, staring ahead unyieldingly and at no one in particular.

The way he exploded shocked me, but I can understand he's been through a lot. I can't hold that against him. "What happened to you?" I inquire softly.

He remains silent for a beat before he looks at me. "The same thing that happened to you, I suppose."

I don't truly get what he means by that, but I decide to let it rest for now. I don't want to scare him off. And yet, I can't resist asking him something else. "What about Sasha?"

"What about her?" Steph sighs.

"I don't know. Something's off about her. Something…"

"What?"

"Something weird is going on."

Steph shrugs. "Nothing's wrong with her, trust me."

Apparently, that's all I'm getting.

Four more hours pass slowly. The dark has embraced us, only interrupted by the pale light of the moon that pours in through the window. Roy has fallen asleep in his chair, being the top-notch sentinel that he is. He's slightly sagging down in his seat, the rifle balancing on his stomach. His colleague doesn't tell him off – he's not far off from falling asleep himself. His eyelids droop lower with each passing second. It's a battle he's bound to lose soon. Not that it matters – it doesn't change our situation in the least. We're trapped in here with no way out. And to be honest, I'm not even trying to figure out how to escape. I can only applaud these people for locking us up, and a part of me is strangely convinced that this council of theirs will see that we pose no threat. They'll let us out of here and make us a part of their tribe.

A soft, murmuring sound pulls me out of the dream world I unwittingly slipped into. I open my eyes and look around in surprise. Luca is curled up into a ball next to me, his nose blowing warm air against my arm. Adam is kicking his little legs in his sleep. Other than that, I see nothing remarkable. Well, by now both Roy and Harvey are out like a light and Roy's almost slipping off his chair... but not Steph. He's staring ahead, fully awake, the moonlight glistening in his eyes.

For a split second, I consider the possibility that the sound was only present in my dream, but then I hear it again. Sharp and gurgling.

"Can you hear it too, Steph?" I whisper.

My brother turns his head to face me and nods. The look in his eyes frightens me – so intense, so fixed on me.

"She's coming."

"Who?"

Before he can reply, the front door slowly swings open with an ominous creak.

Roy and Harvey don't take notice.

In the doorway is one of the guards who was posted outside when we came in. He gives me a glassy look. I eye both him and the world behind the guard suspiciously, holding my breath when I see the shoes and the legs belonging to his colleague appear beside him.

The man opens his mouth to call out to his colleague, reaches out with his hand, then stands rooted to the spot. The moonlight is only illuminating his feet, but I can still see something black running down his chin. Instinctively I know it is blood. When the man tumbles forward and hits the floor with a dull thud, not moving anymore, I let out a shriek. Both Roy and Harvey jump to attention. In a panic, they scan the room, but they miss the dark figure storming into the prison behind their backs. One hand slips over Harvey's mouth to muffle his cries, the other is wielding a knife. Harvey's throat is slit and blood gushes out of the cut. Harvey drops his rifle and claws at his throat, but drops down before his fingers have reached their destination. Roy whips around and aims his rifle at the woman, but she's much quicker. She plunges the knife into his heart and pulls it out with ease, then snatches the keys to the cell doors out of his pocket just before he hits the floor.

Luca's barking frantically. Strangely enough, the ruckus hasn't even woken Adam. Again, I envy his innocent ignorance.

"Here. Make yourself useful." The woman sticks her hand between the bars of Steph's cell and tosses him the keys. Then, she turns around and steps outside to cast a furtive look around before she starts dragging the second guard's lifeless body into the prison building.

"You took your sweet time, Sasha." Steph gets up with a grin. He tries a few keys before finding the right one to free himself. He opens the door and steps outside.

Sasha seems to have no trouble at all with dragging the heavy corpse inside. She's pulling his left leg and in her hand he seems light as a feather. Once she's back inside, she closes the front door. "I had to take out the mountain guards who were keeping an eye on the prison first."

Gasping for breath, I press my back against the wall while my eyes flit from left to right. I'm trying to make sense of the events of the past few minutes, but I'm having a hard time with it. "Steph, what's going on?"

Steph grabs a rifle off the floor and turns around. "Oh, come on, sis. You can't be *that* stupid."

"She's related to you, though," Sasha teases him. She sits down on her haunches and wipes her bloody knife on Roy's shirt. In the dim light, she's nothing more than a vague shadow.

"She's related to Steph, not to me," my brother replies.

Only then do I connect the dots. "You were both pretending. You're *angels*."

"Correct," Steph confirms. He walks over to my cell door, fiddles around with the keys until he finds the right one, and opens the squeaky door for me. "Just like you."

"I'm *not* like you." I put a protective hand on Adam's head, feeling my rage flare up inside. How could I have been this stupid? Why didn't I see this coming?

"Sure you are," Steph replies. "It's just that your soul has managed to suppress the angel in you."

"Touch her, Memphis," Sasha says. "Give her celestial alter ego a hand."

Steph shakes his head. "I don't think that'll help. Will it?" He looks at me inquisitively. In the moonlight all I can make out are his forehead and eyes. His soulless eyes... how did I miss that before? "You're stronger than him, aren't you?"

I don't say anything. Instead, I furtively look around,

searching for a way out. I'm considering the possibility of calling out for help, but I'm afraid of what they will do to me, Luca, and Adam if I do.

"If you're not planning on giving him back control over her body, why didn't you just shoot her earlier today?" Sasha wants to know.

"I don't know about you, but it pains me to kill one of our own kind," comes the reply. "Besides, I was hoping to use her to find out if and where the humans were hiding, and I could sense the angel in her. And then I saw the child and got an even better idea."

"Which is?"

"Easy – we're taking the baby with us. If she ever wants to see him again, she'll have to surrender to her inner angel." He shoots me a devilish grin. "Since only angels can sense where the other angels are located."

"What the hell are we supposed to do with a baby?" Sasha raises her eyebrows.

"*We're* not supposed to do anything with him. *You're* the one who's going to keep him alive."

"Dream on." She gives him a scathing look. "Besides, I don't get it. If she really allowed the angel within to resurface, she'd be able to find him, sure, but what would be the point? The angel trapped inside will kill the baby with his bare hands, given the chance."

"What a predicament to be confronted with, right?" Steph says almost gleefully.

I shoot him a baffled look and feel the adrenaline rushing through my veins. "You gotta be kidding me."

"Not kidding, darling." And with those words, he takes a menacing step forward. Luca growls, snapping his teeth at him, but Steph doesn't seem to care.

"I say we just shoot them." Sasha grabs the other rifle

and points it at me.

"No, you don't." Steph pushes the muzzle away. "Lower your weapon or I'll make you."

Sasha laughs. "You wouldn't dare."

"Pull that trigger and the next bullet's for you, I swear."

Both Sasha and I ogle Steph disbelievingly now. What the hell's he up to? Is it possible that Steph – the real one, my brother's soul, locked up deep within the recesses of his own mind – can still partially control this body and mind? Is this some strange way of protecting me or a cruel way to torture me by giving me hope?

Sasha shakes her head and sighs before lowering the weapon. "Whatever. If you feel like wasting time, be my guest. As soon as we told the others how many people are hiding out here, it won't be long before they come here and kill everyone, including her. And even if no other angels come round, they're still doomed. During the few weeks I spent with these survivors, I've counted at least ten whose teeth were beginning to fall out or whose excrement was mixed with blood. Radiation is a sly killer." She wags an authoritative finger at him as she continues: "And get this: *you'll* be the one carrying the damn baby."

"We'll see about that." Steph approaches me. I utter a cry and flinch. Luca's barking his lungs out. *Surely someone will hear him and come have a look?* I can see Steph raising the stock of his rifle in the air, but I miss the next moment: him slamming it against my temple with brute force. "Good luck making your choice, sweetheart," I hear him say. Pain lances through me, but dissipates just as quickly as it overpowered me.

-27-

I wake up to something licking my face. I open my eyes and the first thing I see is a pair of legs, of a person who's standing next to me in my cell. It's morning, I think to myself. The sun has beaten the moon once more and chased the gloom from this space.

My head feels like my brain's dunked in a tub of water. My vision's blurred and I feel sick.

Another lick. Luca's standing over me, giving me an anxious look. For a moment I lose myself in his eyes.

"Careful now. They knocked you on the head pretty hard."

A second voice chimes in: "He used his fist on her or what?"

I put one hand on the cold, grimy floor and push myself upright. Everything's spinning, but I manage to sit up. "The stock of a rifle," I reply, massaging the bridge of my nose between two fingers. Then I rub my eyes, hoping to clear my vision again. That works, but it takes a few seconds.

Elaine's in front of me, as well as Howard and a few other armed men and women. Several emotions are evident in their eyes – worry, anger, desperation, and fear.

It takes me a while to remember what happened

exactly, but then the images hit my brain like a wrecking ball.

I jump to my feet screaming: "Adam!" Clearly, I'm moving too fast – the room starts to spin again. Elaine dashes forward to support me. A good thing too, because I'd probably have fainted again.

"Easy," she urges me. Her voice is peppered with compassion.

"Where is he?" I yell so loudly that my lungs hurt in my chest. The scream is followed by a hacking bout of coughing. As if on cue, I rest my hands on my knees to draw a few deep breaths. But not too many – I can't allow myself to waste time. "Where's Adam?"

"I'm sorry, Anna," Elaine says. "He's gone – just like your brother."

Tears well up in my eyes. Angered, I ball my fists. "It was Sasha. She set him free and killed the guards."

Elaine nods. "We suspected as much. She's been missing all morning."

"But why would she do this?" one of the men wonders.

"Isn't that obvious?" Howard replies, leaning against one of the walls with his arms crossed. "All this time she was one of *them*."

"No way," one of the three women exclaims. "She's been with us ever since the beginning."

"Yes way," I retort tiredly. "And it's not just her – Steph's no longer human either." Saying the words out loud is like taking a dagger to the heart.

A charged silence follows. Eight pairs of eyes stare at me in surprise.

"What do you mean, no longer human?" Howard inquires. "You mean to say you *know* who or what we're dealing with here?"

His reaction startles me. I'm mentally kicking myself.

Oh wow, nice going, girl. Are you also gonna fess up to having your own personal angel stuck inside you? That they should run for their lives if he ever manages to subdue your soul? Go on then – make sure you get a bullet to the brain.

I worry my lip. Of course I could tell them what's causing the epidemic. They deserve to know the truth – maybe I can tell them what I know without mentioning my connection to the whole thing?

Too risky, you idiot. Chances are they'll distrust you even more than they're already doing now.

I sigh and shrug my shoulders. Luca's sitting next to me and looks around worriedly, as though he's just as aware of the missing person in our party as I am. He's whining. I stroke his fur gently. "Personally I can't believe that this epidemic is just down to thousands of men, women, and children who lost their minds. Do you? There's gotta be more to the story."

"Such as?"

"No idea," I lie. While I shoot Elaine a pleading look, I change the subject. "We have to find them. Adam's…"

Howard lets out a cynical laugh. "They skipped town, believe you me. And even if we wanted to go look for them, we wouldn't know where to start. It's like looking for a needle in a haystack."

"But…" I try.

"I'm afraid he's got a point, Anna," Elaine says. "We really have no way of finding out where they went."

That's not true. There *is* a way to find out, or so Steph told me. Angels can sense each other's presence. I could allow Dean temporary control over my body, but I haven't got the faintest clue how to do that. Besides, it's

240

just like Sasha told me – I'd be a spectator of events while the angel within me tears Adam apart with my own bare hands.

Not if you manage to seize control over your body just as it's about to happen.

Oh, sure. Peanuts.

You've done it before, haven't you?

But I don't know how I did it. It's too risky.

It's also the only chance you'll have of finding Adam back. Isn't that worth the risk?

"What do we do with her?"

The voice brings me back to the here and now. With a start, I look at the woman who spoke those words. I guess she's in her thirties. She has a sunken face and rings under her eyes. "Excuse me?"

"Sia's right," Howard says. "Sasha was infected. What if the same thing is true for Anna?"

"Don't be absurd," another man calls out. He's tall and bearded and he has a fierce look in his eyes. "They wouldn't have left her behind if she were."

"Or maybe they would have," Howard argues, shooting me a suspicious look. It gives me the creeps. "Ever heard of the Trojan horse?"

"You really are a piece of work, aren't you?" Elaine hisses. But the next thing she does is glance at me just as suspiciously. Deep down she must have her doubts too.

The discussion that follows largely passes me by. I just sit there, my jaw slack and my left hand petting Luca. Images pass in front of my eyes. Adam, Hannah, Joey, my parents, Mark. Steph's image lingers for a bit longer. Again, I feel like he's something sharp in my heart. I know I can't blame Steph for what happened – if anything I should pity him. After all, he's nothing more than a prisoner within his own mind, if he's even aware of that anymore. And yet, I can't shake this all-pervading sense of betrayal. Tears roll down my cheeks.

I raise my hand. It immediately shuts up the shouting people around me. "You know what, please stop arguing about what to do with me. You don't get to decide. I'm out of here."

"You're leaving?" Elaine gives me a searching look.

I nod. "Yes. I have to track down Adam."

"And how are you going to do that?"

"I don't know yet," I admit honestly. "But if I stay here, I sure as hell won't find him. Besides, we're not safe here."

"What do you mean?" Sia looks shocked.

"I heard Sasha say something about telling the others about this hideout, and she mentioned it wouldn't be long before they showed up here to kill off the rest of you."

"What?" Howard erupts.

"The others?" Elaine repeats. "What others?"

I shrug. "The fact remains that there is a fair chance of them showing up here by the dozens, and soon."

"We've been at risk of being attacked ever since we settled here," one of the men replies, sounding calmer than I'd expected. "We've got enough people and plenty of guns to defend ourselves. This location is ideal for it. I say let them try."

I look at him nonplussed. "You have no idea who you're dealing with."

"Oh, and you do?"

"No," I lie again. "But I do know what they're capable of. Goddammit, they basically destroyed the entire world within a couple months. You really think they can't take

242

on this village?"

"This is what I mean," Howard snaps. "What if this is what they set out to do? They left Anna here so she could dish up some story about the village being at risk, so we'd pack up and leave. And they'll be waiting for us when we do, trust me."

"Calm down, Howard," Elaine tells him off. "We're not going anywhere for the time being." She addresses me next. "Where else would we go, Anna? The mountains fence us in on the other side of the valley and we'd be sitting ducks. In this place we can at least predict which direction they'll be coming from if they do. Only two tunnels lead to this place, so there's two possibilities."

"And they're both guarded, right?"

Elaine nods.

"And those guards are still alive as we speak?"

She nods.

"Which means they got out by way of the mountains. And if it works one way, surely it can work the other way – they can come back like that."

"Impossible," Howard claims. "The mountains are too steep to climb."

You're underestimating them. But really, can I blame them? Not really. Besides, I can understand where Elaine's coming from. "Well, it's your decision, not mine. I'm leaving here to find Adam no matter what."

And with those words, I head for the front door, only to suddenly slump down to the floor like a sack of potatoes. I temporarily black out and my knees painfully hit the floor. My head is about to be next, but I quickly push myself off with my hands and soften the blow that way.

243

"I'm afraid you're not going anywhere anytime soon, Anna," I hear Elaine say, her echoey voice seeming to come from a large distance. "I think you may have a concussion."

"See if I care." Again, I try to stand up, but fail.

"Take it easy for a couple of days. In your present condition you wouldn't even be able to find a mountain if it thumped you in the face."

"And even if that didn't bother you, we still wouldn't let you go," Howard adds. "Like I said – if *they* find you and torture you for our location…"

"It's a little bit late to consider that now, don't you think?" In my mind I'm shouting the words at him, but they leave my mouth like a whisper. "Adam's in danger. I have to…"

"Honey," Elaine cuts me off. "If their intention was to kill that baby boy of yours, they'll have done it by now."

-28-

"You really want to hold me here against my will?" I'm lying on my bunk and stare up at the ceiling. Luca's cuddled up against me. The cell door is closed. Some hours have passed since I was clubbed down by that rifle, but I don't know how many. Enough for dusk to set in again, at least. Although my headache is getting less, it's still there. I still feel exhausted and nauseous too, which makes Elaine's theory about a concussion pretty plausible.

Elaine is the only other person present in the room. She's looking out the window. "You know why we're doing this, Anna. The others don't want to risk it."

"But that's a load of bull. I wouldn't be surprised if an entire host of maniacs was on their way here right now. I'm telling you – we need to get out of here."

"Maybe..."

"I understand you feel safer here than anywhere else. Those mountains aren't just protecting us all, though..."

"They can be used against us, too," Elaine finishes the sentence.

"Exactly. And when they come – I'm not saying 'if', mind you – then we're all trapped like rats in a cage. Besides, take a look at Sasha, who singlehandedly made it possible for Steph and her to escape. How many men has she killed?"

"Seven."

"Proves my point."

"I know it does. We called a council meeting two hours ago and I told them the same thing. At first I agreed with them. Let them come, I thought to myself. Until one of the men made us face the facts. What if we can't stop them? What if they're too many?"

"And what conclusion did the council reach?"

"That we should take our chances, despite the objections. That's our best option."

I sit up in a rage, but immediately I feel my stomach turn. I have to work really hard not to throw up. Luca barks briefly, then jumps up from the bunk too. I gawk at Elaine wide-eyed. "You're not fucking serious!"

"I'm afraid I am."

"And you support their decision?"

Elaine sighs. "We've taken a vote."

I raise my eyebrows in surprise. "I thought you had some clout in this community."

"I do, but up to a certain point. I'm the one who found this village. It gives me authority, a certain prestige if you will, but this is still a democracy. I wouldn't want it any other way."

"Not even when the situation demands it?"

Elaine keeps quiet.

"And what if some of the people do want to leave? What happens then? The council decides, but surely they can't put people's lives in the balance like that? If some of you decide to run anyway, will you let them?"

Elaine fixes the floor with her stare.

"I guess that's a no, then?" I almost laugh.

"They can compromise our safety, just like you. We

246

can't risk it. But if Steph and Sasha go tell their maniac friends about us, none of this will matter anyway."

"So in other words, if anyone happens to wander into this village, even by accident, they're basically prisoners here?"

Plagued by guilt, Elaine turns her head away to avoid my eyes.

"You must realize that this puts you on the same level as the psycho killers, don't you?"

Elaine says nothing.

"Do the villagers know about this?"

"We never had to tell them before!" Elaine suddenly hisses. She squints her eyes and glares at me. "And let's face it, why would anyone want to leave here? You can't find a place like this for miles around. Where would people find safety, food, and a roof over their heads?"

"And yet you yourself doubt this safety, plus you told me you sent out scouts on a supply run." I laugh scornfully. "As for roofs over people's heads, I can assure you that there's a *lot* of vacant houses out there."

"But here people can live like we used to do before – as part of a community."

"Wake up and smell the coffee, Elaine! Your safety is just make-believe. That world is dead and gone, and we'd better accept it. You stand a far better chance of survival on your own, because it's easier to hide and make sure Hunters don't find you."

"You don't know that."

Was that a tear in the corner of her left eye?

"Even if you're right..." Elaine pins me with her gaze. "Who'd want to live like that?"

"I would, if it means I won't get killed."

"Well, I would rather live happily for one day than

247

survive for years while feeling scared and lonely. Maybe it's better if they end my life anyway. Maybe something better is waiting for us after death.

I shoot her a baffled look. "You're not serious."

She shrugs placidly. "Why wouldn't I be?"

Because Heaven has the No Vacancy sign up, darling. God has closed the fairground for future visitors.

But I don't tell her that. Faith means solace. Back in college I used to have a friend, Dorothy Perkins, who was Bible Belt religious. A bit of a stranger to this world, but I couldn't think of a friendlier, happier person in my circle. I once asked her why she was always so cheerful, and the answer was simple. *"God is with me."* Back then I didn't understand what she meant, but now I do. Living with the firm conviction that something magical is waiting for me after death – that would certainly give me peace.

Silence ensures. After a while, Elaine softly says: "I lost a tooth this morning."

I stare at her uncomprehendingly. She shows me her teeth and the hole in between them. Then, I connect the dots. "Oh, shit."

She nods. "It won't be long now before I find blood in the toilet bowl. My body's dying, Anna."

"The radiation." I swallow.

She nods. "And I'm not the first."

"Sasha told me as much, yes."

Elaine keeps talking as though she hasn't heard my comment. "I also think that is the reason no one here wants to leave. In here, we're together, and nobody wants to die alone. Which is exactly what will happen if we leave here."

"I'm sorry."

"You're still not affected, then? Physically, I mean?"

I shake my head.

"Not even an upset stomach?"

"Yeah, because of that blow to the head, but other than that – no."

"You will. Radiation poisoning takes time to manifest itself, I've read that somewhere. It happens in stages, but the duration and the severity of the symptoms are dependent on the amount of radiation you were exposed to. There's the acute phase in which you feel nauseous, have to throw up, suffer diarrhea and lose all appetite. It can last for days. There's also something called a latent phase – you feel better at first, but then the symptoms come back. Of course, these are all down to the amount of radiation as well as your physical condition. Whether you'll recover or die could become apparent within weeks, but it can also take two years. The problem is that we don't know how much radiation we were exposed to, but it seems a given fact that we *will* get sick. There won't be many places in this worlds that are radiation-free, especially when all these cities and towns were bombed. And of course, there's the polluted rain, spreading the radiation like an infectious disease."

The confident tone of her voice makes me flinch. My thoughts flash back to the dead animals I encountered in the woods before, and I wonder why they had to be punished by God too. I mean, seriously, what could they possibly have done wrong? What makes an animal evil – are they even capable of being evil? Isn't it just in their nature to kill? And if that is the case, doesn't the same go for us humans?

I look at Luca. He can feel the weight of my stare, because he looks up questioningly. What happens to animals when they die? Will they go to Heaven? I do hope so, if God ever decides to open those pearly gates again.

Minutes go by. The darkness intensifies, which causes me to only see Elaine's outline as a shadow.

"Who were you before all this happened?" I ask.

Elaine laughs. "A school teacher. Can you believe it?"

"I can, in a way."

"Oh?"

"Well, you've got a natural authority," I clarify.

"Huh. You should have seen me struggle with those little devils. Sometimes it was impossible to rein them in, even for me."

"Were you married?"

"Yes." She looks at me, but her gaze is fixed on something beyond at the same time. "Patrick and I were in bed when he came."

"He?"

"One of the killers. It's a memory that will forever stalk the corridors of my mind, I'm afraid. It was the sound that woke me – the shuffling of feet. My clock radio said it was 2:13. I was lying on my side and my eyes were scanning our bedroom. The moonlight was bright enough for me to see a few things, but nothing out of the ordinary. So I turned around and spooned Patrick, which was when I felt a sticky substance against my ear. It was warm and like syrup on my neck. Only when I sat up did I see Patrick's mouth, wide open, his glassy eyes, and the knife sticking out of his chest. The man next to the bed only caught my eye when he turned his head toward me like a curious dog. Away from the moonlight he was nothing more than a shadowy outline, although I could have sworn I saw two red eyes glowing in the dark. The man lunged for me and I screamed."

"Jesus," I exclaim, taken aback. "How on earth did you survive?"

"That's what I'm still asking myself today. My recollection's a bit hazy when it comes to that. The next I do clearly remember is the lifeless body of that man being on top of me, with the knife sticking out of his chest. I think I may have yanked it from Patrick's body in a reflex as the man made his move and tried to ward him off with it. I pushed him off me and ran for the annex room, where our three-year-old daughter was asleep, praying that he hadn't hurt her. But he had."

I swallow down the lump in my throat and realize for the first time that there are thousands of these stories, all around the globe. Millions even, and I hate God for it. "I'm so sorry."

She nods appreciatively, looks at me for a second and then clenches a fist. "You know what? They can go to hell, them and their decision-making. You're right. We can't keep people here against their will, because it would make us just as bad. This place should be a safe haven for every person who needs one – or at least, that's how we started out. But we should all be free to choose a different path." And with those words, she rummages around in her pants pocket and pulls out a keyring. She finds the right one and opens my cell door.

Baffled, I stare at her. "Ehm, wow... thanks," I finally stammer. "But I'm afraid I won't get far. I'll be shot at dozens of times before I ever make it to one of the tunnels."

Elaine fixes me with her gaze. A smile plays around her lips. "Not if I accompany you."

-29-

Abel

It's a lonely existence, this roaming around in deserted neighborhoods. The streets are jammed full of parked cars, gardens are now overgrown with weeds, and the houses have been abandoned. It's a peculiar sight.

I step onto a porch, sit down in the rocking chair that's still there, and stare at the horizon.

What am I supposed to do now?

That question has been on my mind for days now. At first, I had this idea of finding people – not in order to kill them this time, but to join them. To those who don't know any better, I look exactly like them, after all. No one would ever have to know the truth. I'd be able to live on earth as a human, but that's not what I want. Not like this. The world is nothing more than a junkyard filled with death and despair. And of course there's the radiation. Besides, an existence like that would be a total lie. Eventually, the truth will come out, especially if my group of people were tracked down by angels. In their eyes I'm nothing more than an Aberration now. Whole divisions will be deployed in order to find me. No – the best thing I can do right now is stay hidden until I find another angel who has the same opinion about this situation. Because there have to be others – right?

Please let that be true.

I watch the sunset and marvel at the colors. The

temperature's dropping, but it doesn't chase me inside.

An hour later, it's dark out and I slip inside the house. Against my better judgment I'm still hoping to find someone, because the silence is driving me crazy. When I hear something fall over in the room next to me, my heart makes a demented little jump, suddenly hopeful. I walk over to the kitchen, on my guard. A scrawny cat looks at me warily from the kitchen top. Its tail is puffed-up and its glassy green eyes keep a close watch on me, glistening in the moonlight. The animal is hardly visible in the dim light.

Slightly disappointed, I approach the cat. "Hey, buddy."

The cat opens its mouth and meows hopefully.

"I bet you're hungry, huh?"

Again, the cat meows.

I nod and start rummaging around in the cupboards to find him something to eat. The only thing in there is junk food, mostly bags of chips. "Sorry, kitty. Nothing for you, I'm afraid."

The cat cocks its head as though asking a question. This furry man is stealing my heart as we speak.

"Okay, hold on. Let me check next door." *I might find some cat food somewhere.* Holding on to that thought, I walk back outside. I do find a box of cat food – in the third house I'm checking – but by the time I return, the cat is gone.

With a sigh I walk over to the kitchen top. I open the cupboard above my head and fish out a small bowl, which I then proceed to fill with some cat food. I put it right underneath the window and shake the half-full box to break the silence before sitting down at the table. It doesn't take long for the cat to return and this time, he's brought a friend. Hesitantly, he looks from the bowl of food to me and back, as though he suspects it's a trap. His tail is still puffed-up. It's not until the second cat – a ginger beast with no fear whatsoever – jumps inside and starts wolfing down the cat munchies that my feline friend decides to throw caution to the wind and joins the red cat at dinner.

With a smile I watch them eat. What a strange sight. I wonder if I can touch them.

Slowly I get to my feet. Like a burglar tiptoeing through a house he's broken into, I head for the two animals. The first cat sees what I'm doing, hisses at me and edges away when I come too close, but his friend shrugs it off and keeps eating. I extend my hand and stroke his fur. The cat doesn't seem to mind – in fact, it starts to purr. I smile again, but the expression dies on my face when I see the hairs that come off at each stroke. When a third cat appears at the scene, this one practically bald apart from a few patches of hair, I understand what's happening. This cat can barely walk and it's clear that he's at death's door.

Instantly, there is this realization:
The radiation.

It's eating away at their intestines like poison. I wouldn't be surprised if these cats have been eating poisoned rats or mice in the past few weeks – animals that succumbed to the radiation poisoning before them.

Is this what you intended, Lord? I glare up at the skies. *How can you allow this to happen?*

"I'm sorry, guys," I whisper.

I fill as many bowls as I can and put them all on top of the countertop. Afterwards I sit back down on my chair and watch the cats with tearful eyes as they're enjoying what is most likely their last supper. I realize I can no longer bear the sight of it and quickly make for the front door, gasping for breath. Crying, I stumble through the streets until I've reached the end of the village. I disappear into the woods.

An eerie sound like rolling thunder makes me look up, but by now it's so dark that there's no telling where it came from. All I see are the trees towering over me.

And then I see the fighter jets. They flash by me and disappear as quickly as they showed up. I scan the sky as best as I can, perking my ears. Before long my feet take over and I run deeper into the forest, following those jets.

-30-

Anna

The past few minutes have seen us sneaking past several houses like thieves in the night. But even in the dark, our movements stand out. The tunnel is only two hundred yards away from here. Luca, who's been sniffing his way up there, is almost at the entrance.

That's when a low voice booms out in the night and cuts my breath short. "What's the meaning of this?"

I whip around, startled. A number of men were patrolling the mountainside and hadn't seen us up till now – which is worrisome, at the very least. Riven Run is supposed to be a well-protected village, but this is the second time already that people have managed to almost slip out unnoticed. Admittedly, these sentinels have no professional experience. In all likelihood, they were butchers, bakers, or sales assistants in their previous lives. Maybe they even doze off on the job more than once. But this one is alert enough. I hear his voice before I see him. The moonlight is the only thing enabling me to make out his scraggly beard, piercing eyes, and grubby clothes, all of this combined with the barrel of a gun aimed at the two of us.

"Josh, don't call out," Elaine tries to stop him, but it's already too late. Taking us both in with his fierce gaze, he shouts: "Breakout! They're breaking out!" His voice bounces off the mountain walls. It is immediately joined by other panicked voices.

I look downhill and see several more figures in River Run Village heading out here.

Not one minute later, we're surrounded by five armed men and women – or at least that's the number of people I can count. More might be lurking in the darkness. It won't be long before those other people from the village have joined them, too.

"What the hell are you trying to do, Elaine?" Josh hisses.

"I'm setting Anna free." To my surprise, Elaine sounds very calm. "She doesn't want to be here. I don't think we can keep her here against her will."

I can hear a woman's scathing laugh, although I can't see her in the dark. "You know, it was *your* idea to make sure no one leaves this place. Those were your orders."

"You said it was for our own safety," a second woman chimes in.

That catches me off guard, and I shoot Elaine a sideward glance. She just shrugs. "Well, I changed my mind."

"Nonsense," Josh yells. "*She's* making you do this!" He points an irate finger at me.

"Partly, yes," Elaine replies quietly. "But she's right, in a way. We're no better than the ones we want to keep out if we take people's free will away ourselves."

"It's for the good of Keystone Valley, for all of us!" another man yells.

"Still doesn't make it right."

From the foot of the mountain come more voices and I see about seven dark figures headed our way. One of the voices I immediately recognize.

Howard.

"Elaine!" He sounds exhausted, clearly gasping for breath. "Goddammit!"

"And you're going with her?" Josh keeps interrogating us without even glancing Howard's way.

Elaine shakes her head. "I belong here, but please understand that…"

A strange sound suddenly cuts through the skies and makes us all look up in surprise. The sound grows louder and it's in fast approach. I squint my eyes and listen carefully, digging around in the little drawers of my memory for this particular sound. Because I know I should recognize it.

All at once I know what's coming for us.

Fuck!

"Take cover!" The words have barely left my mouth or the shockwave of the first explosion flings us all to the ground. The blast is ear-splittingly loud and the orange glow blinds me. The heat of it is unbearable, but it only lasts for a few seconds. It's as though the atmosphere gobbles it right back up.

My ears are ringing and I'm temporarily blinded. I'm screaming but can't hear my own words. My lips, as well as the rest of my body, seem to move in slow motion. I fall to my knees and automatically cover my eyes with my hand before peering through my fingers, down the mountains. A second explosion shudders through the village, causing people and buildings to simply explode. Screams rise up in the air, but they're drowned out by the din of the explosions. I gasp for breath and stare horrified at the place I was trapped in just minutes ago. The prison has been destroyed, just like the buildings surrounding it. A raging fire is all that remains. Black smoke extends its smoldering hand to the stars.

There's no time to react to the scene. Again, the fighter jets pass by overhead and this time, they open fire on everything that moves in Keystone Valley and the surrounding mountains. The sound of bullets whizzing by reminds me of firework, one of those big firecrackers. A never-ending torrent of lethal noise.

"They found us." Those are Josh's last words before he is hit by a volley of bullets. It happens right in front of me. I see his body jerk with every impact, his face contorting in a painful grimace. His mouth falls open, but no more sound comes out. He keels over and hits the ground with a thud. Other bullets hit the mountain road around him. I feel one of them flying past, narrowly missing me. With a scream, I duck for cover with my hands on top of my head.

"Anna, hurry up." Someone hauls me to my feet. I look up and see Elaine, her eyes wide and filled with fear. "They're using goddamned planes, Anna!" she yells. "*Planes!*"

I understand the underlying message. *Despite the electromagnetic pulse caused by the nuclear explosions they still managed to get operational jets. We couldn't win this from the beginning.*

She takes my hand and pulls me along. Above our heads, the jets are tearing through the sky with a shriek of their engines. I let myself be dragged along, barely registering that I'm running. It's a miracle I don't trip and break something, and even more of a miracle that I'm not hit by flying bullets. When I look around me, I see the lifeless bodies of the men and women who had their guns trained on us not one minute ago. Now they're on the ground, dead, with blood still trickling out of their bodies. Their eyes are glassy, their faces contorted in terror. Two men have been hit in the arms and legs and howling in pain. As I scan our surroundings, I suddenly come to a stop and pull Elaine back.

Where's Luca?

"We need to get out of here, Anna," I hear Elaine's voice.

"No. We can't just – we gotta help them…"

"Those planes are making a turn and they'll be back any second now."

"But…" I swallow, my heart beating erratically in my throat. I don't think I've ever felt this much adrenaline before. The yammering and the howling, both here and down in the village, will forever be etched in my memory.

"There's nothing we can do for them." With a decisive tug, she starts dragging me along once more, taking me to the tunnel. I understand where she's headed, but I also intuitively understand that we'll never make it those two hundred yards up alive. It's like a nightmare – every step I take seems to take me further away from the tunnel. Maybe that's what this is: a living nightmare.

By now the jets have come back, opening fire yet again. Their first volley hits River Run, but then they're coming closer to where we are. The popping sounds of their guns make me cower with fear.

"Hurry up, Anna." Terrified, Elaine glances back, at the planes and at me. Her eyes are big like planets, the celestial orbs of her eyeballs seemingly encompassing entire universes. Because she's looking over her shoulder, she can't see where she's going and she stumbles, falling down on the path. I notice it too late and trip over her, hitting the ground behind her. I've barely hit the ground when another barrage of bullets strikes the pavement right behind me. From the corner of my eye, I see Elaine's body spasm with the impact. Drops of blood hit me in the face.

No, no, no!

I look up. Elaine's the sole reason I'm still breathing. Her body is a shield to hide my own.

I seize her by the shoulders and shake her fervently. "No, no, you're okay," I babble. "Nothing's wrong with you." I'm talking to myself, of course, because it's plain as day that she's dead. If the bullets in her chest and lower body weren't fatal yet, the two directly in the forehead certainly are. I shriek, I howl, I slap her cheek. "No, wake up!" I'm in such a daze that I don't even notice the fresh round of gunfire until the bullets hit the ground right next to me. I curl up into a ball, but pull back my leg too late. The liquid pain makes me scream out. I flinch and reach for my thigh, where a bullet penetrated my skin. Warm blood is seeping from the wound, down my hands and leg onto the road. I'm seeing stars, so I bite down on my lip and try to control my pain.

Think of something else.

But the only thing that comes to mind is Adam. A feeling of deep regret and powerlessness overpowers me. I fall backward onto my back, defeated.

I'm so sorry, Adam.

One of the planes zips past me overhead – a merciless killing machine that won't stop until everybody down here is dead. The sound of its engine is interrupted by a bark. I turn my head in surprise.

Luca?

I can't see him in the dark, but the sound is coming

from the tunnel. Most likely he hid in there when the first bomb dropped. Smart dog.

Get up, girl. You can't give up. Not now, not ever!

That voice – for a minute I could swear it's coming from Luca. It's strange what a bullet wound and terrible blood loss can do to your mind. But actually, the voice has a point. I can't give up. It's only over when it's over. So I clench my teeth and scramble up the mountain as fast as I can, to get to Luca. Bullets could rip into my back and head at any moment, but I'm trying to block out that thought just like the pain. My line of vision narrows. This tunnel vision – can I say irony? – puts my focus entirely on Luca and the tunnel entrance. The Labrador keeps barking encouragingly. I see his muzzle work, but no longer hear him. Like all sound around me, he seems to fade with every step I take closer to him. As quickly as I can, I climb up to him, but then darkness takes me out.

-31-

The dark is all-encompassing. The only thing not shrouded by it is the drone of the fighter jets still passing overhead, combined with bullets hitting targets and people shrieking. But my own raspy breath, wildly beating heart and Luca's whining are even louder to my ears. The images burning themselves onto my retinas aren't bothered by the dark. Like I'm stuck in a flashy 3D cinema with Dolby Surround, they're playing on an endless loop. Again and again I see the dead bodies, the bombed buildings, the fire, and most of all: Elaine's lifeless body. The smell of smoke, burning wood, and corpses complete the memory, making it life-like in my mind.

And then, out of nowhere: silence. It comes so quickly that it takes my breath away. Takes my pain away, even.

The darkness is absolute. Curious, I turn around, hoping to see the light of the moon touching the entrance to the tunnel, but there is no entrance... only darkness.

"Luca?" My voice trembles with fear.

Nothing. No bark, no whine.

Ghostly laughter, coming closer and closer. I try to gauge where it's coming from, but I fail. Red eyes light up in the darkness. Tens of them, hundreds of them, like the lights on some creepy Christmas tree.

The temperature drops to a freezing point and chills me down to my soul. I shiver, but I also know that this isn't real – that I've been here before.

I'm dreaming.

I claw at my thigh. No blood, no warmth, no wound!

I'm surrounded. The red eyes are bright enough for me to see who they belong to. I see Hannah and my parents, but I also see the faces of men and women I've never seen before. Elaine and Howard are among them.

"This is all your fault. You led them there. Because of you, we're all dead now!"

The voices hit me like a tidal wave.

"The gates of Heaven are closed. Now we wander through nothingness, now we are nothing!"

I swallow the lump in my throat.

Someone taps me on the shoulder. With a yelp, I turn around.

Steph.

Sasha.

They're standing side by side, only a few paces away.

And Adam – he's in my brother's arms and looks at me with an uncharacteristic, reproachful glare. "Why did you allow them to take me?"

I want to respond, but I can't get the words out. Tears roll down my cheeks. I reach for him with an outstretched hand, but as soon as I do, the group surrounding me steps back into the void.

"No, wait!" I call after Steph, but he grins at me just like the others – that insane smirk of nightmares.

And then they're gone. The red eyes, the sounds, all of it. Only the darkness remains like a jailer guarding my prison cell.

I sob and lie down, rolling onto my side on the icy,

cold floor.

I'm sorry, Adam. So very much.

The chill dissipates, the darkness becoming like a veil as I peer through the slits of my half-closed eyes and notice I'm staring at a white wall. I'm in a canopy bed. My head is gently resting on a fluffy pillow, and my body is covered with two layers of blankets. They smell musty and make me feel all glowy inside. I open my eyes fully now, allowing the sunlight in that pours into the room through the window.

I lift my head a few inches off the pillow and look around me in a daze. A window, a wardrobe, a wooden chair, a narrow, vertical mirror on the wall which shows me myself, lying in bed. And Luca, curled up on the floor sleeping on a pillow.

Where am I?

It takes a while for the memories to come back, the images unclear. For a split second, I dare hope that it was all a nightmare and I am now awake, but then I inadvertently pull up my legs and a terrible pain lances through me. I let out a tense shriek before slipping my hand down to my thigh and feeling the bandage there. Suddenly, the blankets are feeling way too hot. I hastily fling them off me and gasp for breath while groaning. Once the pain subsides, I realize I'm naked. A chilly draft coming from the window that's open to a crack caresses my skin.

Well – color me confused. Did someone find me back there and bring me here? If so, who? And what has this person done to me? I mean, come on – I'm *naked!*

My shriek has woken Luca up. He jumps up, shooting a panicked look around. Then he sees me staring at him and he jumps onto my bed to lick my face. I shove him off me in a rush and snort a bit.

In the hopes of finding out where I've ended up, I look out the window. Only a clear, blue sky with three fluffy clouds is visible.

Downstairs, I hear a door slam, followed by the squeaking of floorboards. As if on cue I haul the blankets back up and over my body. My inner voice tells me to get the hell out of here, to escape, but the knots in my muscles – especially the ones in my injured leg – laugh at that notion. The pain is unbearable and I have to bite my lip to stop myself from screaming. Luca barks loudly.

Ssh. Please, be quiet.

With my ears pricked, I anxiously hold my breath. Loud footfalls on the wooden floor, coughing, and then: silence. Well, apart from my hammering heart and Luca's growling.

I cringe when the footsteps start again – slowly, heavily. Someone's trudging up the stairs! My eyes quickly scan the room in search of an object that might serve as a weapon. Nothing – but even if this bed had been standing right next to a complete arsenal, I still wouldn't have been able to move because of the stabbing pain in my thigh. So I grab the only thing available to me: my pillow.

Obviously. What's this supposed to be, a pillow fight?

For a moment I consider playing dead for a tactic, but before I can act on it, the door swings open and a young man steps inside, his hands holding a tray of food. I see a yellow shirt, blue pants, black boots. He's a bit tall and lanky, but he has a very handsome, sharp face. He's younger than me, but not by much. Eighteen, nineteen maybe? I find myself feeling relieved that at least he's not some old and ugly perv. This guy doesn't look like he wants to hurt me, but on the other hand – the sickest criminals might be wearing the mask of 'perfect son-in-law'.

The guy notices I'm awake, freezes momentarily, then conjures up a smile on his face. "Well, hi there. I was beginning to think you'd never wake up at all."

His voice is low, deep, almost hypnotic. He walks over to me and puts the tray down on the bed, next to me. A glass of soda, an apple, and some toast. The most glorious breakfast I have seen in weeks. My stomach rumbles as I glance at the tray and I try to remember when I last ate. I don't even know. Yet I don't touch the tray and shoot the guy a suspicious look.

"Where am I?" My voice is hoarse.

The boy shrugs. "Does it matter? You're safe." He claps his hands and points to the floor. Luca understanding the command doesn't surprise me – him actually obeying it does. Without any hesitation, he hops off the bed and lies down on the floor.

Do you trust this guy, Luca?

"Who are you?"

"Abel," the guy smiles. Only now do I notice that his eyes are the clearest blue I've ever seen. And he's well-built, too... "And you are?" he prompts.

"The past few years they called me Anna."

He cocks an eyebrow in surprise. "The past few years?"

I shake my head. "Long story." I look around. "Where are my clothes?"

"I threw them away. They were covered in blood – just like you." He nods at the wardrobe. "But there's plenty of clothes in there."

267

I lift the blanket and inspect my naked body. My *clean* body. "You washed me?" I feel heat creeping into my cheeks.

He doesn't bat an eyelid and just nods. "I tended to your injury, too. The bullet's out, but it'll be a while before you can run a marathon again. I hope the bullet didn't damage any nerve endings, because that's beyond my skills."

"You always take girls' clothes off after you find them?"

Abel smiles. "You prudish?"

I turn even redder. "No, I'm not, but..."

"You'd rather I'd let you wear your sticky, bloodied clothes all this time and let the bullet just sit there?"

"No, of course not, but you could have put something else on me, at least."

"I had no idea how long you'd be unconscious for. This way it was easier to get to where I needed to be."

"Excuse me?" *Oh, Lord.*

"To wash you," Abel hastily adds. He sits down on the chair next to my bed and shoots me a self-confident look. "Besides, taking clothes off is easy as pie, but have you ever tried to *dress* someone who's out like a light? It's not like you were cooperating."

"My sincerest apologies," I reply snidely.

Abel shakes his head. "No worries. I just wanted to explain why, uhm..." He sighs. "Look, don't be afraid. I didn't touch you inappropriately or anything."

"You better be speaking the truth." But something in his voice tells me that he is. Still surprised, I glance at Luca. If he trusts this Abel guy, is it safe for me to do so too?

Abel grins, then nods at the tray of food. "Eat, drink.

268

You need to get stronger."

I hesitantly pick up a slice of toast, inspecting it like I'm a biochemist analyzing every single fiber.

"You think I'm out to poison you?" Abel sighs. "Look, if I wanted you dead, you'd be dead by now. I wouldn't have gone to the trouble of nursing you back to health."

The urge to throw the tray – food and all – into his much-too-perfect face seizes me for a moment, but my grumbling stomach stays my hand. *Oh, whatever.* I hastily take a bite. It's dry toast, but the sensation almost makes my taste buds explode on the spot, especially once I combine it with the soda and the apple. "How did you find me?"

"I saw the fighter jets and followed them." He gestures at Luca. "I found you swaggering up the road, with him trailing next to you. Cute dog, by the way. Very loyal. I don't think he's left the room for more than ten minutes combined. Almost had to drag him out to walk him." With a smile, he pets Luca on the head.

His grin makes me wary. It also causes a lump in my throat. How long has it been since I saw someone smile that sincerely?

"I hadn't even made it over to you on the mountain road before you collapsed. I took you into the forest, to a vacation resort I passed by a half hour before I found you."

"How long have I been here for?"

"Four days."

I spit out my bite of the apple and sit up with a jolt. The tray clatters to the floor, plate and all. The glass shatters into tiny pieces. In my panic, I forget about my current physical state, and a new stab of pain makes me gasp for breath and grab at my injured thigh. I'm teetering on the edge of the bed. If not for Abel catching me, I'd have fallen to the floor.

"What's up with you, you whack job?" He shoots me an incredulous look as he shoves me back onto the bed. In a rush, he pulls off the covers and studies my wound. The bandage slowly turns red and I hear him swear. "Keep that up and you'll never heal. Now I have to dress the wound again, and I'm almost out of bandages. What's wrong with you?"

"Adam..." I stutter, still fighting for air. The pain makes tears well up in my eyes. "They took him..."

"Adam?"

"He's just a baby. He's..."

"You have a *kid*?"

I shake my head while holding my leg as still as possible. Slowly, the really agonizing pain subsides. "He's not mine. I helped deliver him before his mom died."

With a sigh, Abel sits down on the edge of the bed. He looks at me sadly. "You've been through a lot, haven't you?"

You don't know the half of it.

"Who took the baby?"

"My brother."

"Brother?"

"He was one of *them*."

"Ah." He nods as though that suddenly makes him understand the situation completely, but then he shakes his head next. "So why did they take him? Aren't they out to eradicate humankind on earth?"

I open my mouth to tell him, then stop. Suddenly it dawns on me that I don't know this guy at all. For all I know he could be one of *them*, too. Okay, so he's kept me

270

alive up till now – but what if he has different plans? How can I possibly trust him? Especially after what happened with Steph.

Abel puts his hand on my arm as though he can read my thoughts. His touch feels warm and sends a pleasant tingle through my body. "I'm not gonna hurt you, I promise."

"That's what I would tell the other person too, if I had a trick up my sleeve."

That gives him pause. "You're probably right, but if I'd still been one of *them*, you'd have been dead by now, believe me."

"Maybe…" His words resonate in my skull. *If I'd still been one of them.* Still. My blood freezes, my eyes grow wide, and I jerk away from him, almost launching myself off the bed again. "You *are* one of them!"

"Of course not," he tries, but the shocked expression on his face clearly tells me that his previous remark was a slip of the tongue.

"Liar."

Making sure I don't crawl any further away from him, he grabs my upper arms. At that moment, I'm convinced he's going to hurt me now that I found out his secret. "Easy, Anna. I told you just now: you can trust me."

"Let go of me." I tear myself out of his grasp with a violent jerk, losing my balance and thudding to the floor. My thigh hits the edge of the bed and I howl. Stars appear in front of my eyes and I feel the adrenaline surging through my body. Luca's barks seem to come from far away, but I know he's still close. Only when the world stops spinning again do I see Abel standing there, towering over me. He clucks disapprovingly, shaking his head. "Happy now? I bet you tore your wound open again."

"Stay the fuck away from me," I hiss.

"Fine." He rolls his eyes and walks over to the door. "I understand you need time to wrap your head around this. I'll leave you for now, take the dog for a walk. But when I get back here, I really need to take a look at your injury."

"You keep your hands off me, *capish*?

"Anna." Abel sighs as he opens the door to head out. "Does the fact that I'm an angel change anything about your present situation?"

"It does if you were going to hide it from me."

"Can you blame me, given your reaction?"

I don't respond.

"Besides," Abel continues, "were you going to tell *me* that you have an angel trapped inside of *you*?" He notices my shock and nods. "Yeah, I know all about it, Anna. I can sense him in you." He nods at Luca and steps onto the landing. "You coming, boy?"

Luca looks at me for approval, then licks my hand before he wags his tail and follows Abel outside.

-32-

Abel

Question: how to scare the living daylights out of a young woman? Answer: let it slip that you're one of the beings responsible for the annihilation of mankind.

You idiot.

Luca is walking around a few steps away, sniffing bushes and looking around him. Leaves whisper as he touches them with his fur. We're on our way back already, but I can hardly remember our walk.

What the hell are you doing, huh? What are you trying to accomplish?

That's a very good question. I'm a rebel without a cause, flying by the seat of my pants. It's a completely new feeling, equal parts terrifying and wonderful. Up in Heaven, being an angel, you don't deal with 'gut feelings'. You're expected to follow orders. Others live your life. Which is fine, because you don't know any better. But now...

It was stupid of you to take care of her. Now you're stuck with the girl.

But honestly, I couldn't leave her behind on that mountain? She would have surely died.

Yeah, so? Not too long ago it was your assignment to kill people. You've gone soft. You want to be part of a group, right? So leave her behind and look for communities to join. She's just going to hold you back, just like that dog of hers.

But what if there are hardly any people left? The radiation must be practically everywhere, and so are the angels. The people still alive will be pushing up the daisies soon. What if she's the only one alive for miles around? No man is an island, and besides, she needs help. It feels good to be able to help.

You've been stuck in this human for too long.

Maybe – but that doesn't change the situation one bit.

The vacation resort is nothing more than a circle of log cabins in the middle of a forest. On the edge, near the main road, is a larger building that used to be the reception area, with a pool and everything. Now it's abandoned and manned merely by ghosts.

The log cabin I picked isn't the biggest one around. Two floors, with a steep pointy roof, and completely made of wood. I whistle at Luca, step up to the front door, and get inside. I'm keeping the door open so the dog can slip inside behind me. That's when I see Anna, lying on her side at the bottom of the stairs, blood dripping from a head wound. She's moaning and flexing her fingers.

"Shit." My eyes grow wide and my breath hitches. I run over to her. Luca follows my lead and starts to run in circles around her like a mad dog.

"Stay away from me." Anna's voice sounds very weak.

"Don't be ridiculous. You still think I want to hurt you? Come on, let me help you."

"If you're one of *them*, I can't trust you. I'm not falling for it again."

"I'm different from the others, believe me."

"Is there an angel trapped inside you too? Is your

human side too strong to subdue?"

"No, but..." I sigh. "Come on, let me help you up." I lean forward to lift her up, but she forcefully shoves my hands away.

"Either explain it to me or get off me."

I curse inwardly. Humans can be a real pain in the ass. "Let's just say I don't believe God has brought us here to kill humanity. And if He did, I don't agree with Him."

"Wow, an angel with a conscience?" Anna laughs cynically.

"If that's what you want to call it. So, may I please help you up now?"

She doesn't reply, but doesn't resist anymore when I pick her up and carry her to the sofa. "What the hell were you trying to do?" I say as I carefully put her down on the couch.

"Adam..." she stammers dejectedly. "They've had him for four days already! I have to find him."

"You think you'll get far in your present condition?" I quickly check her over, taking in the damage. It's obvious she fell down the stairs, but apart from the head wound, I don't see any other injuries.

Anna shrugs. "I have to at least try."

"I hate to break the news to you, but that baby's gone."

With renewed energy, she grabs my shirt and squints her eyes at me. "Don't you *ever* dare say that again." It's followed by a sad and weak: "He's all I have, besides Luca."

"I'm just trying to be realistic. Why would they keep that child alive?"

She yells at me so loudly that the words reverberate through my skull. "Because the bastard who's taken possession of my brother's body is playing some sick game with me!" She then proceeds by giving me the situation in a nutshell.

"But surely you understand that the kid is doomed no matter what you choose to do?" I ask once she's done telling her story. In the meantime I've grabbed the open First Aid kit that was still on the table, and I take a seat next to her. "It's pointless to give your angel control over your body."

"Of course I understand that," she snaps. "But what else am I supposed to do? They could be anywhere. If I don't surrender to the angel, I'll never find them again." Her face contorts with pain when I use a piece of cotton wool drenched in alcohol on her forehead, and the expression intensifies once I take the old bandage off her thigh and replace it with a new one.

All of a sudden, she forcefully grabs my hand and makes me look at her. "Hold on!"

I stare at her nonplussed. "Hold on what?"

"You're an angel."

"So?" But the word has barely left my mouth when it dawns on me. I quickly get to my feet. "Hell, no."

"You can sense other angels, right?"

"True, but…"

"You can take me to Adam."

"I could, in theory, but I'm not going to," I say firmly.

"Why not?"

"Because it'll get us both killed! I don't know about you, but I only get to live one earthly life. I'm not about to chuck it away because of some quest for a baby. And I sincerely doubt I'll be welcomed back by my former angelic friends. I'm the only one who thinks that they're wrong about the Creator and His ideas – they're all still firm believers in their mission. They will single me out as a traitor. Frankly, I wouldn't be surprised if they were ordered to find me, just like I was once ordered to track down Aberrations and kill them. If anything, we should lay low, not walk right into their arms!"

You see, Abel? It was a mistake to save her. Leave her behind and get out while you still can!

Conflicted, I glance at the door. Luca seems to know exactly what's going through my head, because he sits down in front of the exit and bares his teeth at me while growling.

"Coward! Is this how you want to live? By always being on the run?"

"Are you trying to tell me that that's not exactly what *you've* been doing in the past few months? And, yes, this is how I want to live if it means it'll keep me alive." I hear myself saying the words, all the while doubting whether I truly mean them. Living alone is like hell on earth, and it's what I'll have to deal with if I choose to run now. But even that kind of life would be better than dying, right? "And even if I managed to get us to where Adam is, then what? You told me that he's accompanied by two angels. Which means we're outnumbered, because you're no match for a member of my species – certainly not in your condition. Besides, they may have joined a group. Then what? And have you considered what might happen if you lose control over your body, even if it's temporary? I'd be all alone."

"We have to try!"

"Anna, there's no point! Why can't you get that though your head?"

"I can't." She balls her fist and pummels the sofa armrest with it. "Why can't you get that through *yours*?"

277

She throws her hands up. "Oh, what am I doing, anyway? Getting into an argument with an angel, that's what. How could you possibly understand human emotions? From what I've seen, you're all a bunch of unfeeling killing machines."

The comment is like a slap in my face. "That's not true. Not all of us are. I'm not!"

"So prove it!"

I fall silent, bite my tongue and turn my back toward her.

Just walk out now, buddy. Why are you doing this to yourself?

Behind me, I hear the sofa squeak. When I turn my head, I see Anna scrambling up, or trying to. "Where are you going?"

"What do you think? I'm going to look for Adam. With or without your help."

I shake my head disbelievingly. "You won't get far."

"See if I care. I have to try."

"At least wait until your injuries are healed."

"That might take weeks. Adam will be long dead by then."

"They took him four days ago. Even if they kept him alive for that long, which I sincerely doubt, they'll probably keep him alive for a few days longer. Whatever the case, you can't travel when you're feeling like this." I swallow before I utter the next few words. "I won't allow it."

She gives me a withering look. "You'd really keep me here against my will?"

"If necessary, yes."

"And here I was, thinking you had a conscience. Thinking you were trying to act human."

"I am, in my own way."

"People don't do this to each other. Not if they're *good* people, that is."

"It's for your own good."

"Asshole."

I sigh. "Listen, I have an idea. If you stay here until you're healed, kind of, I'll point you in the right direction."

"The right direction?" she huffs.

"That's all I can do for you, I'm afraid. But at least you'll have a better chance of finding them. A far better plan than just walking out the door right now. Your choice."

She looks at me as though she can't quite believe what I've just said, then she drops back onto the cushions with a grimace. "You're gonna regret this."

I nod. *I suspect I will, but for a different reason than you think, darling.*

-33-

Anna

Sometimes he's gone for hours, looking for food. Which makes sense, because the kitchen cupboards are nearly empty and we need to eat something. When I ask him why he doesn't go hunting, he simply replies that he would have liked to, if only there were wild animals nearby. But there aren't – the radiation has killed off most of them. I remember our conversation about it vividly.

"How come we're immune to the radiation?"

"You already know the answer to that," Abel replies.

"Does it have something to do with the angel inside of me?"

"Correct."

"So how about Luca?"

Abel shot the dog sleeping peacefully next to my bed a suspicious look. "Who knows? Dumb luck, I guess. Or…"

"Or what?"

"I don't know. Ever since I first saw him, I feel strangely comforted by his presence."

"Comforted?"

Abel nodded. "Yeah, he feels… familiar."

Abel used to go to the same 7-Eleven I stumbled upon before, but the stuff he could still find there is mostly snack food and isn't nearly enough. So he ventures out beyond the usual territory now, and he sometimes stays away for a full day. In the beginning, his absence was a blessing for me, but frankly, the silence is starting to get to me recently. Especially when Abel takes Luca on his supply runs.

"As long as you're by yourself, chances are slim you'll be found by hunters," he told me two days ago. "Besides, you can hardly walk, and Luca needs to be walked at least a couple times a day."

Such a comforting thought, isn't it? Yeah, right. Maybe that's why when I'm alone, I flinch at every unexpected sound, peering through the bedroom with wide eyes and pricked-up ears. I realize that I'm beyond salvation if Hunters indeed show up here. The only thing I can do if that happens is hide under my bed and keep as quiet as a mouse in the hopes they won't find me and they'll move on. But I'm realistic enough to understand that it won't be that easy. And yet, Abel keeps reassuring me, telling me there are no Hunters nearby. It eases my mind somewhat – since he can actually sense their nearness – but I don't live and die by his promise.

I curse him for bringing me into this situation, and quite often I almost pack my bags to stumble out by myself to go look for Adam. But the sad fact is that I need Abel – in my present condition I don't stand even the smallest chance of getting far, let alone finding Adam.

It's because of this fear and the silence around me that I breathe out in relief when I hear three raps on the door – the sign we agreed to so I know it's Abel – and the pitter-patter of dog paws on the wooden porch steps. The door swings open and Luca cheerfully jumps onto my bed, turning a few rounds before plonking down as close to me as possible. It doesn't take long for Abel to stride into my room too, carrying a full tray of food. He tells me where he's been, what he's found, and asks me how I'm doing.

"The pain's as good as gone," I lie, like every time. "With a bit of luck I'll be able to walk around in a few more days."

Although he knows I'm stretching the truth, he never calls me out on it. He usually just watches me eat, after which we chat non-stop about all kinds of things from my old life. He wants to know everything, so I tell him what life was like for me before D-Day. I tell him about Mark, about the witness protection program, and the lie we had to live from that day onward. About what has happened to me ever since that day the angels went on the war path. Abel asks me questions and somehow reminds me of a scientist who's trying to figure out the meaning of life. But when I put the ball in his court and ask him what life is like for an angel, he dodges the question and makes the conversation come back to me.

"Can't you at least tell me a little bit about what it's like up there?" I ask, annoyed.

He shakes his head with a sigh. "Words cannot express it. You can only understand it when you see it with your own eyes."

But I *did*, I realize. Or at least a part of it, when Einstein grabbed my ankle back at the gas station and projected his memories onto me.

"You got any idea yet how to get Adam back? In case, however unlikely, he is still alive."

I open my mouth to answer him, then shut it again. It's not the first time we're having this debate, and I honestly still don't know what to say. The few times before, I snapped at him and got angry. Sometimes, he wisely drops the subject. Sometimes, though, he's just as stubborn as I am and he keeps grilling me. Today, he chooses door number two.

"I'm serious," he says. "Let's jokingly assume you *do* find them..."

"You really think it's a mission impossible, don't you?" I interrupt him heatedly.

"What do you intend to do once you come face to face with your brother?" he continues unperturbedly. "Best case scenario: only that Sasha girl's with him, but even then you don't stand a chance against them. They'll either make sure your soul loses control over your body, or they'll kill you."

"I don't know, okay?" I growl. "Doesn't mean I won't give it a shot. Whose side are you on, anyway?"

"I'm just trying to understand your point of view. I don't understand why you're so willing to sacrifice your life for a child that isn't even yours. A child that will die, no matter what scenario I come up with. Even if by some miracle you save him from your brother's clutches, little Adam's gotta contend with the radiation after that."

"Of course you wouldn't understand." I suddenly feel the irrepressible urge to punch him on the nose. "You're not even human. You probably think the world is black and white."

He looks at me, shaken as though I've literally slapped him across the face. "That's not true! I like the idea – it's heroic and like tales of old. But no matter how you look at it, it's still a stupid move. Especially if you insist on going alone. It's not so very different from what Jesus tried to do, and look how he ended up."

"Then come with me, dammit. Help me!"

He stomps out of the room and into the hallway. "You're really incorrigible, Anna. Don't you see why I can't? They'll kill me in all scenarios." And with a bang, he slams the bedroom door shut.

Days turn to weeks and only after three full weeks have passed do I hesitantly venture out on foot again without any pain. My rehabilitation is going smoothly. I'm determined to strengthen the muscles in my thigh as quickly as possible, so I practice at least two hours in the morning and three in the afternoon on a daily basis. After diligently sticking to that regime for a few days, I manage to get down the stairs and into the living room unassisted. It's where I like to sit the best. Abel has moved the sofa so I have a clear view of the forest. It's like a relaxing painting. The branches and leaves being caressed by the wind, and the clouds sailing through the sky like ships into a harbor – it's wonderful. Abel has managed to scrounge up enough food for now, so he can stay in today. He's helping me, encouraging me whenever he can. Under his supervision I even manage to walk Luca again, and together we take a forest walk. We find a sturdy branch that acts like a crutch for me and I'm enjoying the fresh forest air once more.

It's during one of those walks that I ask him a question that's been running through my mind for days. "Why do you think Steph's keeping Adam alive?"

Abel shrugs and kicks a branch like's he a child at play. "I hope it is because deep down he realizes that what he's doing can't be good – like I did. I refuse to believe I'm the only angel with common sense."

"So you don't think it's Steph's soul gradually taking over?"

284

"I get why you're hoping for that, but I'm afraid your brother is truly lost. If his soul had been stronger than the angel's, he'd never have been able to seize control over his body. When a soul gets detached from a body for too long, it'll lose the ability to connect and will disappear."

"Disappear?" My eyes widen.

Abel nods. "To heaven or hell. If they were both still open, at least."

"And now?" I gasp for breath, taken aback.

"Now they're wandering spirits, I'm afraid." He sees my reaction and puts a hand on my shoulder. "I'm sorry. Maybe there's something like a gray area there."

"You mean there might be a slight possibility Steph's soul *is* still trapped inside his body?"

He nods. "I don't think so, personally, but of course I hope it's true. For you." Abel pushes aside a branch and extends his hand to help me across a protruding tree root. "But even if that's the case and he's able to influence the angel's feelings and actions sporadically – he's still powerless. In this situation, it's mind over emotion."

"Meaning what?"

"Meaning, the angel knows what's going on and he's still going to do like he sees fit." He pauses for a moment. "But I agree it's a peculiar state of affairs."

One week later, my muscles are strong enough for me to walk long distances without straining them too much. Running is still out of the question, but I'm not planning on it. I decide that it's time – I've waited long enough.

I look at Abel pleadingly. "You sure you're not coming?" We're standing on the threshold of the log cabin's front door. Luca's sniffing some undergrowth a little ways away.

I see the hesitation in his eyes. It makes hope flare up for a second, but then he shakes his head after all. "I'm sorry. I'll be safer all alone."

"Without you it'll be like looking for a needle in a haystack, even if you send me in the right direction."

He fixes the ground with a dejected stare. "You gotta head north. I can't sense people's presence, so I can't tell you whether Adam's still alive, but I do sense at least two angels. A half day's walk away from here, at least."

"At least?"

"They're too far away for me to tell you whether they're going to team up with more angels. Also, I'm not sure it's the two angels you're looking for." He takes my hand and gives me a sad look with his chocolate brown eyes. "Please don't. Just stay here."

"And then what?" I grumpily pull my hand back. "Live here until we, what? Die of old age? Get found by Hunters after all? Because that's what in store for us, Abel. We won't live forever – not even you. It's not about how *long* you live; it's about *how* you live. Don't you get that?" Without looking back, I walk over to Luca and disappear into the forest.

-34-

After walking for a half day – interspersed with quite some breathers – I realize that my decision to head out was taken with too much haste. I should have waited a couple more days. My muscles are on fire, and with every step I'm leaning on a makeshift crutch – a branch I found. I decide to take another break in the ruins of an old mall. I sit down on the floor of a clothes store, directly next to the entrance. It's more than obvious that this mall, like so many others, was completely plundered months ago. There's trash everywhere. Empty bottles, broken glass. Even the clothes stores were looted. There are torn items of clothing and fallen racks all over the floor.

From this vantage point, I have an excellent view of the main mall entrance, as well as all the cars that have been in the parking lot for months. Some of them are parked askew, as though the owners had to come to sudden stops. Some of them have all the doors wide open. Undoubtedly some of them harbor dead bodies, too: rotting corpses or skeletons, even. I also see the freeway behind the lot, waiting for me there like an impossible choice. To go left or right – I have no idea what to do. *Head north*. Well, I did. What next, for God's sake? Although I'm still fully resolved to go ahead with my plan, I'm only now finding out that I don't really have one.

Admit it, girl. This is pointless. You'll never find them. Abel was right.

No. Abel's a coward. If he'd tagged along, at least I would have had a chance to find them.

Rubbing my swollen thigh, I close my eyes. I'm just about to breathe in deeply when a sharp noise startles me. I look up.

What was that?

I furtively glance at the main entrance, then into the mall. Luca stops his restless pacing through the clothes store and comes to stand next to me, tail tucked in and whining softly. I don't see anything coming from outside except the sunlight pouring in through the broken glass of the sliding doors and the windows next to them, chasing the gloom away. The light is accompanied by a gentle breeze, dust motes, and the sour, decaying smell of the destroyed city upwind and the corpses inside this mall.

I hastily grab my walking stick, scrambling up and pressing my back against the wall to keep out of sight as much as I can. I hold my breath and listen intently, hyper-alert to the slightest disturbance. The sound I heard before resembled someone accidentally kicking a glass object – a beer bottle, maybe? A part of me expects to hear the sound again, but no other sound is audible now. I'm beginning to wonder whether I just imagined it.

But Luca heard it too.

Maybe it was some kind of rat.

Or maybe it wasn't.

Again, I'm faced with a choice. Will I stay here, wrapped in the cloak of fear until it strangles me? Should

I investigate? Shouldn't I just get the hell out?

The choice is being made for me when I carefully look around the corner and suddenly feel a hand on my shoulder. The blood in my veins freezes and the hairs on my arms stand on end. I want to scream, but a hand slips over my mouth and smothers my cry. The person roughly yanks me backward, then spins me around.

"Ssh," a voice hisses, but I only recognize it once I see the face belonging to it.

Abel lets go of me and pats Luca on the head before sticking his head around the corner. Luca doesn't even seem to notice him; he's still whining and looking up and down the corridor of the mall. Abel's holding a gun in his hands.

"What are you doing here?" Exhausted, I gasp for breath while shooting him an incredulous look.

"I couldn't let you leave like that," is the simple reply. He doesn't look at me as he says it – his eyes are fixed on the main entrance. "A few hours after you left, I decided to follow you."

"How did you find me here?" My heart skips a beat in euphoria and I feel the tension draining away. I've never been happier to see him in my life, but the expression on his face tells me that there's no reason to throw a party just yet.

"You've got an angel inside of you, remember? I can sense you. But even if I couldn't, you've left quite a trail behind in the forest. Which is also your biggest problem."

"What do you mean?"

He quickly turns around to face me. I don't think I've ever seen more tension in anybody's face than right now. "We're not alone. Luca can smell it too. They've found us."

"Found us? Who?"

"The Hunters."

"Hunters?" My heart skips a beat. "Where?"

"In the mall. I can sense them."

I cast an anxious look around. "How many?"

"At least five."

"Crap."

"No shit." He glares at me. "You happy now?"

"Hey, this is not my fault," I protest. "I tried to be careful and keep a low profile."

"Well, not low enough." As he raises his gun in the air, he takes my hand and drags me along. "We need to get out of here. Fast."

With Luca running in between us, we rush – or actually, I limp – out of the clothes store and past the fronts of the other stores into a courtyard, where some wilting plants in flower boxes block our way. Our footsteps echo off the walls. We pass a dusty escalator that seems to lead to mere darkness, due to the sparse light in here, and I can't help but feel like someone's watching us from there.

My aching muscles make me come to a halt. "Abel, hold up. I can't..."

Before I can even finish my sentence, Abel has already picked me up. He starts to run again, but only ten steps down the way he stops again and puts me down, looking around him.

"What is it?" I snap hysterically.

Without speaking, he searches for a way out.

"Talk to me, Abel. Please."

"I thought I sensed them on the south end of the mall, but they've moved."

"Moved?" I look around us in shock. I don't see anyone. Just deserted stores – remnants of a life long past.

"We're surrounded."

At that moment, Luca starts to bark and my ears pick up the sound of tortuously slow footsteps. The footfalls seem to grow even louder because of the acoustics of the room. They're joined by a voice. "Well, lookee here, my friends. This must be our lucky day." A man emerges from one of the stores. His grimy face is contorted with aggression and for a moment I see a glimpse of madness in his eyes. He claps his hands and keeps doing it until he's right in front of us.

The darkness spits out more figures – three women and two men. With sly grins they close their circle around us. Their glistening eyes and gun-toting hands are the last thing I wanted to see today.

Cold sweat beads on my forehead. I know I've been in situations like these before, but I doubt I'll get out of this one alive.

"And here I was thinking we got them all," one of the women smiles. She's got a firearm but doesn't even truly aim it at us. She knows we don't stand a chance, despite the gun in Abel's hand.

"Leave her alone," Abel commands, threateningly pointing at the people surrounding us one by one. His voice is too shaky for him to be taken seriously, though. Luca barks, bares his teeth, and paces in a circle around us like a lion protecting its cubs.

"Drop your gun and we'll consider it," one of the men to my right speaks up.

"No, we won't." The woman across from me – completely bald and with grimy smears on her face and arms – snarls at us, shaking a fist. "She's human and he is a traitor. I say we kill them right here."

My heart leaps in my chest. *She's shaved off her hair and she's in desperate need of a shower, but I'll be damned if that isn't Sasha.*

Behind her, I see movement in the shadows before another figure emerges.

Steph!

He's cradling a child against his chest, stroking the back of the baby's head almost lovingly.

Adam!

"I have to say I didn't see this coming." Steph's voice is full of wonder. "I was hoping to push you to surrender to your inner angel by doing this, even though it wouldn't have helped the child. But this…"

"Give him to me!" I shout. Adam isn't moving, which makes the blood freeze in my veins. "Please don't tell me he's… he's…" The lump in my throat is so thick it hurts.

"He's not dead. He's sick, though." He tells me this in such a calm and cool voice that it sends shivers down my spine. His words hit me like the strokes of a sledgehammer and take my breath away like he's just punched me in the stomach. My knees start to tremble and I sag to the floor.

"Anna!" Abel tries his best to catch me, but he's too late. One of the angels next to him is quicker than lightning. He sees how Abel's attention shifts to me, dashes forward, kicks an attacking Luca out of the way, snatches the gun from Abel's hand, and forcefully shoves him into me, which makes us both tumble to the floor.

Luca whimpers, but he's back on his feet again already, circling us protectively.

"And it wasn't even because of us," I hear Steph say.

292

It almost sounds plaintive. "It's the radiation. Babies this young have no immune system. I'm sorry."

"You're sorry?" Sasha shoots Steph an incredulous look, just like the other angels gathered here. "Don't tell me you grew soft and feel human emotions, Memphis. Don't tell me you're a traitor like *him*." She nods at Abel, pulling a disgusted face.

"I knew I wasn't the only one," I hear Abel whisper.

But then Steph grins a devilish smile. "Gotta disappoint you there, buddy. Admittedly, I've had mixed feelings about our mission lately. But don't delude yourself into thinking I lost track of God's will."

"What if this isn't God's will?" Determinedly, Abel gets back on his feet.

"Of course it is," the man with the grimy face says. "The Lord was fed up with how things were run here on earth, and to be frank, I can all too well imagine why." He spits on the floor like humanity is some distasteful phlegm in his mouth. "Humans are like roaches – insects that seem to think the world revolves around them."

I hardly register his diatribe. All I can do is stare at Adam and make up plans to snatch him out of Steph's arms. I fail utterly. With all those angels in front of me, I'll never get near my brother.

"ENOUGH!" Sasha hollers, taking a step forward and pointing her rifle at us. "I'm gonna end this right now."

I hear her words, but I don't move. I simply stopped caring. If Adam is really sick with radiation poisoning, he won't live much longer. What's left to live for after he dies? If I can't save him, I want to die alongside him. Because it's clear as day to me that they'll kill the redundant baby in their care once I'm dead. I squeeze my eyes shut and wait for the inevitable.

But the bullet impact doesn't come, and neither does the pain.

"What the hell..?" A surprised voice.

I open my eyes.

Like soldiers retreating on a battlefield, the sunbeams decrease in strength, making way for the dark to advance. Outside, a flash of lightning splits the sky in two. It is accompanied by the roll of thunder – thunder which makes the entire building shake on its foundations. Rain lashes down. No, it's not rain – it's hail. Hailstones the size of pebbles. They shatter the little glass that's left in the windows of the mall with a deafening clash.

And then: silence.

Where Luca was standing not two seconds ago is now a great light, so bright that it temporarily blinds me. Like fireflies, small orbs of light spiral around us like we're trapped inside a tornado. With an earth-shattering noise, the luminous spheres are being sucked in by the column of light, which makes it expand and fight the darkness surrounding it. When the light dims slightly, I see how one of the wilting potted plants is on fire. A booming voice resounds. "Fools!"

My lips are dry. I feel weak and listless. And yet, my fear has mysteriously disappeared completely, just like the angels around us. The only one visible to me is Abel, and he's looking at the burning bush with a face just as baffled as mine. He's the first one who understands what's going on here.

"Lord!"

"I sent you to earth to teach humans about mercy and compassion," the burning bush roars. "Together with them, you were to build up a new society. A community without war, depressions, and decay. You were supposed to teach them how to take care of this planet." The voice resonates in every fiber of my being.

"I don't understand..." Abel stutters.

As though he hasn't interrupted, the voice continues. "It was all a test."

"For humanity?"

"No, for they had already failed. This test was yours. It was for the angels."

"But why didn't you step in, Lord?" Abel wants to know. "You must have seen how things got out of hand."

The ensuing silence makes me think that the voice doesn't quite agree with that observation. But surely all *this* could never be what He intended, could it? That would be ridiculous.

"Upon all creatures in this universe is bestowed free will. That includes the angels. It makes apparent their true nature. But now that they are trapped in human bodies, they, too, will know a Judgment Day. The ones who were not able to look beyond the dark veil of deception despite their faith and obedience to Me. The ones who only listened to the spoken word, not to the words of their hearts and minds. They shall be punished."

Abel is crying. His voice shakes when he pleads: "Forgive me, Lord. I have sinned. I recognized the truth too late."

"Each and every fool can repent. You chose the straight path in time. I have been watching you through the eyes of this quadrupled."

Through Luca? Of course – that explains why he lasted this long, when all other animals have perished by now.

"A new era is dawning," the voice continues to boom. "It will spring from the survivors and those of the angels who refused to believe the lie."

"So I'm *not* the only one?"

"There are more angels like you, although they are far away from here. In the east, just like the survivors I was talking about. There is a secluded area there where the radiation cannot penetrate. A new realm where there will be peace, where sinners will not be allowed to enter, where the sick will be healed if they manage to find this garden of peace, and where the faithful will enjoy My protection. You will have to make your way there too."

The light keeps growing, increasing in strength until the rest of the mall is clearly visible as well. I see the angels, motionlessly on the floor. Dead?

Steph!

My brother's lying flat on his back and he's turned his head to look at me. His pupils are glassy and white and his mouth hangs open. The baby lying on his chest isn't moving either.

"Please," I beg him with a sob. "I have no one left. Give Adam back to me. And my brother…"

"The angel Memphis has killed your brother and he was not strong enough to seek out the truth like Abel did. He is lost."

"Then kill me too!" This may be God I'm talking too, but I've never felt more loathing for anyone than I'm doing now. He sure knows how to spin things, but in my eyes He's still responsible for everything that's happened. He's almighty – He should have stopped it.

My inner voice pipes up. *God moves in mysterious ways.*

"No, I will not. You have a task to fulfil. But I will grant your wish with regards to the child. You have deserved a reward."

The last sentence echoes through the room like a broken record. Again, the light expands, and we're suddenly in the middle of a blank canvas. Everything is gone. The angels, the mall, the burning bush. It's just Abel and me, as though we are the first humans to enter a new world.

"Resist temptation, for it is the road to evil and decay. I shall protect all the chosen ones, as I have done all this time. You will be resistant to radiation and the ailments that come with it."

It takes me a while to process what He's just said. *My struggle to keep control over my body. Luca was there with me. He was the one who killed Einstein and Geraldine, not me. That's why Adam got sick only after he was abducted by Steph. I was under His protection, so the child must have been protected by association?*

And then the voice fades away and we're left with just silence. Or are we? I strain to hear a sound in the distance – is that someone crying?

I look around searchingly. Right next to the spot where the burning bush was, is Luca wagging his tail and looking up at us while panting.

"I will be watching."

The words resonate in my skull. Again, I look around me, until my gaze lands on the little boy.

Adam!

As I stagger towards him, the colors of the world bleed back into my vision. I'm back at the mall, but I don't really care. My attention is solely focused on the child.

Sobbing, I fall to my knees next to him and lift him up. Adam shrieks, but immediately stops as soon as he feels my touch. And then he laughs. It's the most beautiful sound in the world to me.

Inside, I feel empty, but strangely enough this vacuum feels liberating. It's as if something is being extracted from my body. Repentance and shame shiver through my body, and I realize that I'm feeling the emotions belonging to the angel who was trapped inside me. God is literally dragging him back to Heaven by his hair. He's setting me free. The relief I feel is mind-boggling.

Footsteps behind me. A hand on my shoulder. Abel. I grab his hand and lightly squeeze it. I don't quite understand what has just happened – or even what is expected of us – but in this moment, it's not relevant. Nothing is. The only thing that matters is the fact that these two boys and the dog are here with me.

Can you help?

Thank You For Reading My Book!

I really appreciate all of your feedback, and I love hearing what you have to say.

Reviews are very important for an author. My goal is to get my books out to as many readers as I can. One of the ways of doing that is to get a deal with sites like Bookbub. But to get a deal an author needs a certain amount of reviews. So I need your help to get there!

I also need your input to make the next version of this book and my future books better.

So, please leave me an honest review on Amazon letting me know what you thought of the book. I will take you just a minute.

Thanks so much!

J. Sharpe

Wait, there's more?

Yes there is. Eden is not the only novel translated. I have a second book out in English. Its called Syndrome. If you want to know more about that book and/or about me, find me on Amazon, or go to my website.

And remember to sign in for my mailing list to get a free short story and to be the first person to hear about future translations. You can do so by going to my website, www.jsharpebooks.com.

Acknowledgments

Every project I start needs to feel like a challenge to me – it should contain an element I haven't had the pleasure of working with before. This time, I wanted to write an apocalyptic story told in the first-person perspective.

This novel is a tribute to my heroes – authors like Stephen King, Dean Koontz, and Joe Hill. Now, these are men who know exactly how to pen a good story, apocalyptic or otherwise.

You can't write a book all on your own. This is why I want to take the time to thank my publisher, Zilverspoor, for their enduring support, and my editor's Cocky van Dijk, Natascha De Vries-van Limpt, and Inge Pietjouw.
Last but not least, I would like to thank Kelly van der Laan and Milly van der Veen for their comments during proofreading.

About the author

J. Sharpe – a pseudonym for Joris van Leeuwen (1986) – has written several mystery thrillers, fantasy novels, and short stories.

His work is often compared with novels by authors such as Stephen King, Dean Koontz, and Peter Straub.

He was shortlisted for the prestigious Dutch sci-fi and fantasy Harland Award in 2016, for the best fantasy book written in that year.

He is known for not sticking to one genre only. His thrillers, for example, usually contain elements of horror, sci-fi, or fantasy, and vice versa.

Made in the USA
Coppell, TX
09 April 2020

19610576R00176